Convenient Mistruths

A Novel of

Intrigue, Danger, and Global Warming

Geoff Strong

Cover Art Martin Jackson
Editing, layout, and cover design by Esther Hart

Published Geoff Strong

Library and Archives Canada Cataloguing in Publication

Strong, G. S. (Geoffrey Stuart), 1945-, author
    Convenient mistruths : a novel of intrigue, danger, and global warming / Geoff Strong.

Issued in print and electronic formats.
ISBN 978-0-9952883-0-0 (softcover).--ISBN 978-0-9952883-1-7 (ebook)

I. Title.

PS8637.T8435C66 2016   C813'.6   C2016-907856-6
                                                      C2016-907857-4

Disclaimer

This is a work of fiction and all characters portrayed are from the author's imagination, bearing no resemblance to any living person. Exceptions are historical characters and dates, especially in the *Chronology of Climate Change Science* in Appendix II. There I endeavoured to maintain accuracy and truth, since one of the purposes of this novel is to inform the public about the present and potential future disastrous impacts of global warming; and to refute those who continue to deny the reality of anthropogenic climate change, either through ignorance of scientific facts or because they have a vested interest in denial, hence their convenient mistruths.

The climate impacts raised in this novel are already occurring, with one possible exception. The methane threat from offshore drilling and clathrates is mostly contrived; that is, there is no proof that these yet pose a real threat. Still, our lack of knowledge on Arctic Ocean methane emissions is threatening in itself and should be a cautionary warning regarding offshore drilling in the arctic, among other related threats such as oil spills. Other climate impacts portrayed are serious and present dangers, including methane release from melting permafrost, loss of shellfish and corals from ocean acidification, and especially desertification of the African Sahel, Syria, and other sub-tropical regions caused by global warming.

Regardless of the methane threat, rapid increases in atmospheric CO_2 in the past 50 years certainly are a legitimate concern and not simply *doom and gloom* from climate scientists; the concept of a disastrous *tipping point* in our climate is also believed by many climate scientists to be a potential apocalyptic menace to mankind. If that tipping point is reached, all life on Earth would be at great risk. These are the real reasons why I wrote this novel. As Ivan Mazurenko said, "This simply cannot be allowed to happen!"

I sincerely hope you will enjoy the novel, but more importantly, I hope that it will help galvanize more of us to do more to protect planet Earth, the only planet available to us.

Acknowledgements

The author acknowledges the input and encouragement of many people, but especially: Esther Hart, who gave immense moral support while being a concise editor; Dr. Julian Brimelow, for his very helpful scientific comments, as well as our years of working together on counteracting the climate denialist community; friend Bev Cooper, who read the first version and provided helpful feedback and support. Thank you all.

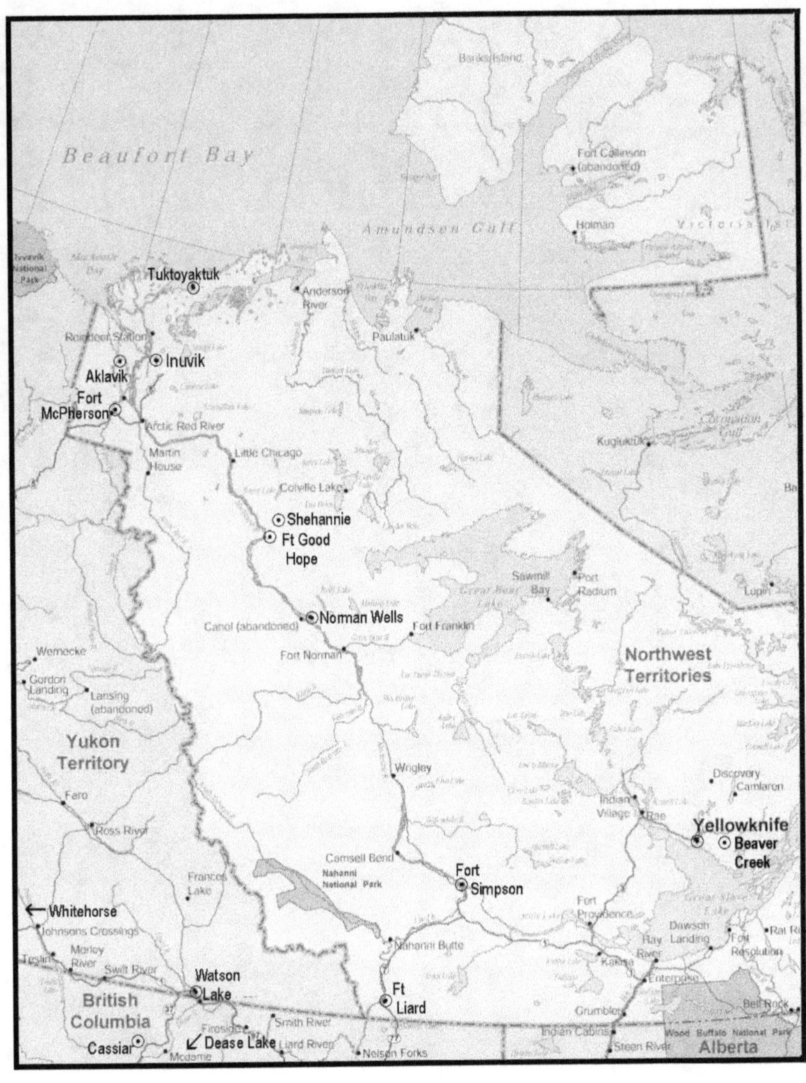

Locations where Julia and John took methane readings in
Northern Canada.

In memoriam to *Chase*, my constant, loyal, Golden Retriever companion, who just moved on from this world. See you in the next, my buddy.

Dedication

Dedicated to Phyllis, my biggest supporter and toughest critic, who also happens to be my wife of more than 50 years; to those working to reverse the present imbalance of atmospheric greenhouse gases and the impacts of global warming on Planet Earth, the only planet available to us; to future generations from whom we have borrowed this land; and especially to my great-grandchildren, as yet unborn, who will live with whatever environmental legacy we leave them. To the latter I say, "I did my best to help ensure your future. I apologize if it was not enough."

Table of Contents

Prologue—Early Signs

Arctic (2011):

Atuat Kunuk looked out over the ice north of Pond Inlet in Nunavut in April 2011. For many of his 55 years he had hunted seal on the ice during spring, but this year much of the ice was not safe. He no longer used dog teams, instead relying on his snowmobile, so he continued around the coast to a location where he knew the ice was thickest. Reaching it, he surveyed the ice. Satisfied that it was safe, he roared out over it, heading eastward toward Baffin Bay. He passed several polar bears along the way, suggesting that there were seal not far off. Finally, he stopped short of an open lead, checking his rifle to make sure it was loaded just in case of an encounter with a polar bear. He did not shoot seal, as bullets ruined the seal's coat, preferring his old harpoon. He stood near the water's edge and patiently waited

An hour later, he saw the water stir, just a little, and tensed with his harpoon ready. Always alert for bears, he suddenly heard a crunching sound behind him. Suspecting a bear, he immediately dropped the harpoon and grabbed his gun. Turning around he realized that the crunching was just a prelude to the very loud crack that followed. To his shock he realized that the ice that he was on had separated from the much larger ice sheet. The water he had just seen stirring was a current. Already his piece of ice had moved 20 feet off the main sheet. He was trapped!

Members of Atuat's band found his frozen body weeks later when the ice floe grounded on the east coast of Baffin Island.

* * *

Philippines (2013):

Manny Rizal was a shopkeeper in Tacloban, Philippines on the evening of November 7, 2013. The Office of Civil Defense had been warning everyone about the danger of Typhoon *Yolanda* that was supposed to hit the east coast of the Philippines the next morning. Manny had reluctantly barred up his shop, careful to nail sheets of plywood over all the windows. He had experienced typhoons before, but the typhoon warning described *Yolanda* to be of record proportions. *Hard to believe*, he thought. *The weather seems so fine. Yet, there is a distant band of dark cloud down on the horizon to the east*, he corrected himself.

The next morning, he woke at 5:00. It was sunny, but the winds had picked up. He quickly ate and went outside. People were stirring all over the city. He could hear horns blaring as many decided to leave the city. By 7 AM, he had checked at his shop. The winds were quite strong and rain had started. As he walked home, he suddenly felt an urge to run, for it was difficult to walk straight with the wind. He realized that he was close to sea level and thought of the possibility of a storm surge onshore. Suddenly he was terrified. People were dashing everywhere, trying to find cover. Behind him he could see roofs lifting off buildings. It was too difficult to stand on his feet. He crawled to a concrete and steel building where someone was motioning him inside. Thankfully he made it. Together they made their way up to the second level, away from any windows, fearful of the storm surge risk. Two hours later, the wind had abated. They went outside and saw the unbelievable devastation of their city. Vehicles had been lifted and thrown about. Not a single wooden structure had a roof intact. They saw bodies lying in the street. They heard a siren behind them, then a loudspeaker telling everyone to get back inside. Manny then realized they were in the calm eye of the typhoon. Further wind and destruction was to follow shortly. Never before had a hurricane of such intensity hit on land. Even Hurricane *Katrina* in 2005 had weakened to Category 3 by the time it was over New Orleans. *Yolanda*, known to the outside world as Typhoon *Haiyan*, remained a Category 5 storm all the way across the Philippines. Later, Manny recalled that scientists had been predicting more frequent and more intense hurricanes as the climate heated up. His shop was destroyed, but some of his goods were salvageable and he still had his life. He could start over again.

* * *

Orona Atoll, South Pacific (2015):
   Jacob Sikua was a fisherman who lived with his family on the Orona Atoll in the South Pacific. Orona was a narrow ribbon of land surrounding a sizable lagoon, covering nine by four kilometres, with a maximum elevation of only nine metres.

Their old home, built on wooden stilts on the shoreline, had gradually been inundated by water, a result of a sea-level rise from thermal expansion as the South Pacific Ocean warmed up. For the last five years they had used their former home as a boathouse for several boats they used for fishing and making their way around the lagoon to pick coconuts.

On March 12, 2015, the crew of an American navy boat arrived to warn Jacob and his family of a developing Cyclone, *Pam,* that could hit their island. The crew offered to take the family on-board their battleship for safety. Jacob resisted at first, but with a little persuasion the Americans managed to take the family on-board and drop them off at the Marshall Islands. Two days later, Jacob was told that their island had been devastated. The Americans flew Jacob back over the island so he could see for himself that the storm had removed all traces of their home and boats. Jacob was given some re-training as a carpenter on the Marshall Islands so that he could continue to support his family in their new home.

* * *

Ahousaht First Nation, West Vancouver Island (2018):

Lewis Sam was looking forward to collecting his first butter clams of the year on March 1, 2018. Lewis was a member of the Ahousaht First Nation band near Bamfield on the west coast of Vancouver Island. His sales of spring butter clams were his main source of income each year. The Ahousaht are the largest Nuu-chah-nulth Nation on the island, and the Sam family were kings of the butter clam trade in the area. Lewis had his own long stretch of beach, accessible only by boat. He started digging in the rough sand and immediately found several clams, but something appeared wrong with them. Their shells were very soft, almost as if they had no shell at all. He placed these back in the hole he'd dug, covered it, then started digging a few feet away, with the same result.

Lewis tried many more holes that day. All he found were butter clams with very soft shells, and none of them appeared healthy. He recalled hearing about ocean acidification, the result of the oceans absorbing more carbon dioxide from the atmosphere, much of it forming carbonic acid in the ocean. Scientists had predicted that this would destroy most corals and shellfish in the world by 2050. *Can't be,* he thought. *They said this might happen within 25 years, but not yet!* He decided to collect several of the sickly clams and have them analyzed by Fisheries and Oceans Canada (DFO). He knew that one of the band members was flying out of Bamfield for Victoria that evening and could deliver his samples to the DFO office at Patricia Bay near the airport.

While waiting for the results, Lewis tried a few more locations the rest of that week, all with the same result. Three days later, a scientist from DFO called Lewis and made arrangements to meet him the following day at Bamfield to visit the site for more samples. He told Lewis that their analysis suggested low pH readings, meaning acidic sea water, and it was likely that the soft shells resulted from this. Together they collected more samples of both clams and offshore water.

Several days later, the same scientist called back to Lewis, confirming their worst fears, that the water was definitely more acidic. DFO was gearing up to collect more samples along the west coast of Vancouver Island and placed an immediate ban on shellfish until final results were available. Those results came quickly, confirming that all shellfish appeared to be affected by the acidic waters, even lobster. A total ban on shell fishing was announced on March 25. This was devastating to the band, as most of their people depended on the shell fishery. In April, the provincial government promised financial assistance for the remainder of the year. Similar results were found later that year all along the west coast of North America, from Mexico all the way to Alaska. Shell fishing was terminated, and with it, the livelihood of fishermen like Lewis Sam.

* * *

Germany (2020):

Mahmoud Wassouf looked across the Rhine River from his apartment in Bonn, Germany. He had recently completed his PhD at the Munich University of Applied Sciences. Predictably, his thesis had focused on climate impacts on Syrian agriculture, and he had just accepted a one-year appointment as a postdoctoral fellow at the German Institute of Agriculture in Bonn. His thoughts were on his father, murdered just prior to the Syrian civil war in 2011. *Now I know what went wrong on our farm, and it was not your fault.*

* * *

It was back in July of 2008 that Mustafa Wassouf had gazed out at his formerly prosperous farm, east of Aleppo in north-central Syria, and sighed. He started to speak to his 12-year old son, Mahmoud, who stood by his side, but his voice caught with emotion.

"What is it, Papa? Something is bothering you?"

"Very much so, son. Something has gone badly wrong in the last five years. Believe it or not, but this piece of desert used to be a beautiful field of wheat. We provided grain for bread for many Syrians, even exported our grain to Europe. And down there," he pointed southwest, "toward the Euphrates River, we had an olive grove, the very best olives in Syria. Turn around toward the northeast. Do you remember five years ago playing in that pond there that no longer has any water? It used to be a watering hole for the cattle we no longer have, and all around it was pasture for the cattle."

"But Papa, it's all desert. You can't grow crops or grass on desert. Even I know that. But I do remember the pond. Maysoon and I used to make mud pies there. Where has all the water gone?"

"That's what's wrong, Mahmoud. All the water has gone, and I don't know why. But it seems that the southern desert," he pointed southward, "has moved into the north here. Perhaps Allah is angry with us because there has been so much trouble in Syria."

Mahmoud shuffled his feet in the sandy soil and looked down. "Am I the cause Papa? Is Allah angry with me? You said the land was good five years ago."

"No, no, no, son. Certainly not! Allah loves all children. I don't know the reason, but I do know that you and your sister, Maysoon, are not the problem. We have been very blessed with you two."

Mustafa paused, then went on, "Mahmoud, there's something else that I need to tell you. Your mother and I have decided to leave Syria. There is nothing left for us to make a living on this land any more. But we did have some good years before, so we have some money invested in Europe, in Germany. There is going to be bad trouble in Syria soon, so we plan to leave early next year. Next week we will all go to the city, to Aleppo first, while I make all our applications. I have contacts in Germany where I used to sell my wheat and olives. I know I can get a job farming there, and you and Maysoon will get a good education. Perhaps you will become a scientist, even, and discover what went wrong in Syria with the land and water. Maybe even come up with a solution to restore things as they were years ago?"

"Yes, Papa. I will. I promise."

* * *

That was twelve years ago, Mahmoud thought. Unfortunately, his father had never made it to Germany. They had moved off the farm to Aleppo while making plans for their big move. But Aleppo had become over-crowded, mostly with people moving in from rural areas where they could no longer farm. Overcrowding in the city helped to provoke social and political unrest. The ruling dictator, Bashar al-Assad, started a major crack-down. When the army started patrolling the streets, it became dangerous to meet in small groups. Just days before they were to board a flight to Germany, Mustafa and his family were shopping for last-minute supplies. A riot broke out nearby. Before they knew what was going on, the army opened fire. Mustafa and Mahmoud were caught in the crossfire. Mustafa was shot while covering his son on the ground. He died instantly. His mother grabbed Mahmoud and Maysoon by their hands and screamed, "Run children, run."

A few days later, they managed to board their flight to Germany, all three of them distraught and in shock over the loss of the head of their family. They had originally planned to settle near Munich in southern Germany, where Mustafa had a job waiting for him to manage a farm. Now that opportunity had been destroyed. However, Mahmoud's mother was well educated and soon found a job as an assistant librarian in Munich. Both Mustafa and Maysoon finished high school there. Maysoon was a talented singer. She entered the German Academy of Fine Arts in Munich where she excelled. Mustafa kept his promise to his father. He went to university in Munich and became an agricultural scientist.

Now as he gazed onto the Rhine, his thoughts turned back to his father of 12 years before. He spoke out loud saying, "How could you know that global warming caused the desert to expand northward and ruin our farm? I can't restore it myself, but I promise you I will work toward solving the problem."

1. Warning Symptoms

Dr. Ivan Mazurenko stared at the data for atmospheric methane concentration and could scarcely believe his eyes. *Surely it can't be,* he thought. *There must be something wrong with our calibration.* He zeroed in on the methane results—4020 ppb, well over double what one should expect. He knew that global values had been rising more rapidly than usual for the past 10 years, but nowhere had anyone reported values higher than 1900 ppb. *Must be just local to our drilling here—has to be,* he thought. Recently the state-owned petroleum company had been confirming lucrative fields of gas and oil at Ice Station Nikita on the Barents Sea, and were under contract to the China-Uzbekistan-US Oil Network (CUUON) to prepare for major production by spring. Ivan called up his field office in Belushya Guba on Novaya Zemlya Island where his graduate student from Moscow University carried out chemical analyses. "Hello Demyan."

"Good morning, Professor Mazurenko. What would you like?"

"How have your methane readings been going? What are you reading just now?"

"As a matter of fact, I was going to ask you the same question, because our methane concentrations have been rising steadily for two days. We are now at 2300 ppb, and I'm wondering whether there's a problem with my instrumentation."

"Exactly what I first thought, but I fear that it's real. I'm getting readings above 4000 ppb on Nikita, and they continue to rise slowly."

"I was speaking with Diana this morning in Murmansk. She said she had readings just over 2100 ppb, so I asked her to re-check all her data. She got back an hour later and said it was then over 2150 ppb."

"I want you to monitor this hourly, and call back Diana to do likewise. If our data prove correct, and these concentrations continue to rise, then the whole world could be in very serious trouble."

"I will. Bye."

Ivan turned to his on-site student, "Nikolai, you know how important this is. I want you to upload *all* our methane data to my Canadian colleague's server in Canada right away."

"Of course, but are we allowed to do that?"

"No, but I'm afraid we cannot keep this secret any longer, and our work might be terminated once our head office in Moscow learns about this. Likely we won't even get to work on the data after that. But the truth must go out, and my friend Dr. Nicholson is my best bet."

"Consider it done within the next hour", replied Nikolai.

"Good. Now I must call Dr. Nicholson and alert him to this. Let's go for coffee after you're done with the upload in an hour or so, and we'll discuss how to approach this with our superiors. I want to be certain that your career, and Demyan's and Diana's will not be affected or tainted in any way, so you and I need to have our story straight."

Ivan knew that these values were unprecedented and that he must alert others, but he also knew that the Russian government would not tolerate any slow-down in their drilling program. Besides, his methane monitoring was not part of the drilling program, and he was using state funds to do this additional work without approval. Ivan was head of the Department of Atmospheric Chemistry, University of Moscow, and years before he had become concerned about the increase in atmospheric greenhouse gases from burning fossil fuels. This led him into climate change research, and eventually he became a member of the Inter-governmental Panel on Climate Change (IPCC), working on the third assessment report (AR-3) released in 2001. One of his team members was Dr. Eric Nicholson. They had become working colleagues, as well as good friends.

Ten minutes later, Ivan was in his office calling Eric via his satellite phone. Ivan knew that Eric had just returned from a climate conference that day. Eric picked up the phone after two rings.

"Good evening; Eric here."

* * *

Carol had arrived home that afternoon in late November, completely exhausted from her stressful weather forecast shift at Vancouver Weather Centre. Her husband, Eric, an internationally recognized climate scientist at the University of

Vancouver (UVan), had preceded Carol's arrival by several hours. Meeting her at the door with their Golden Retriever, Buddy, he recognized Carol's exhausted state. "Here, Hon, you look like you need a good stiff drink. I made your favorite."

"Thanks. You're right, just what I need. I'm really bushed! And how are you, sweetheart", as she patted Buddy. They both sat down in the living room. "How was your climate conference in Denver? Anything new, especially anything on sea surface temperatures?"

"The conference went really well, and yes, there is a lot of concern for those warm sea surface temperatures off the coast of Florida, if that's what you're referring to. It seems to be developing parallel with this latest El Niño in the Pacific. But what happened with you today? You look done in."

"Not just today. It's what's been going on with weather systems these last few weeks—quite unusual—with that warm water off Florida, plus the eastern Pacific El Niño. They seem to be causing strange weather effects all over the continent!"

Eric, sipping his favorite rum and coke, continued, "Those two areas of warm sea surface temperatures were a major topic of discussion throughout our conference. Sea surface temperatures exceeding 25°C off Florida are quite unprecedented for November. But, there is still cold Arctic air driving quite far south through the middle of the continent. And when that cold air mass, with temperatures of only 5-10°C, hits the warm surface water along the southeast coast of the US. *You* know what happens then! The latest global climate model runs support the contention that these sea surface anomalies are an effect of climate warming. After all, over 90% of all the heat generated in the atmosphere goes into warming the oceans."

"Why does this have such a dramatic effect now? Why not one or two decades ago?"

"We've been expecting this to happen eventually. It's simply taken decades to heat deep enough layers of the oceans for it to really start showing up at the surface. Those are not the only warm sea surface anomalies around the globe, although obviously the most striking for North America. The climate models also suggest that this current El Niño will be a record one, likely stronger than either the 1998 or 2015 Super El Niños. But for North America, we're equally concerned about the

Florida anomalies and the fact that the affected area of warm ocean is expanding, even this late in the year."

"Whatever is causing it is impacting on weather patterns everywhere. We've had early snowstorms in the Maritimes, unusually dense fogs in southern Ontario, multiple gawd-awful late tornadoes and severe hailstorms on the prairies last month—in October for crying out loud! And this windstorm on the west coast that has power out all over Vancouver Island. It seemed like we were in teleconference with the numerical weather prediction gurus in Montreal all day today!"

"I'm more concerned about what will happen later this winter as the usual cold air masses develop over the Arctic," Eric added somberly, "because that doesn't bode well for east coast storms this winter if these warm sea temperature anomalies persist. That cold air will explode into storms over the warm water. And if the anomalies then continue through next summer, as they likely will, I shudder to think what energy impulses that might provide to next year's hurricanes, probably ones earlier in the season too!

After a moment's pause, "Changing the topic, where are the kids?"

"Some kids! John has been busy with mid-terms, but he should be home shortly. Julia is at the library, doing some preliminary work for her PhD thesis, on ocean oil spills I believe."

"Good area," said Eric. "We need some young legal minds at work if we're going to prevent more pipeline construction across BC. That proposed northern pipeline terminating at the port of Kitimat is still on the books, but the coastal region around there has some of the most dangerous waters on the globe. An eventual oil spill along that coast would be a high probability if the revived pipeline proposal goes through, despite what government has been telling us for years. But perhaps even worse, they're also planning a double pipeline down the Mackenzie Valley to Tuktoyaktuk, one to carry Beaufort Sea gas south to US markets, the other to bring oil sands heavy crude north for shipping to Asian markets. The energy industry, and in many ways the federal and provincial governments, are paying only lip service to all the environmental concerns that have been raised. It's sheer madness to consider only economic concerns. And so far, the only ones applying any legal resistance on either pipeline are First Nations groups."

"There's an interesting connection there," Carol replied. "Last night on CBC News I heard that your old friend, Matthew Keller, was part of the exploratory group for one of the pipelines, the Mackenzie one I believe. He was interviewed by Jean Simmonds, who asked him why he supported the pipeline project, when, as a climate scientist, he must be aware of the global warming threat caused by burning fossil fuels. Keller maintained the old line that the climate threat is far overblown, and that our economy is absolutely dependent on getting oil and gas to markets in the US and Asia. He alluded to the Companions for Climate Stability website, with the usual claim that it shows proof that fossil fuels are not causing global warming."

"The same old convenient mistruths, and he should know, since he wrote much of that drivel. And yet, many unsuspecting members of the public continue to believe some of that crap, which is why he can get away with it. I'm afraid that, as climate scientists, we have not been doing a very good job of informing the public on the truth about climate change."

Just then, Buddy bounded towards the front door to greet John, who at 21, was a tall, handsome young man in his third year of environmental engineering at UVan. He was serious about his studies, or anything else that he took on. Playing soccer and hockey on his varsity team, he also kept himself in good physical condition. "Hi Dad, Mom, are you two discussing something I shouldn't hear (ha)?"

"We're just catching up on how you and Julia have been behaving this week—ha! How are things going for you?"

"Oh, can't complain. Our semester finals start next week. I'm not really too worried. But I did get some other good news today. I have my preferred Co-op job for the spring term, working on road design and environmental concerns for that new highway through northern BC. And guess what! My buddy Tony has a job with the same company, doing software design and development on the same project."

"That IS great news, John. Ahh, Tony? Oh, I know, you mean Tony Bradley, the software geek."

"Yeah, and the company provides housing and meals so we can save most of our money for next term. Plus, I get to apply some environmental engineering to the task. I'm really happy about that. How was your conference in Denver, Dad?"

"Oh, much of the usual. Maybe some unusual things. There's always something unusual about the atmosphere these days."

"Yeah, Mom was explaining to me last evening about this new ocean temperature warming off Florida, how it will feed more energy to winter storms. Is this another impact from global warming?"

"Almost for certain, although officially we don't say so because there are other factors. But if it persists for very long, we expect severe late-winter snowstorms. It could also help energize Atlantic tropical storms later next summer and fall."

"That reminds me. I have a science-elective course next semester and plan to register for your Climate Change 202 course. I hope that doesn't cause either of us any problem. I need to know as much as possible about future climate for my Environmental Engineering degree."

"Why, that's great, son. Of course I don't mind. You'll just have to do twice as much work as the other students!"

"Great! And you probably mean that, too."

Carol interjected at this point, "Well, you two, what about dinner? Who's cooking?"

"Neither of us," Eric replied. "If you're up to it, I'm taking us all out to dinner."

Julia, coming through the door, "Did I hear the magic words, that Dad is taking us out to dinner? Whoo-hoo!" Julia was an outgoing girl, very pretty, if not outright gorgeous like her mother. She obviously had some of her parents' brains as well. Julia had an almost perpetual smile and laughing eyes that immediately attracted anyone to her, but let her encounter cruelty, selfishness, or injustice of any kind to obtain her disapproval, then her glare could pierce rocks. Competitive swimming and canoeing were her primary physical activities. Julia was a brilliant 25-year old PhD candidate in environmental law at UVan.

Carol replied, "Sounds like it's unanimous then. Let's go!"

* * *

After returning home that evening, The Nicholsons continued their discussions for two hours. Eric was pleased to learn that Julia was keen on picking a topic on environmental law for her PhD degree. And further, that John was interested enough in environmental engineering that he planned to take a course in climate science. *I wonder where all this will lead,* Eric thought.

It was just 10 PM. Carol had headed off to bed a short while before, since she had an early shift at the weather office the next morning. Julia and John were in the kitchen discussing their programs at UVan. Eric turned on the TV to catch the CBC news before heading off to bed. There was an extended report on Russian oil and gas discoveries in the Barents Sea. Apparently a huge new reservoir had been confirmed by a multi-national conglomerate that included Russian, Chinese and American petroleum interests. *Hmm, CUUON, same group that Ivan and Malcolm are involved with.* Just then the phone rang. Eric picked it up right away. "Good evening; Eric here."

"Ah, my good friend, this is Ivan, calling from Ice Station Nakita. I hope you are well, and I hope you don't mind me calling you at home. I believe it is about 10 PM there, is it not?"

"That's right. I am very well indeed, and *you* may call at any time you wish, at my office or at home. It is always good to hear from you, Ivan. I was just listening to the news about the new oil and gas discoveries in your area. And how are you?"

"I'm quite well Eric, but I'm afraid the news is not good. I should clarify, that I believe our data are extremely good, but my situation is more tenuous than I had expected. Before I go further, however, communications are very poor right now as we are in the middle of a solar storm, so in case my satellite phone gets cut off, let me tell you that we have already uploaded our latest results to your server. Please check in the morning that you have received those okay. "

"My post-doc assistant and I will look over the data first thing tomorrow. However, I do hope you can make it to the summit, as we are at a critical stage. Things are about to become rather controversial."

"Perhaps more controversial than even you thought! We're getting very large increases in atmospheric methane concentrations in the area over and around the Barents Sea. We know that oil drilling is releasing methane, but that alone would not explain what we are seeing—values of atmospheric concentrations exceeding 4000 ppb, when maximum global values recorded at Mauna Loa were less than 1900 ppb up to now. The only logical explanation for such high values is the release of methane from clathrates over the continental shelf areas. These methane clathrates are typically confined mostly to off-shore depths of less than 200 m, where the waters are too cold for methane release. But, we've had a few collapses of the continental shelf from all the drilling going on, and perhaps these have been more serious than I thought, resulting in clathrates sinking into the deeper and warmer waters below 200 m."

"That is indeed serious if it's true. I presume you have made all the usual checks of equipment, calibrations, and so on?"

"Yes. No errors."

"So you think the clathrates may be sinking down into that 200-1000 m layer where the denser and warmer Atlantic waters intrude?"

"Exactly! As you know Eric, the influx of more saline and warmer Atlantic and Pacific waters into the Arctic Ocean creates a layer of water of up to 5°C warmer than the surface water just below about the 200 m depth. The same applies to the Barents Sea. Due to its higher salinity, that layer of water is denser and stable enough that it does not mix with the near-surface waters. But if the clathrates are falling down into that layer because drilling is causing the shelf to collapse, then those warmer temperatures could be just enough to trigger the release of huge stores of methane; methane that has been sequestered there for possibly a million years or more. And since our mainland atmospheric concentrations are also increasing rapidly now, I'm concerned that a much more significant collapse may have occurred."

"I see", said Eric, somewhat shocked at what he was hearing.

"That's my suspicion, and if I'm right, then we're playing with a very explosive aspect of nature. We must get a moratorium on the drilling until we obtain more concrete information on all of this. But I doubt that my government will admit to any danger, and they're unlikely to tolerate any slow-down in drilling right now. If I'm unable to speak at the February summit meeting, then you must report on these results and what we have discussed. Imagine what could happen with drilling planned all around the Arctic Ocean by half a dozen or more countries. Perhaps we've just hit one pocket here, but we cannot be sure. Do you have any comparable data from the areas where they are drilling offshore in the Canadian Arctic?"

"Nothing that we're aware of, although I know David is concerned about unusually high values of methane over melting permafrost that they measured last summer."

"Yes, that's true with our Arctic tundra too. And with Arctic sea ice disappearing at increasing rates, we have to be concerned eventually about warmer surface waters too, which would release the clathrate methane in any event. We must get them to stop this drilling madness, at least until more test results are available."

"We'll get right onto the analysis tomorrow," said Eric. "Is there anything in particular you want us to look ...?"

They were interrupted by a heavy knocking at Ivan's office door. "Eric, things are getting very tricky for me. I must hang up immediately. You know what to do. I'll contact you again just as soon as I can. One last thing, be sure you look at the data from Hole 14A, the last two weeks. I've not been able to analyze those in detail yet, but I don't like what I did see. Ivan, out."

"Eric out." As Eric hung up the phone, he had a feeling of impending danger.

2. Family Background

Following Ivan's call, Eric thought about his family and colleagues and marveled at how they had come together, all contributing to the same basic cause, the environment.

Eric had spent his early childhood in Nova Scotia, growing up on the Eastern Shore where he and his dad spent many leisure hours sailing, and where he acquired a huge respect for nature and the elements. Eric completed undergraduate studies in physics and meteorology at Dalhousie University in 1985. He went on to graduate work at McGill University in 1987, where his MSc thesis focused on numerical weather predictions of Arctic storms, supervised by Dr. David Pearce, who was then a relatively new assistant professor at McGill. His numerical model simulated major spring storm events that helped initiate spring breakup, with impacts on melting regions of permafrost, the latter being a specialty of Dr. Pearce. Around that same time, Eric met his future wife, Carol, who was completing weather forecasting studies at McGill. The two became engaged during Christmas 1988. By then Carol was an operational forecaster at the Montreal Forecast Office.

Eric reflected on how his friendship with Matthew Keller had eventually broken down. They had pursued parallel theses at McGill and even co-authored a journal article on their modelling during that period. In spring 1989, the same week that Eric was defending his MSc thesis, Dr. Henry Jackson, a climate scientist from the Washington-based Goddard Institute for Space Studies (GISS), visited McGill to give a talk on climate change. Eric and Matthew Keller both found Jackson's presentation stimulating, as he spoke of global warming in a 2X CO_2 atmosphere. Jackson emphasized the threat of reaching a tipping point in global climate, where the climate could eventually switch from predictable long-term dynamic equilibrium into unpredictable metastable equilibrium. He likened dynamic equilibrium to water sloshing about in a bowl, whereas metastable equilibrium was analogous to tipping the bowl over. Once the tipping point is reached, righting the bowl again does not put the water back in it. In a speech to the US Congress just weeks previously, Jackson had warned that a tipping point in our climate might only be a few decades away.

Mankind needed to drastically reduce carbon emissions into the atmosphere. Jackson had dedicated his life toward this purpose.

After conferring with the two graduate students for several hours, Jackson had invited the pair to pursue PhD studies in climate modelling at the University of Maryland, where he was an adjunct professor and had ready access to the most powerful computing facilities in the world. Eric and Keller had both accepted this opportunity. There followed a few hectic months for Eric and Carol as they tied the knot that summer, then spent their honeymoon looking for accommodations near Washington, DC, making the move in late-August.

Eric's thesis research evolved into modelling the variability of global warming under various carbon emission scenarios. This was a new foray for both Jackson and him. Eric tackled it with great enthusiasm, along with fellow PhD student, Samuel Zwane from Tennessee. Eric and Sam became fast friends, with Sam later accepting a faculty position in Durban, South Africa, while Eric eventually wound up at UVan. Eric was a lead author on several key journal papers during his PhD period in Washington, resulting in several postdoctoral research invitations worldwide.

Keller collaborated for a while with other NASA scientists who were analyzing Antarctic ice core data that dated back half million years. During this time, Keller wrote one paper explaining climate variability and atmospheric carbon cycles strictly in terms of solar cycles, specifically the 11-year cycle. He and Eric had many opposing arguments on their thesis results during this period, climaxing in a particularly vehement verbal attack by Keller on the carbon/global warming link in the fall of 1992. They rarely spoke to each other after that event.

During the spring of 1993, while winding up his PhD thesis, a Chinese colleague of Jackson, Dr. Ching Dao, a climate modeller at Bejing University, was invited to be Eric's external examiner for his PhD defense. While in Washington, Dao invited Eric to spend the following year in Beijing as a postdoctoral fellow (PDF), with continued funding from Jackson's grants. Eric and Carol decided that he would accept the invitation.

Eric and Carol travelled to Beijing in Mid September for his postdoctoral research work with Prof. Dao. They spent many hours with Dao and his family and developed strong personal as well as science-related bonds. And now, many years later, Dao's nephew, Chi-Min Chang, had become Eric's PDF at UVan.

Eric returned briefly to the US in January 1994 to give a keynote address at an American Meteorological Society (AMS) Climate Conference in Nashville Tennessee. He also received a prestigious Climate Modelling Award for his PhD work, as his model runs simulated the current climate very closely when both natural and anthropogenic (CO_2) forcing were included. While there, he once more ran into Matthew Keller, who had accepted a job in the Environment Department of CUUON in Houston, Texas the previous fall. Keller congratulated Eric on his award and indicated that he was doing some PhD follow-up work on solar influences on climate trends.

Eric and Carol returned to Canada in June, giving a presentation at the Canadian Meteorological and Oceanographic Society (CMOS) Congress in Ottawa, where he received yet another award for his PhD work. Carol also rewarded him at this time with the announcement that she was pregnant, the baby due the following February. They flew out to Victoria to announce the good news to Carol's parents. They then stopped over in Vancouver for Eric to be interviewed for a teaching position in the Department of Climate at UVan, where his mentor, Dr. Pearce, was now head of that department. In July, after having returned to Beijing to wrap things up there, Eric was offered the UVan position. He promptly accepted and he and Carol returned to Vancouver in late-August.

That fall, Dr. Pearce alerted him to an article by Matthew Keller in *US Energy Magazine*, wherein Keller provided a convincing argument (for anyone without any climate science background), suggesting that atmospheric carbon dioxide cycles were a result of temperature cycles rather than a cause. The article also claimed that the climate had actually been cooling since 1990. Pearce had quipped, "Keller has turned to the dark side, and I guess he's not yet heard about the Mt. Pinatubo eruption in 1991, eh?" Eric was well aware that when Mt. Pinatubo erupted in the Philippines in 1991, it had spread massive amounts of volcanic dust into the stratosphere. The dust subsequently spread throughout much of the Northern Hemisphere, resulting in a minor global cooling event of a few tenths of a degree for almost two years. Warming quickly resumed after that.

Keller appeared to be a sincere individual on the outside, but those who understood the climate system suspected that he was being deliberately deceptive in his views on climate change. Keller was an ambitious person, who had once boasted that one day he would be the Assistant Deputy Minister of the Meteorological Service of Canada (MSC) and would use that as a stepping stone to eventually head up the World Meteorological Organization (WMO). He never did achieve either position. He continued to be negative toward mainline climate science in general and promoted the climate denialist agenda to dismiss the scientific consensus on the extent of global warming. Eric suspected that Keller was receiving funding from large energy sources to discredit climate science and scientists. Years later, the Alberta government revealed that the energy sector had indeed been channeling money through the University of Southern Alberta (UnSA) specifically to fund unscrupulous Canadian scientists for this purpose. Other institutes were also likely used in this way.

Once Eric started devoting his attention to the global warming problem in the mid-1990s, his friendship with Keller ended. By then, Keller was working within the environmental department of CUUON. Keller later obtained an industrial chair position at North Houston University in Houston, funded by and kept on a retainer with CUUON, effectively still an employee. Keller also became one of the most vocal climate denialists and published several papers on this in a dubious journal called *Energy and Atmosphere*; dubious because most such papers would never pass critical scientific review by referees of a respectable scientific journal. The energy in the journal title reflected the funding sources for it, namely the coal, oil, and gas corporate area. Keller and his friends then formed the cooperative denialist group called Companions for Climate Stability (CCS). The CCS was headed by Tom Bolton, of questionable credentials. Their climate information was portrayed on their very professional-looking website using any and all manner of erroneous and cherry-picked data, misconceptions, and outright mistruths. Here one could find any ammunition one needed to be a climate denialist. It was the ultimate source for convenient mistruths on climate change.

Carol delivered a healthy baby girl in February 1995, whom they named Julia after Carol's mother. During the next 25 years, Eric built his reputation on solid climate science, teaming up with the best experts in the field, publishing several journal articles each year and writing two acclaimed textbooks on climate science. He became an active contributor to the IPCC, both as a writer and reviewer. He developed close scientific ties with other climate scientists including Jackson at GISS; Ching Dao at Bejing University; Ivan Mazurenko at the University of Moscow, Russia; former fellow graduate student Samuel Zwane at the University of KwaZulu-Natal in Durban, South Africa, and especially his mentor, David Pearce at UVan. Despite his dedication to research, Eric always devoted some time toward public education on climate change, giving talks at schools and other public functions, while writing a monthly editorial on climate for the Vancouver Times newspaper, as well as other media. Unlike many climate scientists, Eric was adept at explaining complex scientific subjects in plain language for the public.

The United Nations Climate Change conferences, particularly Copenhagen (2009) and Durban (2011), had been failing in their objectives, primarily because scientific results were being outweighed by political, industrial, and economic interests; meanwhile, the well-organized denialist factions captured undue amounts of public and media attention. Then the 2015 meeting in Paris, billed to be the conference that would start the climate on the road to recovery, once again failed to arrive at explicit binding agreements. While 192 countries signed on to the agreement to limit global warming to 2°C, and while most of those later ratified it, their declared national plans were doomed to fall short of the needs for emission reductions.

Out of sheer frustration with this waffling, Eric and several colleagues organized a parallel set of five-day climate summits to be hosted by the major meteorological societies. The first three days were to be restricted to scientific talks. The fourth day was reserved for special interest groups, and the last day was devoted to speeches by invited government leaders and economic experts. Unlike the previous climate change conferences, the climate denialists had little impact in these scientific meetings. The first of these climate summits, CS-1, was scheduled for Bonn, Germany in the upcoming year. Eric would be chairing this first summit.

Emerging from his reminiscing, Eric mused, *I wonder what Keller and his denialist crowd think about this.*

What Eric did not realize at the time was that Keller, through his parent company, CUUON, was involved in the Fort McMurray oil sands development to try and ensure that the proposed Mackenzie Valley pipeline became a reality—*at any cost.*

* * *

The next morning, Eric met with his post-doc, Chi-Min, to go over Ivan's methane data just received. "Run our test program on these new data, Chi-Min. I'll check back with you after my class in an hour."

After class, Eric stopped by to see Professor David Pearce to alert him to the new data. He then checked in with Chi-Min.

"Here are some pre-analysis results that I just carried out, Dr. Nicholson. They are really quite shocking. Dr. Mazurenko had suggested in his notes that if Arctic drilling continues, and if the ice island records from Barents Sea are typical of what to expect, concentrations might exceed 10,000 ppb or more within five years. However, he wanted to draw your attention to the last two weeks of his data. He didn't have a chance to review these results from Hole 14A before sending them on to us. Those two weeks in the data suggest a big spike in concentrations, giving local atmospheric values already exceeding 5000 ppb. What do you think might have caused the spike?"

"My gosh, that is most scary. Hmm, if it isn't a random error, then we really do have a major problem on our hands. I mean, all of mankind does!"

Just then David dropped by. "Ah, there you are, Eric. How are Ivan's data working out?"

"Everything he said is true, and it maybe even worse," Eric replied, "and Chi-Min has checked the analyses back to front. He found something else quite disturbing—this spike in methane in the last two weeks that Ivan did not have time to analyze before forwarding the data to me.

"Wow, I see what you mean. Now I'm really intrigued, because of that anomaly that my grad student found in our permafrost methane data near Inuvik last summer, a local value over 2300 ppb. As you know, we now have a dozen in-situ methane analyzers at various sites across the northern territories and Alaska. At least 11 are still operational. These continue to show increasing values, some near the coast hitting as high as 2700 ppb. And if I'm not mistaken, a peak occurs about the same time as Ivan's data show here. Would you like to come and take a look?"

"Certainly," Eric replied with interest, "and Chi-Min, please come along too. I'm afraid you're in this just as deep as we are."

"No fear," said Chi-Min, "I want to know what's going on too."

Later, over coffee, the three scientists were still discussing the new results.

"I just don't understand it," said Eric. "The spike in Ivan's offshore methane release exactly corresponds with your permafrost spike, but I don't see the physical connection, given that the two sites are, what, 4000 km apart?"

"Yes, at least", David replied.

"What if," Chi-Min interjected, "these methane sources have some physical connection? After all, we know the oil-gas reserves are huge. Is that possible I wonder?"

"Perhaps," said Eric, "but I hope we don't have that additional complication."

David responded, "We know that the global climate has been much warmer in the distant past, for example, during the Great Permian Extinction some 250 million years ago, and that one theory to explain it involved the release of methane from offshore clathrates, just as Ivan is suggesting. Perhaps that explains why at certain times these methane sources break open to the surface, creating a massive global warming and extinction event."

"Good Lord, David. You make a good point, but we don't want to be tampering with those sources ourselves."

David was pensive—then, "I suggest we bring some geophysics experts into the picture and see if they can enlighten us any further. Meanwhile, I'm going to re-check my own permafrost data. This is too big to risk errors."

Eric added, "I'll drop by to see my friend, Kelvin Nordsen, in Geophysics, and see if he can offer some insight into this problem you've raised."

* * *

Eric arranged to meet Kelvin for lunch at the Faculty Club the next day, Wednesday, with David and Chi-Min joining them. They explained to Kelvin that methane has typically produced about 20% of present day greenhouse gas climate forcing, but that this could change dramatically with northern methane release both from permafrost melt in sub-Arctic latitudes and from oil and gas drilling in Arctic coastal areas and offshore. After explaining the latest results on methane, Eric asked, "So, my question is whether coincidental spikes in methane release from Canadian Northwest Territories permafrost and Barents Sea oil drilling could possibly be physically connected?"

"I suppose it is possible," said Kelvin. "I've seen narrow rifts in the Earth's crust that can extend thousands of kilometres. They can connect gas, oil, and even water sources that far apart. So it's not outside the range of possibility. And we've been drilling in the Beaufort Sea since the early 70s, so it is feasible that the connection is through there. This doesn't look good for undersea drilling in the Arctic, does it?"

"It makes for a truly high potential for a catastrophic and runaway greenhouse effect on our climate. It's imperative that we get a handle on this immediately, before there is significantly more offshore drilling. Can you check in with your contacts for any other information on this?"

"I'll get on that right away", Kelvin replied.

* * *

3. Ice Station Nakita Results

Meanwhile, back on Ice Station Nakita, Ivan faced the Russian Army Major who had knocked on his door. "Hello, Major Bracko, what can I do for you?"

"I've been told to check on your work, since Moscow has reason to believe that you may be conducting unauthorized research on methane emissions. Is this true?"

"It's all part of the gas analysis which they asked me to do. There is nothing secret about that."

"You will have to explain that yourself to the Kremlin Science Ministry, as they want me to accompany you back to Moscow this afternoon."

"Very well," said Ivan, somewhat exasperated. "I'm overdue to see my wife anyway."

"Our helicopter will be ready at 3 PM. Your student will need to come with us as well."

Ivan met with Nikolai for coffee shortly after. "Did you carry out that chore, Nikolai?"

"Yes sir, it's all gone."

"Very good. Listen carefully to what I say, because your future will depend on it."

Several hours later, Ivan and Nikolai got into the back seat of the helicopter that would take them to Belushya Guba. They would fly from there to Moscow by military aircraft.

* * *

At the Kremlin Science Ministry in Moscow the following day, Dr. Klarno of the Science Ministry welcomed Ivan. "Good morning, Dr. Mazurenko. I trust your return from Ice Station Nakita was without incident."

"It could hardly be otherwise," Ivan replied curtly, "thanks to Major Bracko and his henchmen."

"That's hardly a fair assessment, doctor," replied Dr. Klarno, "given that you were using your position for unauthorized research. Regardless, you have been invited here to respond to some questions regarding your work and to defend your actions."

"There is *nothing* to defend, Dr. Klarno," Ivan countered. "I have been monitoring gas emissions from such wells for many years. My publications speak for themselves."

"However," Dr. Klarno continued, "your research work is interfering with the job you were engaged to do, estimating gas pressures in support of oil and gas recovery from the Barents Sea, and you are also monitoring atmospheric methane on the mainland and surrounding islands, is it not so? I should warn you that this is something in which the Russian Federal Security Service (FSS) has taken a great interest. In fact, they will undoubtedly want to speak to you themselves."

"I have nothing whatsoever to hide, and additional monitoring is simply a standard procedure in science" Ivan replied.

"But the FSS may think otherwise, so I would advise you to be very careful in what you say. I understand that you have made some rather disturbing discoveries from the data you've collected. Have you shared any of the results yet?"

Ivan bristled a little, "I've made no secret of the fact that I work with a colleague, Dr. Nicholson, in Canada."

"Does he have these data?"

"Of course, we share all our data."

"Hmm, then that complicates our situation considerably."

"No sir! That simply expedites the release of results that are of the utmost importance to the whole world."

"You clearly do not understand the gravity of the situation. You could be jeopardizing the whole economy of Russia, not to mention of China and the U.S."

"I think not! Dr. Klarno, I believe you have children, as I do. Are you not concerned at all just what type of world we may be creating for them? My only hope is that our results are timely enough to stop all the madness concerning the petroleum industry, and curtail carbon emissions before it is too late, if not already. Everyone knows that existing alternative energy sources are adequate to gradually take over from most fossil fuels. Alternative energy will generate a stronger economy than what fossil fuels now support."

"That may well be, but it won't satisfy either CUUON or the FSS."

Ivan sighed, "I'm prepared to take that risk. The alternative of maintaining the status quo with fossil fuels does not look pretty at all."

* * *

Later Ivan entered the FSS office with some trepidation. However, he was not going to bend easily. Besides, his friend and colleague in Canada would ensure that the world knew about his research results.

"Good morning Dr. Mazurenko," said the waiting FSS officer. "Please sit down. My name is Viktor Gruboff." Two other staff members were present, neither of whom Ivan recognized, and Gruboff chose not to introduce them. Ivan glanced about as he sat. He was well aware that this whole meeting was being videotaped. Even his facial expressions would be reviewed later.

Gruboff continued, "We are here to determine the nature of your research and whether you will be allowed to continue with your project. We are cognizant of the fact that some of your data collection and research was not part of the agreement you had when contracted to Ice Station Nakita. Please tell us, in your own words, exactly the nature of your research."

There followed two hours of explanation and cross-examination of his research methods. The results *had* indicated disturbingly high values of methane release from the offshore drilling test wells. Ivan left nothing of importance out, and did not attempt to soften his view that the drilling in the Barents Sea should stop immediately, at least until a thorough review could be carried out. The FSS officers continually interrupted him with questions and statements, casting whatever doubt they could on the results, but Ivan was not deterred in any way.

Finally, Gruboff stated, "I hope you realize that your research results have put us in an awkward and embarrassing situation. We cannot possibly stop this drilling now, especially when the two largest world powers, China and the US, are involved. We are also very concerned about this upcoming climate summit in Bonn and whether you should even participate. How do you think we should proceed?"

"It seems you have a choice to make here. If I don't turn up at this climate summit, it will look very bad for Russia. On the other hand, if I do go, then the world will believe that Russia is genuinely concerned about global warming and the welfare of the whole planet."

"Hmm, that is a point," Gruboff replied. "However, how could we be sure that you would not bring world opinion against us?"

"You can't know. But I still have to return here, so I am hardly going to attack my mother country now, am I?"

"All right! You win this round, but remember what you just said. You could find yourself confined to a remote lab in Siberia, one not very well equipped!"

"One of the other problems we are facing is the potential of methane release from melting permafrost on the tundra, so Siberia might not be all that bad."

Gruboff stood to end the meeting, "I am prepared to recommend that you attend this summit of yours, but the consequences will rest on your shoulders, should it prove embarrassing for Russia. You do understand this?"

"Only too well, but I have children and grandchildren, as perhaps you do. I want to help ensure that they will have a world fit to live in 50 years from now." Before opening the door, Ivan added, "Gentlemen, I sincerely hope you understand just how precarious the climate situation is. We no longer have the luxury of time to think how we can adapt to this. We must start changing immediately, this year, not even a year or two down the road. Change must start now, mark my words!"

* * *

Later at home, Ivan spent the evening relating everything of the past few weeks to his wife, Nania, a scientist and teacher herself.

"I feel as if I've been cooked on a grill today. However, the powers that be are grudgingly allowing me to attend the climate summit."

"That part seems okay," Nania replied, "but obviously other things are not so good. Yes?"

Ivan replied with intense feeling, "Dear, we should consider whether or not to leave Russia. I am certain that my work will eventually be terminated by the FSS. How would you feel about a move to Canada, if we could even leave at all?"

"Whatever happens, darling," Nania said, "I will always support you. If you think we should leave, then let it be.

However, I trust that God must know how important your work is and will show some way to support you. I think you can still work in Russia. Besides, it would be very difficult to leave our families behind, especially Natasha and our grandchildren."

Ivan glanced up, thoughtful. "I don't understand your God, yet you have such confidence when you speak of him, that surely there must be something to it. I may even have to attend your church and learn something myself about this God."

Nania replied, "You would do well to do so, dear. There is far more in the Bible than most people suspect, even about science!"

"Science in the Bible? Surely you are not serious. Give me an example."

"Just for starters, consider the first three verses of Genesis. Those few words alone run parallel to Edwin Hubble's big bang theory for the creation of the universe. But you need to consider that when those words were first spoken and then passed down through traditional storytelling about 4000 years ago, there was no science or mathematics, nor any form of education. Did that person accidentally come up with those verses, or was it divine inspiration?"

"I don't know if I can accept that or not," said Ivan. "Surely there must be better examples?"

"Try the prophet Isaiah," Nania went on, "who lived almost 3000 years ago. He wrote the words, *Every valley shall be exalted, and every mountain and hill shall be made low: and the crooked shall be made straight, and the rough places plain.*"

"But so what; what's important about such a statement? It could simply be just an analogy, saying that the rich will be made humble and the poor inherit the Earth, or something like that."

"Ah, yes," said Nania, "that is exactly how most priests interpret that passage, but think of the geology within the words. How could Isaiah possibly know about geological processes that take millions of years to come to pass? We have only proven such concepts in the past 100 years, with all of science to bear on it."

"Hmm," said Ivan, "I really must think about that one, although you make a good case. I suppose you attribute that to divine inspiration as well?"

"The interpretation is up to the reader," replied Nania.

"Tell me more."

"Too many Christians and Jews do not pay attention to this divine inspiration. It's probably the only way that a scientist (like yourself) could believe in a faith. Just suppose that ...."

* * *

Later, Ivan decided he would read the Bible, one chapter at a time. He started by reading chapter one of Genesis that evening. After some minutes he thought, *Hmm, the chronology of the evolution of life on Earth is the same as in Charles Darwin's 1859* The Origin of Species. *What a coincidence! Or, is it? Umh, no, it can't be, can it?*

* * *

4. Convenient Mistruths

At UnSA in Calgary in early December, CCS chair Tom Bolton, founding member Matthew Keller, and henchman Nick Savage, were meeting with David Brown, Chief of Environmental Engineering of CUUON. Outside, a severe thunderstorm was raging, a rarity for this time of year.

"How is your speaking tour going, Tom?" asked Brown.

"Extremely well! I'm debunking Michael Mann's 'hockey stick' trends and the long-term carbon dioxide/temperature trends from Antarctic data in these talks. It doesn't take too much fiddling with the trends to suggest that CO_2 follows the temperature trend rather than the reverse. Most people latch right on to that!"

"I take it that our funding channel through UnSA is still working out okay?"

"Very well indeed, thank you. We could use some additional travel funds to hit some of the major centres in Ontario and Quebec," Tom added. "Next month Matthew will be speaking at several Chamber of Commerce luncheons in Red Deer, Edmonton, and McMurray before heading to Yellowknife, and he'll be attending the new climate summit in Bonn in February."

My Russian contacts tell me that Dr. Nicholson of the University of Vancouver has received a copy of data from the Barents Sea project from a Dr. Ivan Mazurenko. Those data include some serious information on methane release from the offshore drilling there. That threatens to derail our Barents Sea drilling as well as the Mackenzie Pipeline that we desperately need. We need you, Keller, to keep close tabs on Nicholson's work. See to it that he does not publish anything on those results, and find a way to relieve him of the data. Perhaps you can find something to discredit him as well."

"I have a student called Andrew Vinson in Nicholson's class at UVan to keep an eye on things," said Keller.

"How safe is it to use inexperienced students?" asked Brown. "What if some smart-ass cop gets onto them and blows us wide open?"

"We don't contract people like that directly. We have a computer expert at UnSA, Ted O'Brien, who handles all the hiring and firing directly. He can also crack virtually any computer security system for us. Anyway, Vinson only knows that he is hired through O'Brien.

Brown continued. "My colleagues in the Kremlin Science Ministry assure me that Mazurenko's work is about to be shut down. All his data and results have been seized. If he has anything else, well, there are other means. Still, there is this other set of data in Nicholson's possession that needs to be destroyed."

"Nicholson is more of a problem than Mazurenko," Keller interjected, "as he is quite popular among Canadian media and all of the environmental organizations; not to mention that damn upstart Green Party."

"God damn tree huggers, the whole bloody lot," Brown replied. "They simply have no understanding of basic economics and the value of the oil industry to Canada. It's too bad we don't still have Parker in Ottawa. That would make our job considerably easier."

"Regarding your plant at UVan, your student, that is," Brown carried on, "you're certain he's well beyond arm's length from you, so that if he is uncovered it won't implicate you?"

"No worries there, and no way to trace him back to us."

"Do whatever you must, but don't discredit or implicate CUUON in any way, or you'll be on your own. I trust you are well aware of that? Okay, gentlemen, time moves on. I'm due back in Houston tomorrow, so I leave you to your vices. Ciao!" Brown was out the door before any further response was possible.

"Hmphh! I guess we know where their loyalties lie," Bolton reflected. "Any ideas what we can do to discredit Nicholson?"

"I've known him since early grad school at McGill. His record is squeaky clean," Keller replied. "If only we could find out some dirt on him, something to bring his honour into question?"

"Maybe we need to be a little creative then ...," Bolton pondered.

"What do you mean?" asked Keller.

"Suppose he got caught cheating with his data? Or maybe fooling around with a grad student? Even fixing his travel claims, like some of those Senators were doing a few years back.

Meanwhile, have you thought of some way to destroy those critical data?"

"Hmm, why not leave me with those thoughts for a while. I have some ideas there. Nick and I already have an alternative plan for Mazurenko just in case the Kremlin chaps can't shut him up, but Nicholson is a trickier problem."

"I can ensure that Nicholson stays quiet," Nick Savage finally spoke up.

"No, not that. At least not yet."

"Okay," Bolton replied, "but we need to come up with something fast, a convenient mistruth to shake his credibility before that climate summit in February. After all, what's one or two fall guys if we can salvage the economy and our company profits, not to mention our own pockets?"

* * *

Later, Keller met with O'Brien at UnSA, "Ted, I need you to hire another casual person, a good-looking chick specifically, who could put the make on a troublesome friend of ours."

"Is this a frame-up you want? Trying to discredit someone?"

"Exactly. It's for Dr. Eric Nicholson in the Climate Department at the University of Vancouver. He needs to be caught in a, well, a compromising situation, if you get my drift. I suspect you can come up with someone from the red light district of Calgary?"

"Oh, I probably can. In fact, I know of a young lady who might enjoy a paid trip to Vancouver and back."

"I knew I could count on you. We need this person to pretend she's a student interested in climate change and request an interview with Nicholson to ask some questions. She will ensure his office door is closed, then get him to ..., you can use your imagination for the rest. Afterward, she should feign innocence and claim that Nicholson tried to seduce her in his office. Perhaps he'll even come through with flying colours on his own. Oh, and the usual condition applies. I know absolutely nothing about this."

"You got it. Leave it to me."

5. Global Warming Impacts
and African Connection

In early-January when classes had resumed at UVan, Eric was lecturing his Climate Change 202 class one morning.

"The source of most atmospheric pollution and of carbon emissions is the industrial world, primarily at middle latitudes. This includes Canada, the US, Europe, Russia, Japan, and China. However, the most obvious global warming impacts to date have been felt on either side of the mid-latitudes, in the Arctic and sub-Arctic and in tropical and subtropical countries. This raises moral and ethical concerns. Among the impacts, let me list the following." Eric displayed a series of slides, starting with North Africa.

"I'll mention first the Sahel region of Africa, where there is evidence of an agricultural economy dating back at least 5000 years. Here, the main problem is desertification, stretching from Senegal and Mauritania in the west, to the Sudan, Eritrea, and Ethiopia in the east. As the climate heats up, the subtropical high pressure belts that maintain the world's great deserts are intensifying, so that these subtropical deserts are also intensifying and slowly expanding. The expansion includes the Sahara Desert north of the Sahel band, squeezing it up against the equatorial rainforest to the south. The result is more frequent and more prolonged droughts in the past 30 years over the Sahel, severe famine, and intense competition for remaining arable land and water. Indirectly it has led to civil wars and millions of refugees. A similar desertification has been occurring in Syria with the northward expansion of the Arabian Desert. This was a major factor in the civil war which broke out there in 2011 and led to five million refugees escaping to neighbouring countries around Syria. Many millions more were displaced within their country."

Displaying a map of the South Pacific east of Australia, Eric continued, "A second impact is sea-level rise due to thermal expansion of tropical ocean waters as they heat up, particularly low-elevation South Pacific islands such as some of the Solomon and Vanuatu Islands. This has already caused some early but permanent evacuations from low-lying islands where people have lived for thousands of years. Sea-level rise will accelerate worldwide in the coming decades, with continued melting of the ice sheets of Greenland and Antarctica."

Showing a satellite image of a series of tropical storms over the Pacific Ocean just north of the equator, Eric pointed out, "The third impact is also due to warming sea-surface temperatures (SSTs) in the subtropics, resulting in more frequent and more severe tropical storms and hurricanes that are spawned over and feed on warm sea surface temperatures, that is, temperatures greater than 26°C. Category 4 and -5 hurricanes such as *Katrina* (2005) and Typhoon *Haiyan* in the Philippines (2013) are becoming more common.

"A fourth major global impact is ocean acidification. This rather insidious problem became evident about 30 years ago. It is due to the increased absorption of atmospheric CO_2 into the oceans, which, mixed with water and following various chemical reactions, produces carbonic acid. The acid breaks down the calcium carbonates of corals and shellfish in tropical oceans. Some studies suggest that corals and shellfish may be non-existent by 2050, contributing to drastic food shortages worldwide.

"And last, but certainly not least, is the warming of the Arctic and sub-Arctic, including the northern regions of Canada, Alaska, and Siberia. This is where warming temperatures have been greatest, but also where the impacts are most varied and widespread. While the mean global temperature has warmed about 0.5°C since 1980, parts of the Arctic are heating up at a rate of 2°C or more per decade! The only positive factor here, if one can call it that, is that these regions are sparsely populated, with little more than one million inhabitants in total and only about 100,000 in Canada's north. However, what happens in the Arctic affects the whole globe and all of mankind. The impacts of Arctic warming include melting permafrost, with multiple effects such as damage to buildings, water and sewage lines, and pipelines; and the release of huge stores of methane (CH_4) from the decay of ancient peat moss bogs lying beneath the melting permafrost. Although less prevalent in the atmosphere than carbon dioxide by about two orders of magnitude, equal masses of methane are about 30 times more effective as a greenhouse gas. It therefore causes a positive feedback to the global warming problem. Methane is also found in natural gas deposits, readily released with fracking operations. And more recently, methane clathrates have been found in marine sediments in the Arctic offshore. These lie in very cold water on the near-shore continental shelf at depths of 100 meters or so.

So methane is released whenever offshore drilling takes place or when coastal waters warm up. We've recently seen dramatic increases of atmospheric methane over northern regions, so this has become a very serious concern.

"Secondary effects of these Arctic impacts include the inability for most vegetation and much of the wildlife to adapt quickly enough, causing whole species to go extinct; the draining of surface ponds and lakes as the underlying permafrost melts, affecting migration patterns of all migratory animal and bird species; the loss of winter ice-roads; earlier spring breakups; and melting Arctic sea ice. The latter decreases the overall summer albedo, another positive feedback to global warming. And finally, we have to contend with the melting ice sheets of Greenland and Antarctica, accelerating the rate of global sea-level rise and changes in ocean currents due to changing ocean temperatures and salinity.

"That's a quick summary. Are there any questions?"
Andrew Vinson raised his hand, "Professor Nicholson, haven't many of these impacts in our climate occurred before? I mean, is the Sahel suffering any more than it has in the past with drought periods?"
"Good question. But while drought and water shortages have always occurred over the Sahel at different times, this particular drought has been ongoing for three or four decades, much longer than any previous drought in recorded history. Climate science has been warning about the increased frequency and severity of these threats since the 1980s. The influence of global warming is now incontrovertible. Most western governments and media generally attribute current local wars and refugee problems to fighting between various ethnic and religious factions, but the root cause is really global warming and the resulting competition for arable land and water. Unless we can reduce emissions and try to reverse climate warming, these impacts are likely to become

permanent. And then there's the danger that we are fast approaching a tipping point in our climate, beyond which natural Earth system processes could cause a rapid and drastic shift in our climate, resulting in unpredictable changes that would cause total havoc to our civilization."

Another student put up her hand, "Yes, Amber?"

"Isn't all of this doom and gloom rather on the pessimistic side?" she asked. "I mean, can the problem of global warming be that bad."

"An experimental biologist, Jean Rostand, once said, 'My pessimism extends to the point of even suspecting the sincerity of the pessimists.' Perhaps that's where I stand at this moment, because our pronouncements to date, that is, by climate scientists, have too long been on the conservative side, so that society has become complacent about climate change, as if assuming that some magic technology will be developed to solve the problem. But there is only one sure solution to the problem. That's for mankind to get off the fossil fuel bandwagon as soon as possible. Twenty years from now will definitely be too late."

"Gosh. You really mean that, don't you?"

"I sure do. I'm very, very concerned, not for myself, but for what you people will have to contend with after my generation is gone."

After a moment's pause, "For your next class, Dr. Pearce will give us a guest lecture on the permafrost problem and show you more details on this issue. Then at the following class we'll consider sources of greenhouse gases and discuss ways of mitigating both these sources and their impacts. If there are no more questions then, thank you for your attention this morning. Let's resume this discussion on Wednesday."

* * *

Just before lunch, Eric answered a phone call, "Good morning, Eric Nicholson speaking."

"Eric, this is Sam Zwane calling from Durban, South Africa. I haven't spoken with you in a year or more. How are you?"

"Sam, for heaven's sake, it's good to hear from you. What can I do for you?" He was delighted to hear from his friend with whom he had collaborated at the United Nations Climate

Change Conference at Durban in 2011, and the COP-21 meeting in Paris in 2015.

"I'm calling you for two reasons actually. First, to mention that I plan to present a paper at your climate summit in Bonn next month, so I hope we shall find some time to connect then. But the main reason I'm calling is because I have a PhD candidate, Nelson Tutu, who is writing his thesis on the impacts of global warming on the African Sahel. I am quite impressed with this student and looking forward to his thesis defense, likely next August. I was wondering if you would be so kind as to be his external examiner."

"How coincidental! Would you believe that I just came from my class where I lectured on that very topic, desertification of the Sahel? I would be delighted, but with an added ulterior motive of learning more about this crucial issue."

"That's wonderful, Eric," replied Sam. "Nelson, incidentally, is related to both Archbishop Tutu and the late Nelson Mandela, but that won't affect our consideration of his PhD."

"You may let Mr. Tutu know that I will look forward to seeing an early draft of his thesis."

"I'll have Nelson forward a copy of his thesis proposal today, which we had already accepted last September. He had completed much of his background research before he even submitted his proposal, which is why he's aiming at completing the thesis by next August. Will an email version of his thesis be okay?"

"Most certainly, and I will look forward to meeting Nelson later."

"And I look forward to speaking with you again, in Bonn this February. Thank you so much, and please pass my greetings on to your good wife."

* * *

Following lunch, Eric was in his office. The department secretary, Melanie, observed a provocative-looking young lady, dressed rather inappropriately with a hiked-up skirt, revealing blouse, etc. walking down the corridor. *Well*, she thought, *it's rather unusual for a student to dress like that.* She watched for a few moments, then noted that the young lady was knocking on

Dr. Nicholson's door. *Hmm,* she thought, *I don't think Eric will be too impressed by that approach.*

Eric heard the knock and responded, "Come in."

The young lady entered and asked, "Professor Nicholson?"

"Yes, what can I do for you?"

"I'm interested in taking climate science next semester, but I thought I should speak with you about it first."

"What would you like to know?"

"I just wanted to know how much work is involved," she answered while closing the door. She immediately strolled across the office, hips swaying, and sat on the corner of Eric's desk before he could even react. Her pose was, to say the least, very revealing.

Eric immediately got up, and while crossing the floor to his door, said, "First, it is not a difficult course, as long as you're prepared to do some study and all of the assigned work," opening his door wide, then crossing back to his desk again. "The chairs right here," pointing to one of the chairs in front of his desk, "are for student interviews, by the way. Second, you need to be aware that there is also a lab involved as part of the Climate 202 course, so you need to be prepared to attend three one-hour classes each week, plus spend one afternoon a week in the lab, running various models for different scenarios. As he sat down, the young lady stood up, rather flustered, as Eric added, "Do you have other questions then?"

'No, I don't think so. I …, well, I believe you answered what I needed to know. Thank you." She hastened out of the office.

Melanie was still observing Eric's door, noting that the student had closed the door as she entered. *Correction, I know Eric will not be impressed.* She waited another half minute, first noting Eric immediately re-opening the door, then the young lady departing in haste a few seconds later.

Curious and amused, she walked up to Eric's door and said, "Eric, you didn't entertain that, ah, young lady very long. Did she cause you any problem?"

"No, and frankly her intentions were not honourable. She said she was a student, but I haven't noticed her around before. Have you?"

"Nope, and to be blunt, I don't believe she is a student, not dressed like that. She reminds me of those 'ladies' one sees in downtown Vancouver on Friday evenings."

"Hmm, maybe you could alert campus security about her. If she repeated that with another professor, she could cause a lot of trouble. Since she claimed to be a student, they have the authority to question her, briefly at least, if they can locate her."

"I'll call right away. In fact I saw them at the front door as I was returning from lunch."

"Good, if they manage to catch up with her, they'll report back to you. Let me know if you hear back. I'm somewhat curious to know what her game was."

Half an hour later, Melanie returned to Eric's office with a campus security officer in tow.

"Eric, this officer did indeed interview our student, who's not a student at all, no surprises there. I thought you might be interested in what he found out.

"Yes," the officer said. "She's not a student at UVan, but in fact, was a temporary employee from the University of Southern Alberta. She admitted that she had instructions to try and embarrass you with her little stunt there."

"Was she hired specifically to do that?"

"She clammed up at that point and would not admit anything further. Since she's not a student here, we couldn't question her further without encroaching on her rights.

"I understand. I'll keep this in mind. Thank you Officer."

* * *

That afternoon Eric dropped by Chi-Min's lab to check on the progress he was making with the analysis of the material Dr. Mazurenko had sent in November. Chi-Min immediately asked, "Professor Nicholson, did you suggest that one of your students, Andrew Vinson, speak to me about Mazurenko's data?"

"Not really, why do you ask"?

"He dropped by this morning after your class. I knew him from those two lectures I gave your climate class while you were at the Denver conference. He said that he had spoken with you about supervising his MSc and using these data."

"That's odd. I don't recall him expressing any interest in an MSc, and he's not really that great a student. He's always in class, mind you, but he has not been doing very well in the course. Still, he did register for the 202 class, so he must have some interest."

"I just thought his comments were a little strange, because he was asking what computer the data resided on, things like that. I was rather coy about it and simply said we keep the data on our department computer. But then he specifically asked whether you kept it on your office computer. I simply said, 'I suppose so,' and did not mention that our main work is carried out on our lab computer here."

"Hmm, well, perhaps he is more interested in the science than I thought. We'll see. Anyway, carry on. This analysis is of the utmost importance and must be our highest priority right now."

"That's something else I wanted to mention. Most of the atmospheric methane concentrations exceed 4,000 ppb, and of course we had that one spike of 5000. I will triple-check the computations before we meet tomorrow, but are methane concentrations of 5000 ppb even possible?" Chi-Min asked.

"Professor Mazurenko warned me that the implications were very serious, and I believe your computations are correct, but do another check all the same. Carry on and I'll get Ivan's further thoughts on it when he calls again."

"Right," Chi-Min replied.

6. Environmental Law and Pipelines

In mid-February, Julia walked briskly through the UVan campus on her way to a meeting with her PhD thesis supervisor, Professor Kane Samson, in the Faculty of Law. Both she and her brother, John, had received a solid grounding in atmospheric and climate science simply by growing up in the Nicholson household. So, despite the fact that Julia's academic interests lay in history and law, it was an easy choice for her to choose to study environmental law at UVan under Dr. Samson, an international expert.

Julia had recently completed her academic courses with straight As. She was trying to choose between several potential thesis topics on environmental law. These included ocean oil spills, workplace asbestos, and the use of pesticides. Professor Samson had also mentioned oil pipeline litigations, but she had not yet managed to investigate that topic. Approaching the Law Building, she wondered why Dr. Samson had left an urgent message for her to see him this morning.

She knocked at his door and heard an immediate, "Please enter."

She entered and Dr. Samson looked up. "Good morning Julia. Thank you for coming in at such short notice. I trust you have recovered from exams and the shock over your grades?"

"It was certainly a pleasant shock, I must say," replied Julia. "But I've been too busy to celebrate, as I'm trying to narrow my focus onto a thesis topic."

"You haven't decided on a topic yet, have you?

"Not really, although I am kind of leaning toward the topic of oil spills; still, I'd like to look a little further into this business of pipelines that you mentioned a few weeks ago."

"Wonderful," Dr. Samson replied, "because that's exactly what I wanted to discuss with you this morning. How would you like to take an all-expense paid trip to an exotic location?"

"Ooh, Tahiti maybe, or China?

"Mmm, well, maybe not that exotic. I was thinking of the Northwest Territories, Yellowknife, Inuvik, perhaps other exotic northern sites. I've been offered some funding from North American Pipeline Incorporated, they're usually referred to as NAPI, to investigate potential legal implications of building a northern pipeline from Fort McMurray down the Mackenzie to Tuktoyaktuk, paying particular attention to First Nations concerns. Although they have cleared most of the legal hurdles and are gearing up to build the pipeline, they want to know how valid the concerns of the Dehcho First Nations people may be. I think NAPI's concerns are genuine. In any case, there are no strings attached to the funding, other than for us to provide monthly updates and a detailed report later. Now here's perhaps the difficult part, but which is most important perhaps for your PhD thesis: At some point you will have to evaluate the legal aspects of all this. My advice is to 'take lots of notes', and perhaps not write any evaluation until the trip is over. I suspect that's when your real work will begin."

"I think I understand. I'll be hearing a lot of opinions, and will even have some of my own, but my job is to incorporate what I learn into the legal ramifications."

"I knew you would understand. That's partly why you are my preference for this job. I realize that this pipeline is an issue of your father's, but that need not be a concern in itself. We are not, after all, under any obligation to NAPI in this study other than to file our report. Whoever takes on this project has my word that what they report is entirely their choice."

Looking thoughtful, Julia replied, "Hmm, well, exactly what would I be doing on this trip?"

Samson went on, "You would meet with company experts in Yellowknife. They would brief you on their plans for the pipeline construction and all the safeguards they are building in, as well as on the numerous public enquiries and briefings that they have had in Alberta and the Northwest Territories. Then you would need to make your own arrangements to visit with various First Nations groups, especially the Dehcho, who represent both Dene and Métis people in the Northwest Territories. I have a few contacts you could start with in Yellowknife, Fort Simpson, and Inuvik. I understand that you've been in the Northwest Territories several times with your family."

"Yes, our whole family vacationed there for three summers, two near Yellowknife, most of the other near Fort Simpson. To be honest, that makes it attractive because I love the north. In general the people there are friendly, always willing to help. When Dad was working with Dr. Pearce on permafrost melt, we all decided to make a holiday out of their field work. It was wonderful, because the whole family was able to help them set up data collection sites while having a fantastic holiday. We canoed on many of the lakes east of Yellowknife, among other areas, although I've never been as far north as Inuvik. We also met many of the First Nations people; in fact, one of them was our guide during all three trips. I even learned a little of the Dene language."

Julia went on, "If I took this study on, what if the results appeared negative toward the pipeline? Are you sure there is no obligation to the company *at all*?"

"The answer is an emphatic *no*. I raised that matter with NAPI myself. They assured me that our reports would not be edited by the company, nor are we under any obligation to slant the reporting. I was very specific on that point, since, as part of the law society, we cannot be seen to favour one side or another. I did not mention you specifically, since I don't know whether you wish to take this on. I didn't inform them of any association with your dad, who I know is adamantly opposed to northern pipelines, especially one alongside the mighty Mackenzie. On a purely personal note, I fully agree with your dad, but that does not come into consideration here. NAPI wants my yay or nay to their offer by the end of next week. It would certainly make a great thesis topic. So, would you like to take a few days to think about this, do some investigation?"

"No way!" Julia replied. "This is a fantastic opportunity for me. I'd love to take this on."

"That's wonderful! But first, here is a file I had already made up on the project. I suspected that it would not be difficult to find a law student interested in this, but given your family background, not to mention your great grades, you are my first choice. Have a look through this, then let's see what other questions you might have. We have a couple of months to spare, because spring breakup on the Mackenzie River won't start before April. I suggest that you not depart for Yellowknife before early May. If you're okay with that, I'll have our secretary make the initial flight arrangements."

Julia immersed herself in this material and much more over the next three months. It was a steep learning curve for her.

Following the discovery of oil in Leduc, Alberta in 1947, oil engineers began studying routes over the Rocky Mountains to build a pipeline between Edmonton and Vancouver. This resulted in the Trans Mountain Pipeline, which began transporting crude oil from northern Alberta to Burnaby, BC in 1953. Sixty years later, Kinder Morgan announced plans to expand this pipeline, building a larger twin to transport diluted bitumen from the oil sands project. Various environmental groups and First Nations opposed this, noting that BC's population had quadrupled to five million since the 1953 Trans Mountain pipeline was built. The new line would have to transect some busy urban areas, seven provincial parks and 13 First Nations reserves. Raising the environmental stakes, it would also cross 500 rivers and streams, add 14 new bulk-oil storage tanks on the waterfront in Burnaby, and provide berths where up to 34 tankers a month would be loaded with diluted bitumen for shipment through Vancouver harbour and past Vancouver Island. Despite all the opposition, both federal and provincial governments approved the project and it went ahead in 2017. A similar proposal for an all-new Enbridge Northern Gateway pipeline from the Edmonton area to Kitimat, BC received much more attention and opposition. This route was also approved by the federal government in 2014, but was still stalled by various court cases. While there had not yet been any coastal oil spills of the magnitude of the Alaska Exxon Valdez spill in 1989, there had been numerous smaller spills that had closed several areas to fishing.

Meanwhile, oil producers in land-locked Alberta were still desperate for new routes to markets. The large oil corporations were anxious to have dual oil and gas pipelines down the length of the Mackenzie River Basin, connecting to the Alberta oil sands and on to the proposed Keystone XL Pipeline into the US. They also proposed a west-east pipeline across Canada.

The controversy on the Mackenzie Valley pipeline went back to the 1970s, when there was a strong proposal to build a gas pipeline from the Beaufort Sea down through either the Yukon or the Mackenzie Valley to link with others in northern Alberta. This culminated with the Berger Report by Justice Thomas Berger in 1977, which recommended that no pipeline be built through the northern Yukon, and that a pipeline through the Mackenzie Valley should be delayed at least 10 years. One comment by Justice Berger in his final report stuck in her mind. *I listened to a brief by northern businessmen in Yellowknife, who favour a pipeline through the North. Later, in a native village far away, I heard virtually the whole community express vehement opposition to such a pipeline. Both were talking about the same pipeline; both were talking about the same region—but for one group it is a frontier, for the other a homeland.* In fact, Berger's report was appropriately titled *Northern Frontier, Northern Homeland.*

The debate had been continually revived since then. A Mackenzie Gas Impacts Project Fund of $500 million was set up in 2006. This was dusted off by the Federal Conservative government in 2013 with calls for pipelines south, west, north, and east from the Fort McMurray oil sands reaching frenzied levels. The Berger report had cautioned that a gas pipeline north-south would be a precursor to an oil pipeline going the other direction. Now this caution was a reality. It appeared that the northern pipeline might go ahead despite public opposition, especially from First Nations groups. She thought, *I guess I can forget any hope of universal agreement on the pipeline,* and started preparing herself to listen to opposing opinions.

7. Bonn Climate Summit

Eric was in Bonn to chair the First International Climate Impacts Summit. During the first session, Sam Zwane gave a presentation of his student's results on desertification of the Sahel. It was followed by a similar presentation on desertification of Syria by an agricultural scientist, Mahmoud Wassouf. Following the session, Eric and Sam met briefly with Mahmoud. He was interested in drought studies on the Canadian prairies, given the increasing importance of prairie agriculture with so many crop failures worldwide. Eric introduced Mahmoud to the chair of the Department of Climate Impacts of the University of Prairie Agriculture in Saskatoon, who happened to be there to find faculty for his new department. Before the conference ended, Mahmoud was interviewed for one of the research positions in Saskatoon and was offered the position the following month, to start that September.

The following day, Eric was wrapping up his plenary address titled "Climate Results of the Past Decade".

"...I must reiterate, in the strongest terms possible, that observations and field measurements during this past year confirm that the last IPCC assessment report (AR-5) was very conservative in its estimates of climate impacts, as all previous assessments have been. We have quite deliberately stayed on the conservative side in all the IPCC reports, as no one wants to cry wolf on an issue that threatens all mankind.

"To summarize the main impacts," pointing to his slide, "and these I direct specifically to those of our audience from industry, the media, and government. First, we sincerely hope that no one would still argue against the relation between carbon emissions from burning fossil fuels and global warming—that's become a non-issue with 99.99% consensus among scientists, according to James Powell in 2016.

"We've also shown that global carbon emissions, instead of stabilizing or slightly decreasing, have continued to accelerate over the past five years. Earth *can no longer* sustain this systematic destruction of the environment in which we all live! Period!"

Pointing to another summary slide, "Arctic regions are warming at rates of 2-4°C per decade, well above the global average. Subsequent melting of sea ice and polar ice sheets has increased exponentially during the past five years. The great polar ice sheets are no longer building in their centres. Most recent deep ice cores confirm that rapid melting is taking place at their base as well as along the surface peripheries. That's because the immense summer melt ponds contain huge moulins, where water cascades right down to the ice sheet base, helping to melt the base as well as lubricating it for motion. Global sea levels are now predicted to rise four to eight metres by 2100, a catastrophe in itself, because many coastal cities on the globe simply will not be able to build dykes that can withstand the added pressure of future storm surges."

"My fourth summation point is this," bringing up a slide showing desperate Syrian refugees in over-crowded boats, "we've already seen climate refugees for the past 30 years attempting to escape the deadly droughts across central Africa, especially in the Sahel region. With the expansion of the inter-tropical high pressure belts and continued desertification of the African Sahel region, we can confidently predict that this can only get worse. And in the last decade, we saw this repeated in Syria as the Arabian Desert crept northward. For millennia, even back beyond biblical times, Syria has been at the northern part of what's been known as the Fertile Crescent, watered by the Tigris, Euphrates, Jordan, and Nile Rivers. Syria was a food exporting country in 2000, but between 2005 and 2010 became a food importer. As rural people lost their ability to farm, they moved into the cities, some one and a half million of them, creating housing and food shortages, followed by social and political unrest. Eventually, civil war broke out in 2011. Many civilians fled for their lives. The result has been around five million Syrian refugees outside their country, another ten million or more displaced within the country. But the worst may be yet to come, because we believe that within a few years we will begin to see this disaster replicate itself in Mexico, the southern US, Australia, southern Africa, and other subtropical countries.

"My fifth point concerned the increasing numbers of severe storms at all scales, from tornadic thunderstorms to category

4/5 hurricanes to severe winter snowstorms; no need for me to repeat the importance of these."

"My sixth and final point involves ocean acidification, virtually ignored by the western world, but which is being observed in varying degrees in all coastal regions. Earth's coral reefs are literally crumbling before our eyes. We are losing fish breeding grounds and most shellfish, now banned from being fished in Canadian west coast waters, are doomed to extinction. Already, other fish stocks are disappearing at an alarming rate.

"There is much more to say on global warming impacts. If you think that this is just too much doom and gloom for the public to digest, then, pardon the pun, but this is but the tip of the iceberg.

"My colleague at the University of Vancouver, Dr. David Pearce, will next update you on melting permafrost impacts in our Arctic regions, including methane release. And after that, our esteemed colleague from Russia, Dr. Mazurenko, will update us on perhaps the newest and most disquieting results of all, dramatic increases of methane emissions from other sources in the Arctic. I *implore* you to listen very carefully to what these two eminent scientists have to say this morning. Thank you."

Loud applause. "Ladies and gentlemen," the session chair announced, "we have time for a few questions or comments."

A distinguished-looking gentleman was the first one to a microphone and introduced himself, "I am David Brown, Chief of Environmental Engineering for CUUON in Houston. Professor Nicholson, contrary to your confidence in the relation between carbon emissions and global warming, a recent paper by the esteemed Dr. Ray Spender proves that observed climate variability can most easily be explained by the 11-year sunspot cycle of solar radiation. Why do you continue to say otherwise?"

Eric replied respectfully, "The 11-year solar cycle is indeed reflected in the global temperature variations of the last 100 years or so, but it is just that—a cycle. Global temperatures have always returned to whatever is normal following such a solar cycle. In other words, the solar cycle *does not* explain the observed slow, but steady, upward trend in global temperatures. Of climate scientists who publish in the refereed literature, 99.99% concur that this upward trend can only be explained by the greenhouse effect resulting from carbon emissions. Dr. Spender is part of that one one-hundredth of 1% who disagree, whose opinion the denialist community chooses to accept while ignoring the scientific consensus.

"The denialists disagree with the consensus opinion because the truth is inconvenient to their viewpoint. Most do not attempt to publish their opposing views in the refereed literature simply because those views would not pass scientific scrutiny. So instead, they take the easy route of publishing convenient mistruths on climate information on the Internet and in newspapers and magazines, as well as stating their misconceptions on popular radio talk shows. None of these are edited for scientific accuracy, and most importantly, are readily available to the public. We should be questioning their motives and ethics, particularly since many are known to accept funding to deliberately raise uncertainties concerning climate change. The gloves are off. I do not apologize for these statements because the climate situation is already far too serious for a debate that has no justification whatsoever. Your question is therefore irrelevant."

Interrupted by a second question from an unidentified government official, a bristling David Brown stomped from the room.

"Professor Nicholson, what are the disquieting results from Dr. Mazurenko that you seem so concerned about?"

"I beg to defer to my colleague, who will address that very subject after our morning break."

The session chairperson cut in with, "I think we should move on to hear the second plenary talk from Dr. Pearce; then, following a short break for refreshments, we will go on to the other sessions for today. I give you a person who needs no introduction, Dr. David Pearce, professor emeritus from the University of Vancouver, whose keynote paper is titled 'The Dangers of Melting Permafrost in the Arctic.' Dr. Pearce?"

"Ladies and Gentlemen," David began, "I came to this summit quite prepared to present the paper indicated by our chairperson. However, last night, on arriving in Bonn, I learned of very recent results from joint research by Drs. Mazurenko and Nicholson on methane, that my friend and colleague from Vancouver alluded to just now. Eric has, in fact, teamed with Ivan Mazurenko to study this in more detail. On conferring with Ivan last night, I offered to shorten my own presentation to allow him more time to elucidate his results, the potential impacts of which, I assure you, are extremely serious and of the utmost importance to all mankind. In any event, my friend Eric has summarized the primary results of the past decade, while my paper is available in your preprints. I earlier alerted our chair of this, so Mr. Chair, I suggest that we break early for refreshments, give Dr. Mazurenko the additional time for his presentation, then open the floor for more discussion than would normally occur."

"I concur with your gracious offer, Dr. Pearce. So let us break now. We will return in 30 minutes, at precisely 10:30, to hear from Dr. Mazurenko."

* * *

Half an hour later, "Order please. We would like to get this very important session underway by introducing our first speaker of this session, Dr. Ivan Mazurenko of the Department of Atmospheric Chemistry, University of Moscow. Before I pass the session over to Dr. Mazurenko, however, I have something to share with you that is unusual and important. That is the fact that certain corporations attempted to disbar Dr. Mazurenko's presentation at this conference, unsuccessfully I might add, which underscores just how important this presentation will be to all of us. The title of Dr. Mazurenko's paper is 'Atmospheric Methane Concentration Sources from the Near-Shore Arctic Ocean.' Dr. Mazurenko?"

"Thank you Mr. Chairperson, ladies and gentlemen and my esteemed colleagues, thank you for this opportunity to present results from our investigations of methane concentrations. And especially, I thank my friend, Dr. Pearce, who has kindly deferred his talk to give me additional time for presentation and audience discussion. I must add that it was Dr. Pearce's earlier research on permafrost melt that largely prompted my own research. And now, I must tell you that the abstract of my talk, co-authored by Dr. Nicholson and appearing in your preprints, is no longer quite complete, as we have obtained new and very disturbing results from the deeper Arctic Ocean bottom." Showing a map of the Barents Sea region, Ivan continued, "These results are from an area where major oil exploration has already begun. I have therefore scrambled to re-focus my talk on these new results, so you may appreciate that these results are preliminary, but are important enough that we *must* focus on them. I am indebted to my co-author, Dr. Nicholson, who has provided much of the analysis work on these new data and has agreed to spend time with my team later this year, that is, if my employer allows me to continue."

"First, for the benefit of those from the media and government at this meeting, I cannot emphasize enough that, with these latest field results, our scientific community will likely agree, unanimously, that we face both a window of opportunity, and a window of vulnerability. The two may overlap, but once our vulnerability in this instance is exposed, absolute disaster will just be the next step for humanity. After that the opportunity will disappear. *Gaia*, the term used by Richard Lovelock some decades past, will then take its revenge on mankind.

"Let me review Gaia in simpler terms. There are two basic types of equilibrium by which Earth systems (Gaia, if you wish) maintain the status quo. First, there is dynamic equilibrium, which occurs when all acting processes eventually cancel each other out, resulting in a stable, balanced, or unchanging system; i.e., the rate of loss is equal to the rate of gain. A very good example of this is how weather systems, at all scales, restore equilibrium wherever and whenever there is an excess of heat and moisture, forming large synoptic scale systems, tropical storms, or thunderstorms, depending on the scale of the imbalance.

"The second type we call metastable equilibrium. This occurs when a system is on a prolonged trend, upward or down, reaches a threshold or a tipping point, and can no longer maintain its character. Nature, or Gaia, then says, 'Enough,' and the system then lurches relatively suddenly to some new operational level. The difference from dynamic equilibrium is that the system is then changed completely. The best example of this type is an explosive volcano. For example, when Mount St. Helen's, in Washington State, erupted in 1980, it completely changed the mountain visually, taking 500 m off the top and altering the mountain's shape, as well as destroying all life within 10-20 km.

"You most likely understand the difference between these two forms of equilibrium. For the past million years at least, atmospheric carbon dioxide, and by inference, our climate, has been in long-term dynamic equilibrium. Great glaciations have come and gone, on average every 100,000 years, but atmospheric carbon always remained, for at least the last million years, between 180 and 280 ppm by volume, except for one or two spikes up to 300 ppm—until the industrial revolution, that is. Once humans became addicted to fossil fuels, we upset that dynamic balance and atmospheric carbon steadily increased, passing 300 ppm for good by about 1910, then accelerating markedly in the past 30 years to its present level of 416 ppm, well above the previous high of 300. During the 1980s, atmospheric CO_2 increased at a rate of 1 ppm per year, but then accelerated to 2 ppm per year by 2000; and for the past ten years, it has continued to accelerate by an average of 3 ppm annually. We are now at 1½ times pre-industrial CO_2 levels, and at present rates would reach the $2XCO_2$ level in 15-20 years. With all respect to government and industry leaders who may be present, constant statements that tell the public that we have reduced emissions are not just in error, such statements are simply propaganda, for our data do not lie!" Loud murmurs and shouts pervade the auditorium. Mazurenko has to wait several minutes before continuing.

"Water vapour is by far the most prevalent greenhouse gas in the atmosphere, but it is always capped by the saturation-precipitation process, so that its residence time in the atmosphere can be measured in days, or at most, a few weeks. The other greenhouse gases, including carbon dioxide and methane, have no such cap and have continued to increase exponentially in the past 30-40 years. What I'm trying to say, is that over the past century, atmospheric carbon has gone from long-term dynamic equilibrium into metastable equilibrium,"—a little louder and with emphasis—"*and, with this quite dramatic change, global mean temperatures are following suit, with warmer temperatures lagging the greenhouse gas increases by only a decade or two.*

"So, what is the danger? Recall that I just said that our greenhouse gases have moved from dynamic equilibrium into metastable equilibrium, much like a volcano. And now, just as a volcano reaches a tipping point, atmospheric carbon will also reach some tipping point—perhaps it already has, in which case humanity is already in serious trouble. I say this because the atmospheric residence times for CO_2 is centuries. For CH_4 it is decades. So even if we curtailed all emissions today, our climate would continue to warm throughout this century.

"Now I come to the most important part of my talk, and perhaps the most threatening. You are all aware that when we talk about greenhouse gases in the context of global warming, we tend to focus mostly on CO_2 because it is by far the most prevalent greenhouse gas, other than water vapour and it has the longest residency time in the atmosphere. Also, most climate modelling work is highly dependent on the input values of CO_2 and on estimates of emissions of same during the present century. You may also be aware that methane is a more volatile greenhouse gas than CO_2, by a factor of almost 30 times. But it has a shorter residence time in the atmosphere, plus its atmospheric concentrations have been generally two orders of magnitude smaller than CO_2. *This last fact may be about to change in a very dramatic way!* So let me bring you up to date on our most recent field results.

"Fifteen years ago, my interest in atmospheric chemistry shifted to greenhouse gases after hearing a talk by a visiting scientist to Moscow, none other than our esteemed Dr. Pearce," He acknowledged Pearce sitting nearby. "I found that atmospheric CO_2 is well-covered in the literature and its concentrations are predictable based on our present consumption of fossil fuels. Dr. Pearce had talked about how the Arctic was warming in Canada at a much higher rate than the global average. He also discussed the problems of permafrost melt, particularly the release of methane from decaying peat mosses underlying the permafrost. The problem is that we have had little *quantitative* knowledge about the underground stores of methane that were thought to occur mostly in tundra land covers. Recent estimates of methane storage have caused great concern, especially in our vast Siberian tundra. These stores of methane below the permafrost could throw a hideous wrench in our estimates of global warming in this century.

"You may assume that, for the past decade, those of us in the climate field, aware of and disturbed by carbon dioxide emissions, have become equally concerned about atmospheric methane. Methane concentrations, which started to rise sharply in 2007, recently exceeded 1900 ppb, or just under 2 ppm, compared with CO_2 at over 400 ppm. But remember that this 2 ppm is equivalent to about 60 ppm of CO_2 in terms of warming potential. That is a very threatening addition to the global warming concern as is. *But,* it turns out that the permafrost methane problem, real and threatening though it is, is overshadowed by an even greater threat.

"We have found that the sub-sea region of the continental shelf in the Arctic, at least in and around the Barents Sea, contains enormous reserves, billions of tons, of methane hydrates. These have been locked beneath the east Siberian Arctic Shelf for hundreds of thousands, perhaps even millions, of years. We've been aware of these methyl hydrates for several decades, but never did we suspect the huge quantities that we've discovered. If these are disturbed, either through continued drilling for oil and gas, or by continued warming of the Arctic Ocean, the atmosphere would receive a sizeable dose of methane in a relatively short time.

"Already in the Barents Sea this last few months, we've recorded local concentrations of CH_4 as high as 5000 ppb, or 5 ppm. These numbers could easily exceed 10,000 ppb or more within five years. *That amount of increase threatens the very survivability of mankind itself,* for this alone has the potential to increase global temperatures by several degrees within just a few decades, on top of the anticipated warming from carbon dioxide increases. This simply", raising his voice again, "... *cannot ... be allowed ... to happen!*

"It is also well-known that methane is concentrated with raw petroleum sources. But near-shore and offshore drilling for oil and natural gas in the Arctic has raised the ante tremendously with this discovery of methane hydrates. Since little research had been done in this area, when I was offered research funding from our national oil conglomerate to carry out gas emission analysis for test drilling for oil reserves, adding methane to my personal objectives was a no-brainer. Admittedly, this objective was not part of my mandate, or of my budget. However, last year I reported some disturbing results on methane release from submarine clathrates at near-shore drill sites on the continental shelf of Siberia along the Arctic Ocean. The potential for methane release that we uncovered from the near-shore area alone would result in a large additional component of warming in climate model results. But then, over the past months I have had a team of technicians and graduate students studying the samples from drilling 500 metres below the ocean floor. Our preliminary findings suggest additional methane emissions. When added to that from near-shore clathrates, it can only be described as catastrophic in their future impact on climate. Let me show you these preliminary results now."

* * *

"In conclusion, the very real potential for methane release from offshore drilling, added to global CO_2 emissions, could result in global warming of between 10 and 12°C by sometime between 2050 and 2070. In actual fact, whether this warming is 8°C or 12°C is totally irrelevant, because even a 5 or 6°C increase would doom civilization as we know it, so that potential small errors in these preliminary estimates are a moot point. Ladies and gentlemen, we are standing on the precipice of the extinction of the human species! I am going to conclude the formal part of my talk with this proclamation." At this point, Mazurenko proclaims loudly, "WE MUST NOT, UNDER ANY CIRCUMSTANCES, ALLOW ANY FURTHER DRILLING FOR OIL OR GAS IN THE ARCTIC OCEAN FOR THE FORESEEABLE FUTURE, EITHER NEAR-SHORE OR OFFSHORE!" Brief pause as the audience once again creates a loud murmur; then, more quietly, Mazurenko wraps up with "The consequences—for mankind—go beyond any other disaster we could possibly conceive. Thank you."

Pandemonium breaks out—the chairperson yells, "The floor is now open for questions and comments." A race to the audience microphones ensues, and the chairperson loses control for a few moments.

"Please identify yourself before you address Dr. Mazurenko."

"Yes, I am Matthew Keller of North Houston University. Dr. Mazurenko, you admit that your results are preliminary; yet, you have the audacity to demand that all drilling in the Arctic be terminated at once, an act which would paralyze the world's economy right now, imperiling the livelihood of billions in the third world who need oil and gas to fuel their industries, bring produce to market, heat their homes, etc., which could result in further starvation and other stresses on third world peoples the world over. Are you answerable for this?"

Mazurenko, slowly, "Dr. Keller, I am well aware of the energy needs of our global economy. My appeal to stop drilling in the Arctic is not made lightly, I assure you. As a former climate scientist *yourself*, you must be aware that allowing the huge amounts of methane that we have discovered to be released into the atmosphere could be catastrophic. Once out, like the proverbial cat out of the bag, we won't be able to put the cat back in with today's technology. Moreover, your reference to third-world people is hardly relevant. Most of the starving peoples of Africa, Asia, and Latin America use only minimal amounts of oil and gas compared to the western and eastern bloc. Furthermore, many tropical and sub-tropical developing countries have been suffering the consequences of our emissions from the mid-latitudes for decades already. We in the western and eastern bloc countries, including China, Japan, and India, are the larger users of fossil fuels, by far. This adds an ethical issue to the whole problem I should think. All I am saying is that Arctic drilling for oil and gas needs to stop, *at the very least* until we are able to better assess the situation. This may take weeks, months, or years, I simply don't know. Regardless, surely it is better if Big Oil would control their greed long enough to cooperate with us to get the right solutions. All humanity is in this together."

"Mr. Chair …. Mr. Chair …. Mr. Chair …." A further hour of vociferous discussion took place.

* * *

Later, Prof. Mazurenko returned to his room and found a message slid under his door. He read:

Dr. Mazurenko, your presentation today represents a crime against your fatherland. You must return to Moscow immediately without any further contact with your colleagues. Otherwise, the lives of your wife and children will be forfeit. This is not an idle threat.

He slowly folded the note. *So,* he thought, *it has come down to this. These people have no scruples or morals whatsoever.* He picked up the phone and called home. Trying not to reveal his fears, he pleaded with his wife to leave immediately for his parents' home in a nearby suburb. Then he quickly called Aeroflot to change his reservation to catch the next flight out of Cologne Bonn Airport.

* * *

At 5 PM, David and Eric were meeting in a nearby lounge over a glass of wine. "Eric," David began after a few moments, "you spoke briefly with Ivan following that session. What was his impression from the pointed questions from the industrial community and that ratty senator from the US?"

Eric, contemplatively, "He didn't make much comment, since that attitude is predictable. However, he did emphasize that the new information is extremely critical. He asked if I could meet him in Moscow this month. We both thought it would be useful for you to join us. Is that possible?"

"Absolutely, yes!"

"Let's discuss this further over dinner. I'll see if I can get Ivan to join us."

"Good idea. How about we take a cab to the Reduttchen Restaurant on the Kurfurstenallee? I hear the food is excellent."

"Sounds great," said Eric. "But first, I think I'll go to my room and call home." As he left the lounge, he caught site of Ivan with his bags in the lobby elevator, noting that he was headed down to the underground car park. *Hmm*, thought Eric, *looks like David and I will dine alone. I wonder if something has gone wrong.*

Back in his room, Eric called his Vancouver home number. Carol, just getting up shortly after 8 AM, answered immediately, knowing it was Eric from the caller ID. "Hi dear. How's the climate summit going?"

"Somewhat tense would be the short answer, but that would be an understatement," Eric replied. "How are things there?"

"At the weather office, we're following the first major winter storm, which is causing havoc all along the east coast, from Virginia all the way up to Newfoundland. It's a classic Atlantic bomb. Two feet of snow in New York City, would you believe, and already they're calling it the new storm of the century. They've named it *Diablo*. Nova Scotia and New

Brunswick have both declared states of emergency and there have been a terrible number of multi-vehicle accidents on the highways. It's not affecting us directly on the west coast, but we're all wondering when the shoe will drop here."

"I heard about the east coast storm," Eric replied, "and one of the NASA scientists blames its intensity directly on those warm SST anomalies from Florida north to Virginia that started last fall."

"I'm thankful that things are quiet enough here. John and Tony are still doing fine at school and are excited about their upcoming summer jobs in Dease Lake in northern BC. It's good that those two can spend the summer together if they're going to a remote area."

"How about Julia? I had a very positive email from her supervisor, Kane Samson, last evening."

"Julia finds the legal mumbo-jumbo fascinating. She's still doing background work for her thesis on ocean oil spills I believe."

"She may be changing her thesis topic," Eric said. "Dr. Samson asked me what I thought of Julia doing some background investigation on the resurrected Mackenzie Valley pipeline proposal. He contacted me because it would involve her spending some time in Yellowknife and several other northern locations, where things are getting rather testy between First Nations and the pipeline industry in some areas. He knew that we'd spent a few summers in the Northwest Territories, and that Julia was used to roughing it. I told him I thought the idea was great, *if* Julia was interested, as I'm sure she will be, and if she's careful there."

"I didn't hear about that from Julia. Maybe because she was in bed when I got home from my evening shift, and was gone back to school when I got up just now. I'm sure I'll hear more this evening. But, what do you mean by First Nations people being testy?" Carol asked with some concern.

"That goes way back to the early 1970s, when a Mackenzie Valley pipeline was first proposed. There were no promises of anything for First Nations then and no guarantees of safety with the pipeline. At that time they wanted a gas pipeline for the North American market. That's still on the books, but they also want a second pipeline from McMurray to the north coast, for the Asian market, along with the second pipeline across BC to

Kitimat, which is still not settled. The risks are tremendous, especially the Mackenzie Valley route, because they'll be working over very unstable ground with melting permafrost. You recall the work that David was doing on permafrost years ago. His results are far more significant today, because we suspect a huge reserve of methane in the peat bogs below the permafrost. Methane is a more volatile greenhouse gas than carbon dioxide, 30 times more effective in fact, so that introduces another nagging complication to the global warming question."

"Which is?" Carol replied.

"The methane factor is becoming more critical because of the Arctic offshore data that my Russian colleague, Ivan, is collecting. Because of warming Arctic waters, the continental shelf is releasing huge amounts of methane. The rate of release is being accelerated by drilling there. We are wondering if the same thing may be happening in the Canadian Arctic, but to date it has been difficult to obtain data because the oil companies are rather reluctant to allow data collection within their drilling lease areas."

"So, what role would Julia play in this?"

"With the proposed new pipelines, the risks of breaks are much greater than for southern pipelines because of the unstable permafrost, while the difficulties for emergency repairs are also far more complex, because there is virtually no surface transportation, except during winter over winter roads. They want to move McMurray oil north with a second pipeline as well. Julia's role would be to collect opinions from both sides of the issue, that is, from the petroleum industry and from First Nations, and then evaluate the legal implications."

"Do you think that Julia would be at risk going north at this time?"

"I don't really think so. Investigating the legal implications of pipelines is extremely important right now. The only concern I might have is that NAPI are providing the funding for the study through the UVan Law School. But I've known Kane for years. He won't allow any biases because of the funding source to influence the results, and for sure we know Julia won't either. Her results could eventually turn out to be a breakthrough for our northern climate concerns. Julia has those three summer vacation experiences up north, and we have our own First Nations contacts, not to mention David, to assist her."

Carol cautioned, "Let's keep quiet about this until Julia decides on her own. We don't want to influence her especially if she hasn't even heard about it herself yet. It has to be her decision."

"For sure," Eric agreed. "In any event, you should know later today, because she was meeting with Dr. Samson this morning…. Dear, I have to run now. On my way to my room, I saw Ivan disappear out the door with his bags, presumably headed home early. I'm concerned because I'm sure he would have spoken to me first if things were okay. I need to speak with David to see if he knows anything further. We're meeting for dinner shortly. I'll say good bye for now."

"I hope things are okay with him. Let me know. Bye for now."

* * *

As Eric hung up the phone, he noticed that his phone message indicator was flashing. The recorded message turned out to be a request from Canada's federal Environment Minister, Webb Andrews, who was attending the Bonn Summit, for a briefing on the Arctic situation at Eric's earliest convenience. He called back, and yes, the Minister was available immediately. The Minister was an MP for the Green Party, presently in a minority coalition government with the New Democrats, a welcome departure from earlier years when environmental issues were furthest from the concern of the Canadian government.

Following the update briefing, the Minister gave Eric a private number with the assurance that Eric could call him at any time when there was new information. He would appreciate hearing anything new prior to the media getting hold of it. Eric agreed that this would be wise, given that media were prone to overemphasize any bad news, often without checking their sources. Besides, having the minister's ear may yet prove extremely valuable once permafrost and offshore methane estimates were confirmed.

8. The Accident

Ivan Mazurenko was greatly disturbed by the threat he had received against his family in Moscow. He was so distracted as he drove his rental car to Cologne Bonn Airport, that he did not notice the large truck that suddenly appeared from a side street on his driver's side until it was too late to avoid the collision. The truck careened into his door. Pain and blackness immediately overcame the Russian scientist.

Some minutes later, he revived briefly. He felt a sudden stab of additional pain as someone tried to move him, "Professor, where is your data, because you're not gonna need it anymore."

With difficulty, Ivan replied, "Don't be foolish … man … my colleagues … have copies … of the data and analyses. Stealing from me … will get you nowhere."

"Keller, he has no data sticks on him. There are only papers in his briefcase."

Keller almost screamed, "Don't mention my name again. Take the briefcase and let's get out of here before the police or witnesses arrive. It's obvious he won't survive this, so leave him." As Ivan passed out again, Keller added, "I'm not too worried, since I have someone in place to look after the copy that Nicholson has. I doubt they've had time to spread these any further."

* * *

Ivan revived later in hospital in extreme pain. Doctors and nurses hovered over him. "I must …," he began.

The attending doctor cautioned him, "Please try to relax, Dr. Mazurenko. You have been seriously injured in a car accident. Everything will be okay."

"No, I won't … be okay," he stammered, "don't kid with me. It was no accident … and I must … speak with … Dr. Nicholson …. Is he here?"

The doctor glanced at his colleague, who was shaking his head. They knew that Mazurenko's time was very short. "We will try to contact Dr. Nicholson. Do you wish to speak with the police? There is a Detective Stahl here who is anxious to ask you a few questions."

"Yes, yes, I must ..., before it is too late." They stepped aside to allow the detective near his bedside.

The detective moved in and introduced himself. "Dr. Mazurenko, I am Detective Hans Stahl from the Bonn Police Department. I'm in charge of security for your climate summit. Is there anything about this accident that you possibly observed? You see, we have reason to suspect that it may not have been accidental."

"I share ... your suspicion .... I revived before the ambulance arrived," Ivan began. "There was ... this chap standing over me, searching my pockets ... a scar ... on his right cheek. He spoke ... to a partner. He addressed him as ... Keller. Then ... this Keller demanded to know ... where my data analysis was .... I told him not to be so foolish. ... I had already passed copies ... of the data and analysis ... on to Dr. Nicholson and others. It all ... sounded ... so suspicious. Then ... I passed out again."

"There was a Dr. Matthew Keller who asked a very leading question following your presentation this morning" said Hans. "Do you think it could be the same Keller?"

"I shouldn't think so ... ohhh." Ivan started to lose consciousness again, then recovered, "I did not see his face ... only the second person ... and I had never seen him before."

With so many important people at your conference, our security is very tight. Unfortunately we cannot protect everyone at all times. I am sorry we could not have prevented your *accident*."

"Look ... I have ... no time left. You must ... warn Dr. Nicholson ... that his own life is in danger ... because he is ... part of this team ... and will ... have to take the lead. And please ... can you ... pass a message to my family ... that I love them very much. ... Tell my wife, Nania ... that I have thought very much about her God ... and maybe I shall meet him soon, eh!"

The doctor interrupts, "Detective Stahl, please leave. We must operate on Dr. Mazurenko immediately."

"Yes," Hans replied. "Dr. Mazurenko, I promise to get your messages to your wife and to Dr. Nicholson. Please, try to relax. The medical team will look after you."

"Too ... late ... for tha ...," and Ivan stopped breathing, his life drained from him.

9. Investigation and Threat

Hans Stahl made enquiries about Matthew Keller, the only suspect he had so far. While there was no real proof that the collision with Mazurenko's vehicle was not accidental, it was clearly a hit-and-run, which immediately made the incident a criminal investigation. The truck involved had been rented by someone called Nils Scheer with a false driver's license and false address in Hamburg. Hans suspected Scheer was an alias, although German police would continue an all-points search for him. The removal of Mazurenko's briefcase, and his testimony right before his death, left no doubt at all in Hans' mind. Just, where to look?

Hans had no illusions about finding the briefcase in Keller's hands. Earlier in the day, Keller had checked out of his hotel. A quick check of airlines indicated Keller was scheduled on a Delta Airlines flight back to the US that evening. Hans quickly arranged for a thorough but discrete US CIA inspection of Keller's checked-in and carry-on baggage. As expected, nothing suspicious had turned up. Many of the conference delegates were interviewed to try and determine who Keller may have associated with during the conference, but this process also turned up negative. If he was guilty, then Keller had certainly covered his tracks well.

* * *

Meanwhile, Eric and David were discussing Ivan's findings over a late dinner at the Reduttchen Restaurant. "You know," David said, "Ivan's results are potentially catastrophic in their implications and are just the evidence we need right now. I've been concerned about permafrost melt and methane release for years, but these drilling results suggest something far more disastrous and more immediate."

Eric replied, "Yes, and the devil is that we have so little time to stop the madness. I think we should clear the wrap-up session agenda tomorrow and get complete consensus from the summit concerning the seriousness of this. I think you and I need to draft a press release right after dinner to present tomorrow for immediate approval. This needs to get out to the media before the energy gurus get their PR experts working over the public."

David said, "I wish we knew why Ivan checked out so suddenly this afternoon, especially without contacting you. Something is in the wind for sure. He presumably headed back to Moscow?"

At that moment, they were interrupted by a mild disturbance at the front of the restaurant.

"I'm sorry, Detective Stahl, but Drs. Nicholson and Pearce gave explicit instructions not to be disturbed during their dinner meeting," said the head waiter rather sharply.

"Disturb them I will," Hans replied emphatically, "since I doubt that anything takes precedence over this investigation. Besides, I see them sitting over at that corner table—excuse me."

Eric and David became concerned as Hans walked up to their table.

"I apologize for the interruption, Dr. Nicholson and Dr. Pearce. My name is Detective Hans Stahl of the Bonn Police Department, a liaison with Interpol. I think you'll both agree that this is important."

"No problem," Eric replied. "What can we do for you, Detective?"

"Because of the many high-profile politicians and industry representatives present at your climate summit, I'm in charge of security there."

Eric said, "Yes, I saw your name listed as head of security. Your team has done an excellent job. I'm pleased to meet you."

Stahl replied, "I wish the circumstances for meeting were better, because unfortunately your Russian colleague, Dr. Mazurenko, has met an untimely end."

"Good Lord!" Eric and David, responded simultaneously.

"Whatever happened?" continued Eric. "I saw him leave the hotel unexpectedly about three hours ago and never even got a chance to speak with him."

"He was involved in a collision, a hit-and-run accident," said Hans, "although we have reason to believe it may not have been accidental. Since you know him well, do you have any suspicions at all about who could be involved in this?"

Eric replied, "He was under considerable pressure from Russian security, the FSS, regarding his release of data to me from their offshore drilling operations. He barely got permission to attend this summit. Surely, though, the FSS would not go that far?"

"It's not outside the realm of possibility, given the influence that the energy industry has today," replied Hans. "Have you heard of anyone by the name of Nils Scheer before?"

"No, not at all," Eric and David replied simultaneously.

"I didn't really think so. The truck involved in the accident with Dr. Mazurenko was rented by someone using that name, but I suspect it was an alias. However, before your friend died, he mentioned that one of the people involved had a prominent scar across his right cheek." A few moments' silence, then Hans continued, "What do you know about this Matthew Keller then? I was present this morning when he raised that objection to Dr. Mazurenko who was calling for an immediate halt to Arctic drilling operations."

Eric answered, "I've known Keller for many years; in fact, since we were graduate students together back at McGill University in Montreal during the late 1980s; we even worked on a project together. Then we were both accepted for PhD studies at the University of Maryland. Our thesis results on climate change clashed. We had a falling out altogether in 1992. After our PhDs, I did postdoctoral work in China, while Keller went on to work for CUUON, later taking a faculty position at North Houston University in Houston, also funded by CUUON. That's more than 30 years ago. We've hardly had a dozen words between us since. He has become one of the foremost climate denialists, and they run a very active website through a group called Companions for Climate Stability out of Houston. While I have suspicions about his research results, I've never had any cause to suspect him of any criminal activity. Why do you ask about Keller?"

Hans answered, "I want you both to keep this to yourselves for now, but I was able to speak briefly to Dr. Mazurenko at the hospital moments before he died. He mentioned two people were at the accident scene when he came to, before any ambulance arrived; one of them, the chap with the scar, called the other person Keller. We have no proof that it was the same Keller, especially when it's a common enough name in Germany, so no arrests can be made. Dr. Mazurenko's briefcase was also taken by these individuals. Your friend, Keller, has checked out of his hotel. He changed his flight reservation to return to the US this evening, arriving in New York, with a connecting flight to Houston. Since we have no reason to detain him, the CIA will check his bags thoroughly in New York. Meanwhile, we have no further leads on the two individuals who were present at the so-called accident scene."

"Oh my," David whispered.

"Dr. Nicholson," Hans went on, "as a working colleague of Dr. Mazurenko, I regret to say that your life may also be in danger. Mazurenko also suggested this. We are providing you with a security guard for the remainder of your stay in Bonn; in fact, he is here right now," pointing at a burly-looking plain-clothes officer by the door. "He'll drive you back to your hotel and remain with you at all times here in Bonn. I'll be discussing this with your authorities back in Canada to provide similar protection for you and your family. You will likely need protection for the next few weeks at least. May I keep in close contact with you until this is resolved, even after you return to Canada?"

"Certainly!" Eric replied. "I am quite shocked over losing a colleague and personal friend in this way."

Hans then related the remainder of what Ivan had said before passing, including the message for his wife. Eric said that he would phone Nania and pass Ivan's last message on to her.

"One last thing," Hans said before departing, "if this is a deliberate act to delay or stop altogether the release of the results from the Russian drilling activities, they may not make any attempt on your own life, but you should be aware that they may threaten you in other ways."

"What do you recommend that I do?" asked Eric.

"Perhaps two things," Hans replied. "Once the results of Ivan's work are published, it's then too late for them to forestall public opinion. So, you may want to push this to the forefront and get the information out as soon as possible. Second, I think you need to inform anyone close to you, family, close friends or working colleagues, that there may be some danger to them as well, certainly including your colleague, Dr. Pearce. You should advise all to take care. I will need to speak to you again before you leave. Here is my card with cell number and other contact information. If anything at all occurs that you suspect might be related, I want you to call me immediately, regardless of the time."

"Thank you, I will, you can be sure of that. One more point, however, actually a request," Eric added hurriedly. "If at all possible, could you be present at tomorrow morning's final plenary session when we announce Dr. Mazurenko's death?"

"Yes, that may be helpful in our investigation, as I will have our security staff in full force to maintain order and observe the participants for any signs of reaction to the news of the accident."

"I gather then, that you want us to announce it as just that for now, an accident?"

"By all means, please. We have no real evidence yet that it is anything but. The longer we maintain that stand, the better chance we have to find the culprits."

Hans then left.

With a sigh, David said, "So disturbing. This kind of puts new emphasis on things, doesn't it?"

"Understatement of the year! I think we both need to warn our families back in Vancouver. I'll also call our offices and warn them to be on the lookout for any trouble. We're nine hours ahead of Vancouver, so it's late-morning there. I think we should get back to the hotel. First let's go meet our friend over there."

They paid their bill, then met Cpl Garan Liebermann, who drove them back to their hotel. Liebermann spoke perfect English with only a trace of a German accent. He informed Eric that he or his relief would be accompanying Eric everywhere for the remainder of his stay. Another officer would take over at midnight, keeping guard at his room. Liebermann would be back after noon to take over again.

* * *

Back in his room, Eric called his wife again.

"Hello dear," answered Carol. "Wh" + "at's up?"

"Something extremely important, I'm afraid," said Eric.

"Afraid? You're okay, aren't you?

"Fine, but you need to listen carefully, Carol …."

Eric related the events of the past few hours to Carol, telling her to contact Julia and John and warn them to stay safe with friends until contacted by the police. He assured Carol that these were standard precautions, that there were no direct threats against him and he did not think it would go any further. "Meanwhile," he added, "everything is being done to keep the summit meeting secure. German police take such threats very seriously, they don't fool around. And you should be contacted by Vancouver police this afternoon."

Next, Eric called Melanie,

"Hello, Climate Department" she answered.

Eric quickly repeated the events of the day, then asked if anyone had contacted them from the Police Department yet.

"No," she replied, "but we've had to contact them. I'm afraid your office was ransacked last night and basically trashed."

"Good Lord," he exclaimed, "what exactly was trashed? Did they break into the lab or Chi-Min's office?"

"No, just your office, but they really made quite a mess, your papers and books scattered, your computer destroyed. Whoever did it, it does not appear that they went after either Chi-Min's office or the lab. I trust you had backed up your computer?"

"Yes, we have everything backing up automatically to the central university computer. Would you please alert Chi-Min to the possibility that they may have gotten at his computer, to check out all our recent data and to get back to me as soon as possible."

"I understand he is doing that just now," replied Melanie.

"All right. Please keep me posted on things there and how the police are handling this."

"Right-o. Please look after yourself. It doesn't sound very good at all over there."

"It's not," said Eric. "But we'll get through this. Good-bye for now."

Eric hung up the phone. He tried to think over the events and to plan what was to transpire the following morning. Just then, the phone message recorder flashed red. He picked it up and listened to the message from the hotel desk, indicating that there was an envelope waiting for him at the front desk. *Hmm, wonder what that's about. I'd better go check.* He opened his door, finding Cpl Liebermann there.

"Are you going out, Dr. Nicholson," he enquired?

"Just to pick up a message at the front desk," he replied.

"Fine, I'll just watch your back along the way."

Eric opened the envelope at the desk. It was unsigned, but its intent was clear. He showed it to Cpl Liebermann.

Dr. Nicholson,

I strongly advise you not to publish any results from the Barents Sea Project. We know where you live, and we know that you have a son and daughter. The decision is yours.

"I'll contact Det. Stahl immediately sir," Liebermann said. "He will want this examined for fingerprints and held for evidence."

"Yes, of course," Eric replied grimly. His thoughts were entirely on his family. He picked up the house phone to call David. "David," he said, "are you in bed yet? Something else has come up."

"Come on up to my room," David replied.

Eric and David talked over the events for an hour. In the end, Eric decided that his family may be at risk regardless of whether the results were published or not. They then spent another hour discussing strategy for the closing session the next day and drafted a brief press release to be voted on by the delegates.

Eric and David met for breakfast at 7 AM the following morning, with the relief guard in close attendance. David had picked up a newspaper and showed Eric an article, which translated, read,

Major Oil/Gas Discovery in Barents Sea

The Russian-Chinese-US consortium CUUON announced a major oil/gas discovery in the Barents Sea on Thursday. The giant corporation indicated that test wells drilled over the past six months have confirmed oil reserves at least equal to that of Saudi Arabia, Operational drilling will start in May, or as soon as current ice conditions allow. Early trading on Wall Street was wild ...

"There's our target," said Eric. "We have to stop this somehow."

"Agreed, but *how* is the question," replied David.

"The press release is the first step. WMO and IPCC will likely take it from there. They cannot afford to make conservative statements any longer. This needs to be out there on every newscast and on the mind of every person on the planet. The madness must stop!"

Just then, Det. Stahl came through the door, and Eric invited him to join them. "I'm glad I caught you before your next session starts," he announced. "I need to update you. Last evening I alerted Vancouver Police. They have a watch on your house. Your family will have inconspicuous escorts along wherever they go for a while, I'm afraid. With Mazurenko's death under so much suspicion, this has become an Interpol issue. Since I am the primary liaison for Interpol here, I've been tabbed to take over their part of the investigation. You may likely see a little of me in Canada as well."

Eric said, "If it's any consolation, that news actually relieves my personal stress a little."

"I'll ditto that!" said David.

Eric went on, "I trust we can use first names with each other from now on?"

"Yes," said the detective. "For one thing, that will make our meetings less conspicuous in public. I'm Hans, so hello, Eric and David. The Russian Embassy has been informed. They will look after contacts with Mazurenko's family."

"Has any new evidence turned up yet?"

"Not much," replied Hans. "Not surprisingly, when the CIA checked Keller's baggage, nothing incriminating was found. We have no other leads yet, I'm afraid. But Keller will be watched. Oh, one other item of note for you; we have someone looking into funding sources for the Companions for Climate Stability group you mentioned, which may eventually provide other leads."

David, passing his newspaper over to Hans, said, "Hans, since you're aware of some of the discussions going on at this climate summit, have you noticed the headlines this morning regarding the Barents Sea oil drilling?"

"Yes," he answered, "that's what prompted us to consider funding sources for the denialist group. We need to know if CUUON is directly involved in this."

Eric said, "David and I have to get on with the Summit proceedings. Today will be rather interesting, I'm sure." The three of them left together.

* * *

Eric called the final plenary to order at 8:30, then made the announcement.

"Colleagues, I have some very, very sad news to pass on at this moment. Yesterday afternoon our esteemed colleague, Dr. Mazurenko departed for home early without giving a reason. He was driving a rental vehicle to the airport when he was involved in a horrible accident. Dr. Mazurenko was fatally injured and passed away a few hours later in hospital."

The session erupted in murmurs of sorrow. After a few moments, Eric continued. "We do not yet have any further details of the accident. But I do know you will all agree that this is a terribly unfortunate occurrence. Our thoughts and condolences go out to his family in Moscow. Dr. Pearce and I, in particular, are feeling great shock at this turn of events, as Ivan was our colleague and close friend. I should like to delay the start of this session for 30 minutes as we each give thought to this event. May I please point out our Chief of Security, Det. Hans Stahl," pointing to Hans. "If anyone has any information at all as to why Dr. Mazurenko left so early yesterday, or if you observed any small detail of his departure, Det. Stahl would very much like to speak with you. Let us take a short break now. Please return at nine o'clock."

The final plenary session wound up that afternoon with all scientists agreeing on the importance of having a moratorium on all Arctic drilling for oil or gas. The press release, signed by all summit delegates, pleaded with all governments through the United Nations for an initial nine-month hiatus, with a review following the second climate summit the following January in Beijing. Eric and David agreed to spearhead the analysis of Mazurenko's data, assisted by the major climate modelling groups in Canada, the US, UK, Germany, Russia, Japan, and China. There was unanimous agreement among the remaining scientists that the situation was potentially disastrous for mankind. They further agreed that a second summit meeting was necessary within a year, once Dr. Mazurenko's results could be duplicated and some preliminary estimates of permafrost and offshore Arctic methane could be ascertained.

A colleague and friend of Eric, Professor Ching Dao, chair of the Climate Department of Beijing University, had already offered their facilities in Beijing for the next meeting. A motion to this effect was quickly passed. The summit was then adjourned.

Eric and David left Bonn early on Sunday morning.

10. Back Home

The following day, Eric was met by his family when he arrived back in Vancouver, accompanied by RCMP and local plainclothes police. He decided to forego any work at his office until the following day, as there was much catching-up and family planning to be done, with police involvement.

On Tuesday, Eric and David briefed all staff at their UVan offices. Fortunately, most of the damage to his office and papers had been tidied up by Chi-Min and Melanie after police had checked for fingerprints and any other clues. Chi-Min had set up a new computer for Eric, all ready to go. He had also confirmed Mazurenko's results, even using different analysis techniques.

The impact on the global climate could be staggering if Arctic drilling could not be stopped. It might even threaten Earth with a runaway greenhouse effect. It was essential to obtain reproducible data from other drill sites. Eric had a feeling that the data might already exist, but in confidential files.

* * *

Following his climate class several weeks later, Eric answered his phone, "Hello," Eric Nicholson here."

"Hello, Eric, this is Hans Stahl, in your hometown."

"Hello indeed, Hans. You said you might see us here. Are you close to the university right now? I'd like to get updated on your investigation and fill you in on some details here."

"Yes, at the moment I'm at Vancouver Police headquarters downtown, near the former Olympic Village. If you're going to be at your office for a while, could we get together today? I could be there in half an hour."

"Most certainly, Hans. I'm in the Climate Building at the north side of the campus, Room 2170."

"Fine, I'll see you shortly."

Just 20 minutes later, Hans appeared at Eric's door.

"So good to see you, Hans," Eric said as he got up from his desk.

"And you, Eric. Vancouver Police filled me in on your break-in and drove me here special delivery. I trust you did not lose much valuable data. It appears you have recovered your office."

"Actually, we didn't lose any data, thanks to our backup systems and my PDF, Chi-Min Chang, here. Chi-Min, this is Detective Hans Stahl, who has been working on Dr. Mazurenko's murder case and is assigned to Interpol on the larger issues."

"My pleasure," said Hans.

"Let's get a coffee, Hans, while we talk about the latest. I'm interested in anything you can tell me about those horrible events."

A few minutes later, they were seated at a corner table in the cafeteria. Hans glanced around, out of habit, as he began, "We have a number of leads, but nothing to start making any arrests that would stand up in court. The two suspects used a rented truck, registered to this Nils Scheer, as I mentioned back in Germany. As we suspected, that was an alias; at least, there is no trace whatsoever of anyone by that name and nobody at the rental agency had any recollection of Scheer, either. So there was no paperwork to identify them. They were also very careful about fingerprints, obviously wearing gloves. All we know about Scheer is this scar on his right cheek, while the Keller individual remains a mystery for the moment. Dr. Mazurenko's briefcase has not been recovered either, not that it would provide much useful information. As for your Matthew Keller friend, he travelled back to Houston alone. We checked individuals on all flights back to the US for the following few days. No suspicious males turned up. It appears that one or both individuals were locals, whether or not Keller was involved. I say appears, because personally I don't think either was a local, at least to Bonn."

"I can't imagine that Keller would be involved in something like this, Hans. Yet, you say that Ivan heard the name Keller mentioned at the accident scene? Has the CIA turned up anything?"

"Nothing, not even a link in Germany comes up in his contacts," replied Hans. It appears as if he is clean. However, here's something that may be of interest to you. You'll recall that we had someone looking into funding sources for the Companions for Climate Stability group in Houston that you mentioned. It turns out that CUUON does indeed fund them, by a round-about means. CUUON provides two million dollars a year to the Climate Change Policy Think Tank in Washington, specifically to fund climate change research. The think tank, in turn, has been granting the CCS around a million of that every year; plus they have also funded Keller's research by about $250,000 per year for the last five years at least. Considering that these groups use little in the way of expensive instrumentation or field work, they seem fairly flush. Keller also receives $500,000 in grants directly from CUUON. Other than four graduate students that he supports, he appears to use most of his funds for travel and giving climate presentations, most of which, incidentally, are organized by CUUON's Environment Department."

"Hmm, that *is* interesting," said Eric. "I've seen the odd notice posted for his talks in Canada, but I didn't realize it was so extensive."

"One other thing, Eric," added Hans. "Vancouver detectives have traced fingerprints from your office to Andrew Vinson, a student in one of your climate classes I believe?"

"Climate Change 202, that's the course. I noticed he was not in class this morning."

"That's because they've charged him and are questioning him concerning his motives. The young man simply refused to talk, but they think he might break down by tomorrow. They invited me to sit in on their questioning tomorrow morning."

"That's too bad," replied Eric. "Not that he was a great student, but I hate to see any young student's life turned upside down by something like this."

"I may be able to tell you more after tomorrow. Meanwhile, I must get back to my hotel and check for messages. There may be more information from either Interpol or the FBI, or even your RCMP."

"If you're not too busy tomorrow evening, since it's Friday and I'm barbecuing, perhaps you'd like to come to our place for a family dinner. Carol and the kids would love to meet you, I'm sure."

"That sounds terrific. Perhaps we'll have more evidence by then. I'm hoping for a breakthrough with this student. What time?"

"Try for five, but don't worry if you have to be late. I won't start the barbeque until you arrive. Here's our address," passing a card to Hans, "but we could also pick you up?"

"No need, as I've already arranged for a rental car. It should be delivered to my hotel by now. I'll supply the wine. There's a decent-looking wine store next to my hotel. See you about five tomorrow."

Eric dropped by David's office and invited him and his wife, Thelma, to the barbeque as well.

* * *

That evening, the Nicholsons had a family meeting about security.

Julia had informed the family weeks earlier that she was taking on the pipeline issue for her PhD thesis work. Eric had greeted the news with fatherly pride, while internally he was ecstatic. Julia was planning a three-week trip to the Northwest Territories in May to start her survey, while John was preparing for his Co-op job in northern BC. Eric hoped that their current security arrangements would not interfere with Julia's and John's work plans.

"Besides," Eric confided to Carol later, "we have almost two months before they leave. I expect this will all have blown over by then. By the way, we have extra guests for our family barbeque tomorrow. Hans Stahl, our German detective, is here. I've also taken the liberty of asking David and Thelma."

"Wonderful, I haven't seen Thelma in weeks. We need to catch up," Carol answered. "Julia has no classes tomorrow, so she and I planned to go shopping in the morning. She needs some new duds for her trip north in May."

"And thanks to your perfect forecast," Eric continued, "we are supposed to have a way-above-normal, global-warming 25 degrees tomorrow, with no wind; perfect for sitting outside on the patio."

Eric was able to leave his office by 2 PM on Friday, stopping by their local supermarket to pick up steaks and other food for the barbeque that evening. David and Thelma were at the door at 5:10 just as Hans drove up the driveway.

"Come on in, everybody," Eric called from the backyard. "I'm just lighting the barbeque and the beer's cold. Hans, meet my better half, Carol, David's wife, Thelma, and our main family protector, Buddy." Buddy approached Hans, with his tail wagging and a tennis ball in his mouth.

Carol said "I'm delighted to meet you, Hans. I've heard a lot about you. Our two kids, Julia and John, will be along in a couple of minutes, eager to meet you as well. Mind you, they're hardly kids anymore."

"It's certainly my pleasure to meet you all. And here, Carol, if I may call you all by first names, I'll let you look after this wine."

"Are you a prophet too, Hans? This is one of my favorite French reds, and I see you have Thelma's favorite white."

"Now Mom, don't you drink too much," John teased as the two siblings came out the back door. "You know we have a cop here! Hello, Detective Stahl, I'm John. This is Sis, Julia."

"Please call me Hans. I see your mom and dad sure have good genes." Turning to Carol, he added, "You have handsome grown-up children."

Eric interjected with, "And reasonably bright, too. Julia is starting her PhD thesis work in environmental law, while John is completing his bachelor degree in environmental engineering and considering starting a master's degree in September. They're both headed north next month for their summer work. And did I tell you, Hans, that Carol works with Environment Canada as a senior forecaster. She arranged for this beautiful day today."

"Ha," chuckled Hans, "Truly a total environmental family!"

"And our dearest friends too," added Thelma.

During dinner, Eric asked Hans, "Did you learn anything new about Andrew Vinson's motives in trashing my office and computers?" Eric asked.

"Yes," replied Hans, "he did admit to being hired to spy on your research, so that they would have some advance notice of your results, presumably so that they might be able to stop your publicizing anything. The trouble is, we don't know who *they* are. The kid is really genuinely scared and won't tell us who his contact is. He said that he was afraid they would kill him. No doubt he has that threat hanging over him, but whether they would go that far or not, who knows? However, we've brought the RCMP security branch, CSIS, in on this. They have a search warrant to go through his apartment on campus. They are probably doing that as we speak. They have experts who can trace anything on any computers that Vinson has."

"Okay, you men, are you prepared to take on dessert and coffee?" Carol interrupted. "We have my special Banana Cake Supremo."

"Oh Lord," said Eric, "Hans, you'd better be careful of that one. It's deadly on the belt-line!"

"I can attest to that," said David.

Later, Hans groaned, "I'll never pass security myself if I don't run five miles after that cake."

"You were warned," said David.

Just then, Hans' cell phone rang. "Hello … I see. Is there anything at all left that your boys can work with? … Okay, I'll do that. Thank you. I'll see you tomorrow."

Hans looked contemplative, so Eric asked, "Some bad news from CSIS?"

"Yes," said Hans. "Apparently *they* got to Vinson's apartment before we did. It's completely trashed and two computers destroyed."

"I guess that suggests that some larger organization is involved here, doesn't it," said David?

"Yes, it does. But we won't discount the abilities of CSIS. They may yet find something on the hard drives. The drives themselves are no longer usable, but they have their ways of retrieving data. I'm to meet them tomorrow. Meanwhile, you need to increase security on your own office and home, I'm sorry to say."

"I'd already deduced that one. I think the same may go for you, David, since you've been cooperating on this project, especially with the most recent results from your permafrost data."

"Eric, I followed some of the talks at the climate summit last month", Hans interposed. "It might help if you could give me the layman's summary of what you two brilliant scientists are talking about?"

"Yes," said Eric. "You see, David's permafrost data show similar trends to …."

The next day, Hans met with CSIS experts, who thought they might retrieve some of the information on the Vinson hard drives, but the drives needed to be sent to their labs in Ottawa. It would take a few days before any news came back.

* * *

The following Thursday morning, Hans made another visit to Eric's office.

"I see your office door has been changed," said Hans as he sat in front of Eric's desk.

"Yes, they've beefed up security considerably. That door is solid steel, works only with my security card. You'll note extra security cameras around the department as well. Just as you recommended."

"Good, well, we do have some good news from those hard drives of your student. Vinson apparently had a local contact in Vancouver, somebody called Smith, who has disappeared without any trace so far. There is also some evidence that he was paid from an account out of Calgary, with a further link to the Climate Change Policy Think Tank in Washington."

"Is that the organization that also funds Keller's research?" asked Eric.

"One and the same," replied Hans.

"Well, well, then things are starting to gel in this case?"

"Not enough to charge anyone yet, but they are pointing in the right direction, I believe," said Hans. "Something else that's just of interest for the moment. Do the names Todd Barton or Nick Savage mean anything to you?"

"No, never heard of them that I can recall," replied Eric.

"Barton's name appears on Vinson's drive, nothing that we can connect directly to your office trashing, but a clue all the same. And, a check with the FBI indicates that they both work for Keller, are supervised by him anyway. They are presently in Alberta giving some talks, on climate change—from their perspective of course. We'll be keeping an eye on their movements for a while."

"Anything known on their background?"

"Savage was part of Special Forces with the US Marines during the Iraq war in 2003-04. At one point he was accused of conduct unbecoming with respect to the killing of a number of Iraqi soldiers. He was acquitted, given an honorable discharge, and later wound up working with CUUON. That's all we know so far."

Hans went on, "I have to be off. I have a flight to Washington this afternoon to meet FBI and other Interpol operatives. Then back to Europe. I plan to return next month, but I'll be in touch in the meantime. Don't relax your vigil on security. Your science is big, really big, and it's obviously caught the attention of the whole petroleum industry. Are you planning any further travel this year?"

"My only plans at the moment are for a PhD defence that I need to attend in Durban, South Africa in August, and a conference in New York in October. There are always a few impromptu meetings that arise, but no other travel plans after New York until the next climate summit next January in Beijing. David and I will be giving plenary talks at that one. We need time back here to complete our analysis of the Barents Sea ice island data and David's Arctic permafrost data. We'll need tight security while in Beijing. Although the Chinese will handle the domestic scene, I hope Interpol will provide the international security."

"We're already working on that and yours truly will be in charge again."

"That pleases me greatly. It's good to know ahead of time. The Beijing summit is crucial, because we absolutely need to keep China onside with global warming issues.

As Hans rose to leave, Eric added, "Good luck in Washington. I sure hope this case gets cracked soon. If there is a clear link to the petroleum industry, maybe then we can get some politicians in the western world to listen and be more proactive on climate issues. To date, they have failed to provide the leadership we need." They shook hands, and Hans departed.

* * *

The following morning, Eric had a call from his colleague, Samuel Zwane. "Eric, this is Sam calling from Durban, South Africa. How are you? Recovered from the Bonn Climate Summit I trust?

"Yes, I am well. It's good to hear from you, Sam. What can I do for you?"

"Since you are the external examiner for Nelson Tutu's thesis in August, I was wondering if you might find time to visit us earlier, discuss what he has done so far and give our department a lecture or two on your own work. I realize, however, how much your time is in demand, so please do not feel bad if you must decline right now. After all, you will be coming here for the defence in August. A visit right now, while we have students in classes, would be extremely valuable, as a number of the undergraduates are contemplating graduate school on climate change topics. I'd also like you to take a 2-day tour with me, to see something I'm sure will interest you."

"I would find it difficult to refuse a valuable old friend. Let me see if I can clear a week off my schedule. Our winter classes are winding down, with final exams in early April. Would a week to 10 days in May work for you?"

"I think so. Students come back from mid-term break after April 10th. If you could come any time after that, it would be perfect. I have funding to pay your travel expenses."

"I think that is possible," replied Eric, "but I'll get back to you tomorrow to confirm."

11. Africa Liaison

In early-May, Eric was on the way to Durban, site of the COP-17 climate conference of 2011. Among all the scientific presentations and political posturing at COP-17, Eric recalled the impassioned speech on the final day by the young student from Maine, Anjali Appadurai, whose plea garnered attention world-wide. *That's what we really need,* thought Eric, *more young people to get active on climate. Passion like that spreads among youth. Just a small percentage of them carrying that into their careers could change this world for the better.*

Eric arrived in Durban on a Monday afternoon. The next day, after adjusting to the time zone change, he met Samuel Zwane in the Atmospheric Science Department at the University of KwaZulu-Natal. Samuel had been a black activist in Tennessee in the 1980s, but moved to South Africa following his PhD graduation and on the heels of the Mandela movement in the early-1990s. Eric had agreed to spend one week in Durban, including the weekend when Samuel had promised him a special trip to view climate impacts.

Eric spent most of the week discussing climate impacts with Samuel and Nelson Tutu.

Nelson's thesis showed that the Sahel climate had warmed by almost half a degree in the past 50 years, and rainfall had decreased by 50% in the same period. Two in six trees had died across the Sahel, evidence of the desertification of this former agricultural belt of northern Africa. "Millions of Sahel people have been displaced by drought and the ensuing wars," Nelson explained. "It is particularly hard on native and domestic animals. Watering holes can be separated by tens of kilometres, so thirsty wildlife often cannot find water. And because farmers generally don't own land in most African countries, they use community land and community watering holes. If their community water hole dries up, often they are not welcome to take their cattle or goats to a neighboring hole."

Addressing Samuel and Nelson, Eric emphasized, "Too often the western world thinks of climate change in terms of warming temperatures in Arctic regions. They don't recognize just how badly global warming impacts are felt in these densely-populated subtropics, where the actual temperature increase may even be unnoticeable. I hope you are able to attend the next climate summit in Beijing in January. There needs to be more emphasis on the impacts of global warming, especially here."

"Yes," Samuel replied. "Both Nelson and I plan to be there. We've already submitted two abstracts to the summit planning committee and these have been accepted."

On Thursday, Eric said to Samuel, "Tomorrow I would like to present some of our recent results on methane release from permafrost and the Arctic Ocean drilling sites. It's becoming more apparent that methane could be the Achilles heel in climate model predictions. Unless we can put a stop to the madness around Arctic drilling for oil and gas, we may be faced with a catastrophic failure of our civilization by the end of the century. It's imperative that results like Nelson's work get higher visibility, for it's the impacts, such as the amount of heat being added to the atmosphere and oceans, and desertification, not just the higher temperatures, that can cause catastrophe to humans in the end."

Eric's talk received wide attention, including major TV networks from the US, Europe and China. There was particular interest in the methane results from the Barents Sea, especially the possible connection to methane from melting permafrost in northern Canada.

After lunch, Nelson brought their attention to news from Chad. During the past 50 years, the shallow Lake Chad had lost about 98% of its water due to excessive evaporation and desertification, coupled with poor irrigation methods. The news indicated a complete breakdown of surface water flow around Lake Chad. Samuel informed Eric that the special trip to view climate impacts that he had promised involved the three of them taking a flight to Chad to view the Sahel disaster there first-hand. Eric agreed enthusiastically. They set off on Saturday morning, the flight taking them northward along the coast, then northwest through Kenya and the Sudan to Chad. The effects of drought from northern Kenya on were dramatic and disturbing.

Landing at N'djamena, the capital city of Chad, they were met by one of Samuel's colleagues from the University of N'djamena for lunch. He then directed them to a smaller aircraft to fly the 100 km to Lake Chad. As they flew along what used to be the eastern shore of Lake Chad, Eric was amazed at the huge sand dunes where just a few years before there had been lake water. They flew east to west across what was supposed to be Lake Chad, but observed only a few patches of parched wetland vegetation, with no visible open water remaining. The southward expansion of the Sahara had virtually completed the job of desertification.

They then flew southwest into northeast Nigeria and over a refugee camp, which, Samuel's colleague informed them, had 50,000 refugees. "True climate refugees," he remarked, "and in a very dangerous part of Nigeria." Eric was shocked by the camp conditions which, even from 500 feet above ground, were visibly squalid at best. A huge graveyard just a few hundred metres southeast of the camp completed the disturbingly sordid picture.

"These desertification conditions," observed Samuel, "are responsible for more than five million known refugees across the southern Sahel, from Senegal through to Eritrea. And God only knows how many more hundreds of thousands perished before they could make it to a refugee camp, not to mention those killed by roving bands of armed thugs."

Eric commented, "This is an absolute blight upon mankind. The industrialized world must bear much of the blame because it's a direct result of global warming at its worst!"

"Aid agencies can no longer handle all the needs of these camps," Samuel replied. "There are hundreds of refugee camps like this one, and they desperately need massive inputs of aid from western governments. Eric, I wanted you to see this first-hand, because you know that words alone cannot describe the tragedy that is unfolding here. Moreover, an even worse scenario appears to be happening as the desertification is reaching a full horrific climax. You see, many Sahel countries draw most of their water from deep wells, but our latest estimates suggest that the primary aquifer, beneath Chad and Niger, at present rates of withdrawal will be essentially dry before mid-century."

"To say that that is shocking is a gross understatement," said Eric.

"Yes," was all that Samuel could reply.

Following an overnight stay in N'djamena, Eric, Samuel, and Nelson flew back to Durban. Eric emphasized to Nelson the importance of his research, from both the socio-economic and political viewpoints, and urged him to start publication of his results even while he was completing his thesis. "Following your PhD confirmation, I can offer you a postdoctoral position for at least a year at the University of Vancouver. It would be very useful if you could carry out similar socio-economic analyses of conditions in Canada's north."

"That would be wonderful," replied Nelson. "I hope my final thesis will confirm your present view of my results to date."

Eric delayed his return to Canada to explore a little of South Africa on Monday with Samuel as his guide. On Tuesday, he departed for the return trip to Canada, with a stopover in London. He felt that the time spent in Africa had enormous importance in the fight against global warming. Still, he wondered what the dissidents and climate denialist movement might next have up their sleeves.

12. Friends in Yellowknife and Arctic Impacts

While Eric was in Durban, Julia had headed to the Northwest Territories. She was thinking back over events as her flight was approaching Yellowknife. She had spent the last few weeks learning as much as she could about oil and gas pipelines and the various pros and cons. Having listened to her dad talking about recent spikes in methane over both permafrost and the Arctic continental shelf, Julia had even ordered her own methane detection sensor on the assumption that it might be useful around either pipelines or permafrost-melt zones. Her dad agreed that this would be very helpful to them as well. Julia wondered who she might meet on her northern trip. Being outgoing, the prospect of new friends excited her. *I brought along a dozen UVan T-shirts to give out as gifts.*

Several weeks before, Julia had discussed the details of her trip and proposed thesis with her mom and dad. They were just as excited as she was. Eric had suggested several First Nations contacts of his own, including an RCMP Corporal Bob (Great Bear) Jackson in Inuvik, who could introduce her to others. There was also John's UVan friend, Paul Anawak, who was working back home in Inuvik for the summer break. John had given his traditional, "whoop, whoop, whoop," and had pleaded, "Could you take me as an assistant, Sis, please?" though in reality, he was headed for his Co-op work term. Not to be outdone by his sister, John too had ordered a methane detector to use in northern BC.

God, what a fantastic family I have, she thought as the Canadian North flight touched down in Yellowknife. *I am so fortunate. I love them so much.*

* * *

At that moment, Calvin Hollsworth, Chief of Field Operations for NAPI, Yellowknife, was meeting with his executive VP, Dr. Andrew Long.

"Calvin, I'm sure you realize just how sensitive these legal implications of building the northern pipeline could turn out to be. We're out on a limb offering money to the UVan Law Department for the investigation, but we're hoping it will generate some good will on both sides."

"Chief, I'm well aware of the risks. As long as we don't get some hothead involved, on either side, we should be all right."

"Regardless, we have to bear in mind that the feds are not keen on the Mackenzie Valley pipeline going through. So they might cancel all permits with just a minimum of disturbance. The student arriving today may be small potatoes, but the tone of her report could be a big stick either way. Give her whatever help she needs, but try to steer her away from any First Nations agitators. Will you have Keller show her some of the operations? Isn't his dad that gung-ho climate denialist with CUUON?"

"Yes, but Malcolm's nothing like his dad. In fact, I understand that they haven't talked in years."

"Hmmm, but CUUON is involved in the oil sands and is one of our own major partners. It wouldn't help if Keller Sr. decided to get involved up here."

"We'll watch out for that. I have my own spies in McMurray, so I'll make a few quiet calls."

"Okay, I leave Ms. Nicholson in your hands then. Drop by with her tomorrow for the usual courtesy call."

* * *

Even as they spoke, Matthew Keller was visiting Fort McMurray with his partner, Todd Barton, with orders from security within CUUON to check on the progress of the Mackenzie Valley Pipeline negotiations, and to grease the wheels a little to move things along. Having determined from Fort McMurray sources that there were holdups because of talks with First Nations people, he had decided they would visit some northern sites to use some friendly persuasion. Aware of his son, Malcolm's, involvement with NAPI, he would stay well clear of Yellowknife himself. Instead, he gave explicit instructions to Todd to see that the natives got a firm idea of who's in control in the north. He also found out about the seed money that NAPI had granted UVan to investigate the legal implications and that the daughter of none other than his nemesis, Eric Nicholson, was leading this. *She needs a little scare too*, he was thinking, *just so she knows what the stakes are.*

"Todd," Keller said, "this is your game. If necessary, use the same tactics that we used on the bloody Indians in Texas on the shale reserves last year. Ya have to use intimidation sometimes!"

Barton replied, "Once Savage and I finish with them, they'll see the light. Ha!"

* * *

The next morning, Julia had a call from NAPI offices advising her that they would have a company car pick her up at 10 AM to take her to their offices in downtown Yellowknife.

Hollsworth got out of the car to greet Julia as she stepped out of the hotel, recognizing Julia from a description that Professor Samson had given him. "Hi, I'm Calvin Hollsworth, Chief of Field Operations for NAPI. I believe you must be Ms. Nicholson?

'I am", replied Julia.

"I trust you had a restful night at the Yellowknife Inn?"

"I did, thank you," said Julia, "although I must confess that I turned in late after reading lots of material on the proposed pipeline. Before I first started reading up on this a couple of months ago, I hadn't realized that northern pipeline proposals go back to the early 1970s."

"I was surprised at that too when I joined the company five years ago. I also discovered that First Nations people can be quite difficult on this issue, although you can understand their viewpoint, given their traditional background of hunting, fishing, and simply being a part of their environment. It's a different world here from growing up in a city as I did."

Julia picked up on this, "And where did you grow up?"

"Houston, Texas, M'am. I come from a long line of Hollsworths involved in this industry. My granddaddy made some of the first oil finds in Texas, while my dad was an executive with Texas Oil, just retired recently. How about you? Where are you from?"

"Vancouver. I'm still there, at the University of Vancouver, that is. I'm studying environmental law and hope to include what I learn from this trip as part of my PhD thesis. Our family spent a couple of summer holidays in and around Yellowknife, camping and canoeing on the lakes and rivers, plus one summer near Fort Simpson. So I've come to know some of the First Nations people."

"Good," Calvin replied, "that will help you when you speak with them next week. For our part, we'd like to spend today with you, familiarizing you with our operations and plans for the Mackenzie Valley. Then, Monday we could have someone show you some of our nearby field operation sites. Seeing the real thing often gives one a different slant from us just talking at you. We thought you'd like the weekend to yourself to get familiar with Yellowknife. We can provide you with the loan of a company vehicle if you wish."

"That would be perfect," said Julia, "I'm hoping to use part of the weekend to make contacts and set up meetings with First Nations here, in Fort Simpson and around Inuvik next week."

As they approached offices, Julia could see that NAPI was no small-time field operation. A brand spanking new five-storey building, it had not existed when she last visited Yellowknife four years previous on that last wonderful vacation. Since then studies and summer jobs had tied her down. Inside, the building was even more impressive, commensurate with its owners. Calvin first introduced Julia to Dr. Long, the company Vice-President of NAPI Northern Operations, then led her to a meeting room where a display of maps and company posters had been set up. For the next two hours, Julia immersed herself in briefings from several NAPI employees on existing and planned northern pipelines, some of the engineering details, then the economic benefits to the Northwest Territories, especially to First Nations people.

Shortly after noon, Calvin suggested, "I'm getting the growlies; how about we go for a bite to eat?

Julia replied, "Sounds excellent to me. My brain is getting overloaded and needs a short break."

As they ate, Calvin suddenly said, "Julia, I'm not going to try and give you a perfect picture about this pipeline business. We're well aware of most of the issues around it. Just between you and me, I feel that some of the First Nations claims are justified. Also, I should tell you that I did look into your history, not in a prying way, but I know that your father is a climate scientist and his primary concerns deal with atmospheric emissions and global warming. Regardless, I want you to know that I support you completely in the job you are setting out to do."

"Then you should also know," Julia replied, "that I am studying environmental law. While I believe in the work my dad does, I take an unbiased view when it comes down to legal issues."

"Of course, but I also want to point out that the petroleum industry, all industries in fact, simply respond to the demands of the public, users like you and me. And, to shareholders, some of whom I must admit, will stop at nothing to see quarterly and annual profits increase."

"Why are you telling me this?"

"Simply because I understand the pressures in the corporate world, including those within my own corporation, and I don't want you to feel pressured to make your results sound all wine and roses."

Julia was taken aback a bit. "I certainly appreciate your frankness. Thank you. I assure you that I won't taint my results with pressure from any side."

"At the same time, don't think I won't emphasize all the positives with respect to this pipeline operation whenever I can. On the other hand, I will confess, just to you, that I have been reading up all I can on global warming to familiarize myself with the science. My own background is in physics, so the climate science material is not overly difficult for me to understand. Too often in this business, oil people pay little or no attention to the science, or even to the environment where they are working, concentrating on the geology, engineering, and simple economics; but I'd like you to know that at least I do pay attention."

They finished their lunch with a more general conversation about northern lifestyles, weather, climate, and each other's hobbies. Once back at NAPI offices, Julia again threw herself into learning as much as possible about the corporation, its various operations, and the planned pipeline. Calvin had mentioned that a NAPI technician, Malcolm Keller, would be available to guide Julia to some pipeline locations in and around Yellowknife during the following week. Julia thought his name sounded familiar and made a note to enquire later.

Just before breaking for the day, Calvin introduced Julia to a First Nations NAPI employee, Nancy Wedzin, who carried out hydrological measurements for NAPI. Nancy was a member of the Yellowknives, one of the five main groups of the

Dene indigenous people that live in the Northwest Territories. She and Julia clicked immediately. Nancy readily agreed to Julia's offer to take her out to dinner. In turn, Nancy offered to show Julia around Yellowknife on the weekend.

As Julia and Nancy headed out for the day, Calvin was thinking about the material he had been reading on global warming impacts. He had long ago ceased being a climate change denialist; the science connecting global warming to carbon emissions was simply too strong. One article was a review article that Julia's father had written for the *Canadian Geographic* the previous year. The part on northern impacts connected to melting permafrost was causing him some concern, but the recent evidence of methane emissions from offshore drilling in the Arctic Ocean was indeed very disturbing—and he was part of that operation! He thought of his family, especially his recently-married daughter in Winnipeg. *What are we doing for my grandchildren?* was his recurring thought.

* * *

As they left NAPI offices, Julia asked, "Can you suggest a good restaurant?"

"What would you like to eat?" said Nancy.

"Arctic char," Julia replied without hesitating. "We can't get the real thing in Vancouver, only farmed char."

"Ah," said Nancy, "you've hit on my favorite fish too, in which case, we'll go to the Hub Restaurant, definitely one of the best, but not too expensive, plus they also serve a wicked char chowder."

"Lead on," said Julia.

During dinner, Julia and Nancy shared stories about their respective families. Julia told Nancy how everyone in her family was involved in environmental issues in one way or another and that their interests had partly evolved from the summer holidays they'd taken in the Northwest Territories. When the chance to study environmental law related to the pipelines came up, she had jumped at it. Nancy mentioned that, after high school, she had attended Aurora College in Inuvik for two years, later transferring to the University of Prairie Agriculture in Saskatoon where she obtained a BSc in Hydrology. Following graduation, she was offered a job with

NAPI and had been with the company for three years. Nancy asked Julia what exactly was the topic of her PhD research.

Julia began, "Primarily I'm investigating the legal aspects of building the northern pipeline down the Mackenzie Valley, paying particular attention to any First Nations concerns. First, I thought I would learn about your company operations here in the north, then try and meet with some First Nations groups, possibly here, then in Fort Simpson and up around Inuvik. Perhaps you have some contacts you could introduce me to?"

"Oh, I think I probably could all right. I assume you want to get opinions from the other side, so to speak?"

"So to speak," Julia confirmed.

"Can I be frank with you and off the record?" asked Nancy.

"Absolutely," replied Julia. "And if you think at any time that our discussion might get you in trouble with NAPI, please say so and we'll change the topic. Ok?"

"Fair enough," said Nancy. "Here's the basic problem. Most company and federal government officials think that the Dene are mainly concerned about land claims and what jobs might be available for them with the pipeline construction and later operations. In fact, our people are more concerned about damage to the environment and to their traditional way of life. There are funds available to the Dene for housing, medical, and the educational needs of our people, so jobs are not really all that much of a concern, well, not the major concern anyway. In fact, if jobs were our major concern, why wouldn't we move south to where the jobs are? Climate change has already altered life throughout the north, and mostly not in a positive way. Our people are concerned about even more dramatic changes in future."

"What sort of changes are you talking about," Julia asked? "My dad is a climate scientist at the University of Vancouver, so I'm aware of things like Arctic sea ice melt and possible shipping through the northwest passage, the melting of the Greenland ice sheet and future sea-level rise, and even permafrost melt that may cause an increase in methane emissions. But what impacts do these factors cause in the north?"

"Plenty," replied Nancy. "We have already lost most traditional hunting of seal, walrus, and polar bears on Arctic sea ice. The ice is rarely safe enough to take dog sleds or skidoos over any more, so most sea fishing has terminated as well, because you don't take small fishing boats into ice floes around here. The great caribou herds are obviously affected by the warmer climate as well, and their numbers are way down. And with a longer period of open water on the Beaufort Sea, the northern coastlines are rapidly disappearing just from permafrost melt and coastal erosion. We no longer find fish where they used to be, even when it is safe to go out. We may actually have to import your farmed char in a few years."

"That would be a disaster," said Julia.

"I wish those were the only impacts we had to worry about," said Nancy. "There are plenty of other issues. You're aware that most transport of goods in the north is over winter roads?

"Yes."

"The seasonal window for winter roads is narrowing, with later falls and earlier springs. And it's not at all feasible to build many year-round roads over tundra up here, other than near larger centres like Yellowknife and Inuvik. Spring ice melt, especially on the Mackenzie, has been occurring several weeks earlier than it did 10 or 20 years ago. That causes further disruption in river transportation and crossings. Most crossings on the Mackenzie are either over solid ice or by river ferry, and they can't operate during spring breakup, or for a month or so after that when the flow is too strong. And in the main centres, we have permafrost melt to contend with. That's already caused plenty of damage to some building foundations and walls in Yellowknife. Just last week, they had to condemn the old post office building. In Inuvik, they are getting quite concerned about water and sewage line breaks. All their lines in Inuvik have to be built above ground. But they've had permafrost melt for several years, even that far north. Ask some people in Simpson and Inuvik to show you what is happening to inland lakes over the permafrost. That's affecting all animals, not to mention the vegetation."

Nancy paused, then, "How many other climate change impacts would you like to hear about?"

Julia exclaimed, "Wow, I've heard rumours of some of these things, but I didn't realize just how much climate change was impacting northern lives. We have our winter problems down south, but nothing like you are describing."

"Actually, there's more to it than I'm telling you. That's why you really do need to speak to more First Nations people before you return to the south. I can get you in touch with some contacts—what is your plan for next week?"

"Mr. Hollsworth has arranged for his technician to show me around on Monday. I think I may then head to Fort Simpson on Tuesday morning, then further down the Mackenzie. Beyond that, I'm open to anything and anyone you recommend."

"Why not come over to my apartment after dinner and we'll phone around to some of my contacts for you."

Two hours later, with Nancy's help, Julia had made some key contacts in Fort Simpson, Norman Wells, Fort Good Hope, Inuvik, Tuktoyaktuk, and Aklavik. They pulled up Google-Earth on Julia's laptop to start planning her trip in more detail.

"Perhaps you might also like to visit Fort Liard in the southwest to see a different variety of impacts," said Nancy.

"That seems to be on the way to the Yukon. I planned to visit the northern archives at Yukon College in Whitehorse to check any additional local information about a World War II pipeline that they built from Norman Wells across to Whitehorse. Apparently it was shut down after the war. I'd like to know why."

"In that case," said Nancy, "you should also take in Watson Lake, halfway between Fort Liard and Whitehorse. Didn't you say that your brother works at Dease Lake? That's just a couple of hundred kilometres from Watson Lake."

"There's a thought," Julia countered. "I might get to meet up with John on this trip."

Later, while driving Julia back to her hotel, Nancy suggested, "How would you like to visit my home village of Beaver Creek east of Yellowknife tomorrow. You could meet my family and see some of the country out that way?"

"My gosh, I'd love to, but I don't want to take up all your time."

"No problem, since tomorrow is Saturday and I planned to visit my parents anyway. I have some things to drop off that Mom wanted. Plus, Mom and Dad are always asking me about my friends and why I don't bring them out to see them.

Dad fishes, traps, hunts, and does some guiding. Mom is starting up her big vegetable garden. They love it out there. My mom and dad, my brother, Jack, and I are all proud Yellowknives Dene First Nations."

"I'd love to drive out there and meet your family, but only if you let me pay all your gas and buy dinner and lunch."

"You're on! How about I pick you up about 9:30?"

"Perfect. See you then," Julia replied as she got out of Nancy's truck.

Julia decided to check in with Dr. Samson that evening. When he answered his phone, Julia said, "Hello, Dr. Samson, it's Julia. I just thought I'd let you know that I've arrived safe and sound. Already the trip is paying off. I'm getting lots of information; in fact, it's a good thing that I brought along a voice recorder."

"That's just great, Julia, and thank you for calling," Dr. Samson responded, clearly happy to hear from her. "You know, I've been thinking that maybe you should have taken someone else along with you, for safety's sake, but also someone who could pick up additional information for you. It's almost too late, but if you find someone you can trust, please don't hesitate to offer to pay their travel expenses and even a reasonable fee for assisting. Is there someone who might be interested, do you think?"

"I hadn't really thought of that, but now that you mention it, there might be. I'll think about it. Let's leave it at that for now. I have my departmental credit card, so I guess I could use that for any additional travel expenses, right?"

"Absolutely," Dr. Samson sounded relieved, "and that would ease my mind as well. The north can be dangerous for travel, as there are not always emergency people available, as I'm sure you're aware. You do have the advantage of having travelled up there with your family, but please feel free to take advantage of this, as well."

"Thanks for mentioning that possibility. I'll keep you posted as I go along. Monday I'll still be in Yellowknife. I have reservations to fly to Simpson on Tuesday and Inuvik on Thursday morning." After a little more small talk, they hung up, with Julia agreeing to call back Tuesday evening from Fort Simpson.

* * *

The next morning was surprisingly warm for May. On the way out to Beaver Creek, Julia and Nancy saw numerous species of wildlife, including moose, caribou, rabbits, beaver, wolves and a family of black bears. Julia was pleasantly surprised and remarked, "I'm always impressed by how this area teems with so much wildlife. You just don't see as much down south, except in major parks like Jasper or YoHo. And while the terrain is rough, it's still so beautiful here."

"The land here is part of the Canadian Shield, with some of the oldest rocks in the world. Too bad that most people working for NAPI don't seem to like it here, as you do," replied Nancy. "But then, most are from the far south, especially the Americans. They've had no other northern experience. You said you spent some summers with your family in the Northwest Territories?"

"Yeah, three summers in all. We spent much of the time canoeing, quite a bit of it east of Yellowknife in fact, and one summer around Fort Simpson. I love the Shield landscape."

They were about 20 km east of Yellowknife when Nancy pulled onto the roadside. "Let me show you something interesting just off the road here." They got out and climbed a nearby hill where they had a stunning view of the country to the south. Nancy pointed out a system of ponds and small rivers and said, "See the last pond to the left there? Now notice a bit further left and you see a large brown area?"

"Yes," said Julia, "what is that brown area?"

"It's one of thousands of former ponds that you'll see all through the north. It's caused by melting permafrost that allows the pond to completely drain as one end or the other melts. A pond can drain completely in just a couple of hours. My dad used to fish trout on that pond five years ago. It really affects wildlife when that happens."

"Have we got time to walk over there? I'd like to try out my methane detection sensor near that drained pond."

"Sure, why not?" replied Nancy.

Julia grabbed her backpack from the back seat, then they worked their way down across to the dead pond. Reaching there, Julia pulled her detector from her backpack and turned it on. Immediately it started beeping. Julia glanced at the digital read-out, "Hmm, needs calibration I suppose, because it's indicating 2900 ppb. I understand that the global atmospheric value is only around 2000 ppb, so that's really quite high!"

"Why don't we check it a few times away from the pond, kind of get the background count for this area and that particular sensor?" queried Nancy.

"Good idea," Julia agreed.

On the way back to Nancy's truck, they stopped once more and checked the readout. "Still over 2850 ppb," said Julia.

Back at the truck, the sensor was still reading over 2800 ppb. "It must be out of calibration like you suggested," said Nancy. "Or maybe we're not using it correctly?"

"Perhaps, but I've done everything according to the manual. It's pretty straightforward. Interesting, the manual says that it is factory tested to ensure accuracy within 25 ppb absolute, while its relative sensitivity is rated at 5 ppb."

They continued driving for another half hour, each lost in her thoughts. When they arrived at Nancy's parents' home, her mother immediately came out to the car to greet them, followed by her dad. After introductions all around, her mom invited them inside. "I have lunch all ready, your favorite meal, Arctic char. Oh yes, Nancy told me lots about you and said you craved char!"

Lunch was delicious, followed by coffee and tasty buttered raisin bread that Nancy's mom had just pulled from the oven. Later, Julia brought out some UVan t-shirts for Nancy and her parents. The four of them wore these the rest of the day. Nancy's dad took them on a short canoe trip that afternoon. During a quiet moment in the middle of a beautiful lake, they listened to a family of loons calling. Julia felt perfect peace and said so. Nancy's dad replied, "This is the way it's always been here. We worry that the big oil people may come and spoil all of this. Although we're right into the Canadian Shield, so I understand there's little chance of finding oil or gas here." Julia talked about the rest of her tour of the north with Nancy's parents.

After lunch, Julia and Nancy checked methane readings again—the sensor now indicated 2420 ppb. "Hmm, we must have met a pocket of it around here; that value is still high, but maybe it's coming down closer to the global values," said Julia.

"Let's remember to check again back in Yellowknife," added Nancy.

About 4:30, after hugs all around and a firm promise from Julia for a return visit soon, they started their drive back to Yellowknife.

"Wow, you have great parents just like me, Nancy. You're very lucky."

"I sure am, but after today, I'm not sure whether they love you more than me. You should have heard how Mom and Dad raved about you while you washed up before leaving. I felt a bit jealous," she joked.

* * *

Arriving back in Yellowknife at 7 PM, Julia remarked, "I'm ready for a light dinner and a glass of wine. What do you say?"

"I was thinking the same thing. The Hub's just around the corner. Oh, what about checking your sensor again?"

Julia pulled out the sensor and waited for it to warm up. "Wow, it's reading high again, 2850 ppb. I must mention this to Dad when I'm talking to him. I'm sure he'll have an explanation for it."

A few minutes later they were each enjoying a glass of wine. Nancy looked pensive.

"A penny for your thoughts, Nancy," said Julia.

"I was just thinking. I have several weeks leave coming to me. How would you like for me to accompany you to Simpson and Inuvik? I've been thinking of visiting friends and relatives there anyway, so there'd be no cost to you."

"Actually, I have to confess that all day I've been trying to think of a way that I might entice you to come along," said Julia. "I was reporting back to my university supervisor Friday evening and he suggested that I bring along an assistant, at project expense."

"If you like, I could also arrange some side trips to visit other First Nations bands who may be most affected by the pipeline. Would that be of use to you? Plus my uncle, dad's brother, Tim Wedzin used to work for the oil company in Norman Wells, if you want to stop there. Although he's most likely up Fort Good Hope way where he runs a camp and guiding outfit during the summer. He could give you a perspective from both the energy industry and First Nations."

"That would be fantastic. I really must get more feedback from your people up here."

"But I'd better first ask my NAPI supervisor, Calvin, on Monday morning if I can take some leave, just in case they think there might be some conflict of interest. If it's okay, then I'll make a few more contacts. Are you up for some canoeing? I know of some very reliable guides north of Fort Simpson who we could engage for a small fee; actually, for nothing, since they are relatives."

"Excellent. You make the arrangements and I'm all for it." Julia paused, then added, "Here's to us. Cheers!" They clinked glasses.

* * *

Julia spent most of Sunday reading the material she had collected on Friday. She arrived at NAPI offices early on Monday morning. Calvin Hollsworth introduced her to Malcolm Keller, who was to be her guide for that day.

"I don't think we've met before, Mr. Keller, although your name seems familiar," Julia offered.

Keller replied, "I think your dad and mine, Matthew Keller, were colleagues in graduate school at McGill University in the 1980s."

"Ahh, I seem to recall hearing Dad mentioning his name when talking about his grad school days."

"Yeah, my father is with CUUON these days. I worked a couple of summer jobs with CUUON while studying at Texas A&M, which led to my full-time work in Yellowknife with NAPI. So ..., what's your plan for today? Would you like to see some of our field operations nearby?"

Julia smiled, "That would be great, especially since you have the wheels."

"You bet. How about we head a bit west of here for starters? There's an oil pipeline junction point about 30 km west. You grab a coffee and I'll meet you outside in, say 20 minutes, after I pick up some equipment and a company truck."

Julia went for coffee with Nancy, who informed her that Calvin had said it would be useful to NAPI for her to accompany Julia on the trip, and to consider it company time, not vacation leave.

"Perfect! If it's okay by you, then," said Julia, "would you like to make up our itinerary and reservations for the next week? Take my university credit card and I can confirm any reservations you make, if necessary. Obviously you know the country and contacts far better than I. The only contacts I have for sure are Cpl Bob Jackson of the Inuvik RCMP, whom Dad recommended to me, and my brother's friend, Paul Anawak, who is from Inuvik and is working there for his summer job with the Northwest Territories Environment & Natural Resources Department.

"Oh, you mean Great Bear Jackson," replied Nancy. "I went to school with Bob at Aurora College. And I know Paul too. He also did his first two years' study at Aurora, then took a job with the Beaufort offshore development for a couple of years. After making a bundle, he went back to school at UVan.

"Great Scott! It's a small world. You seem to know everyone in the Northwest Territories."

"When you think about it, the total population is less than 50,000. And everyone helps everyone else up here, so you get to know more people that way."

* * *

On the drive west out of Yellowknife that afternoon with Malcolm Keller, Julia started with some small-talk. "So, how come you came this far north for work, Malcolm? I would have thought your dad could easily lead you into a similar or better position in Texas."

"Ahm …," Malcolm said, "actually, I, uh, don't get along well with my father, not since he and Mom divorced a long time ago. Mom moved back to Montreal and I wanted to get as far away as possible from Dad."

"Oh, I'm sorry," Julia apologized, "I didn't mean to pry; I was just curious."

"It's okay, I'm used to it," Malcolm replied. "How about you? You get along with your parents?"

"Gosh," Julia said. "I honestly don't know what I'd do without my mom and dad, and my kid brother, John. We're all very close."

For a few moments, both were silent. Julia broke the uncomfortable silence with a change of topic. "What's your take on relations between NAPI and First Nations?"

"To be honest, I don't pay too much attention to that, just try to do my job and keep my own nose clean, so I can't be of much help to you there."

Julia accepted this as an honest response. She went on, "Fair enough. How much further to this pipeline junction?"

"About another 10 km, just beyond that next distant hill you see. Have you seen much of this country yet?"

"Our family used to vacation up here when John and I were teenagers; we spent two summers mostly on canoe trips east of Yellowknife. And yesterday, Nancy took me out east to visit her family. Rugged but spectacular country out that way."

A few minutes later they turned left onto a dirt road, went another half kilometre, and arrived at the pipeline junction.

"There's not a lot to see here, just the pipeline and this junction station," said Malcolm. "One thing you might want to know is that all NAPI pipelines are Class 2."

"Umm, what does that mean exactly?" asked Julia.

"When the project length (in kilometres) multiplied by the outside pipe diameter (in mm) equals or is greater than an index value of 2,690, the pipeline requires a Conservation and Reclamation approval under the Environmental Protection and Enhancement Act. All of ours have an index less than 2,690 and don't require that level of approval. The Environmental Protection Guidelines for pipelines address all project planning, construction, operations, maintenance, and reclamation. On public land, an approval under the Public Lands Act is also required."

"I guess that's why you have these junction stations then, with the index value being computed between junctions?"

"That's part of the reason for junctions, another being that they are useful for extra distribution."

Julia decided to try out her methane detector again. It was still indicating just over 2800 ppb. She mentioned it to Malcolm. "Must be instrument error," he said. "This is an oil pipeline into Yellowknife, not gas, so there shouldn't be any methane spikes. But, I'll mention it to the techs and have them do some checks."

"How serious a threat is melting permafrost, in terms of causing possible disastrous breaks in a pipeline, in your personal view?" enquired Julia?

Malcolm hesitated, then answered, "Our company takes it seriously, but our design folks seem pretty sure that they have the engineering mastered. Around here, around Yellowknife, that is, it's not a major concern, partly because we are building over mostly shield country, which is rock solid, no pun there, so shifting permafrost is not as much of a concern here; also, we have good electronic warning systems and really rapid access by roads, so even if a break occurred, our repair and clean-up teams could be on it within a couple of hours."

"And for the proposed Mackenzie Valley pipeline?"

"Off the record?—Scary! The problems there are plenty of permafrost area and not great access time, since we don't have much in the way of decent roads up there, at certain times of the year. Any pipeline break could seriously affect the Mackenzie River and everything downstream. But again, our engineering people are confident that they have any potential problems licked. They're doing lots of field tests and employing First Nations people in those tests by the way."

"Are the Environmental Protection Act rules any different for those permafrost areas or the Mackenzie Valley than here"?

Malcolm hesitated again, then, "I understand that NAPI has asked Environment Canada about that, but they haven't come up with anything different. Which is a concern for us because if we go ahead and build the pipeline, are they going to change the rules later?"

Julia agreed, "Good point."

"That's why NAPI is seriously considering tightening up the guidelines themselves, regardless of the increased costs. It's a kind of a no-win situation for us, dammed if we do and dammed if we don't."

"I understand. Is there anything else I should see around here?"

"Maybe the controversial fracking test site back closer to Yellowknife."

"Why do you say it is controversial?"

"Yellowknifers have been very much against it for the last six or seven years, marches, the lot. Because of the public opposition, NAPI has decided to dissociate itself from fracking altogether."

On the way, Malcolm explained, from his perspective, how much local people might benefit from the new pipeline.

* * *

Back at NAPI offices, Calvin met them and the three sat down for coffee. Calvin opened with, "Has Malcolm answered all your questions?"

"Yes, although I have a couple more to ask you right now. I'll possibly have others later as I digest everything."

"Shoot!"

"Has NAPI developed emergency plans for any potential pipeline break?"

"Yes, we have," replied Calvin, "even though we think the chances are small. I suppose Malcolm told you that we have planned for Class 2 pipelines, meaning that our pipeline sections will exceed all present requirements."

Julia countered with, "But what experience does the industry have with pipelines over permafrost where there might be more precarious circumstances?"

"Granted, there are some unknowns there, but we do have the experience of the Trans-Alaska pipeline from Prudhoe Bay to Valdez, Alaska, which has been operational since 1977. That pipeline was built to withstand earthquakes, forest fires, and other natural disasters. The only pipeline breaks have been through malicious damage—gunshots, that sort of thing.

"Even the 2002 Denali earthquake did not cause a break, although it damaged some of the pipeline sliders designed to absorb similar quakes. It caused the pipeline to shut down for more than 66 hours as a precaution. In 2004, wildfires overran portions of the pipeline, but it was not damaged and did not shut down. Our Mackenzie Valley pipeline will have even more stringent precautions and should be able to withstand any gunshot damage. It would virtually take a missile launch or a much more severe earthquake than Denali to crack this one. Those are construction precautions, and we are also developing emergency measures plans to account for anything unforeseen."

"Would that include plans for a major permafrost melt over a long section of pipeline over the next 50 years?" Julia added.

Calvin's responded confidently, "We are watching that problem closely. In fact, I have personally overseen the installation of some of our own instrumentation to monitor permafrost. So the answer to that is yes, we have contingency plans and will update these on an annual basis."

"Jumping further along, a what-if; in other words, what if a break did occur at the worst possible time of year and in the worst possible location, close to the Mackenzie River?"

"We've thought of that scenario as well. While we would not anticipate that happening, we're conducting an extensive probability analysis based on all available data, time of year, locations, and so on, and establishing an aerial probabilistic analysis of the weakest location along the proposed line. Those areas will get extra attention during construction and will have detailed emergency measures planning."

"I really appreciate your being candid on this. I have one more question at the moment. This concerns tanker ports at the end of the pipeline. How does NAPI propose to avoid an Exxon Valdez-type incident, that is, beyond the pipeline?"

Calvin hesitated a little, then, "As you know, that's beyond the scope of the pipeline construction. The industry must plan for that, yes, but not NAPI, as our responsibility stops at the pipeline endpoints. That's where CUUON and others come in. I have to say that that possibility does concern us, as it should everyone. You should also realize that two pipelines are a possibility, one from the Beaufort Sea to carry liquefied natural gas southward to North American markets. The other possibility is a dual pipeline that would carry McMurray crude oil northward to a Mackenzie Delta port, likely Tuktoyaktuk. From there it would be shipped by tanker to Asian markets."

"In that case," said Julia, "there must be emergency measures planning for a potential shipping disaster. Are you aware of what their emergency plans are?"

"Just in their broadest details," Calvin replied. "You may need to arrange discussions with them later."

"That's all I have to ask at the moment. May I call you as other issues come up?"

"You certainly may. My secretary has a package of information made up for you, including my business card. Please call me at any time."

Julia stood up and said, "Thank you so much for your cooperation. Thank you, Malcolm, as well. You have both been very helpful."

"Always our pleasure," said Calvin, "and I believe Malcolm can give you a ride back to your hotel. And by the way, I'm delighted that you and Nancy have clicked together and that you've invited her along for your northern tour this week. I was tempted to suggest that myself, but thought it might come out as being too self-serving for NAPI, almost as if we were spying on you. She is quite free to go. We won't even ask her for a report later, since you are doing that under contract. I hope that the two of you have fun as well as good results for your study."

"Thanks, I do appreciate that, especially since Nancy knows so much about the country and her people. It will be helpful to me to have her along for work, for safety, and for friendship. Plus Nancy is making all our reservations."

* * *

Julia met up with Nancy for dinner at the Hub, where both ordered their favorite again, oven-baked Arctic char. "What kind of itinerary did you set up for us?"

"We're going to have a busy couple of weeks, let me tell you," Nancy replied. "Tomorrow we fly to Fort Simpson. We'll meet with Chief Margaret Roche the next day to get her views on the present pipeline that runs from Norman Wells to northern Alberta through Fort Simpson. Then on to Norman Wells on Day 3 to see why that pipeline exists. There we'll meet Chief Daniel Mackenzie of the Dene, as well as a representative from Esso.

"Esso in Norman Wells?" queried Julia.

"Yes, Wells refers to oil wells. Esso, and its predecessor, have been drilling oil there since 1920 or so. They even built a refinery during World War II and shipped oil across the mountains to Whitehorse by pipeline. The pipeline was only operational for a year or so before it shut down. They built the present pipeline to Zama, Alberta in the 1980s.

"I had no idea that there was oil production in the middle of the Northwest Territories," said Julia.

"Alexander Mackenzie noted that he had seen oil seeping from the river's banks at Norman Wells in the 1780s, but the Dene knew about the oil long before that. In fact, the name of the town's location in the Dene language means, 'where there is oil.' They say that Chief Daniel Mackenzie is related in some way to Sir Alexander, or at least his family took their name from him."

"I'm impressed with your knowledge of history, Nancy," said Julia.

"I studied mostly northern history and geography at Aurora College, before taking up hydrology at the University of Prairie Agriculture in Saskatoon. After Norman Wells, we take a local flight north to Fort Good Hope, where we'll meet my first cousin, Tim Light Foot Wedzin, who will take us to the Shehanni settlement of the Dene nation about 20 km from Fort Good Hope. It's a bit out of the way, but Jack worked on that pipeline out of Norman Wells, so he can provide a different perspective. He and his family fish at Shehanni during the summer, where he also operates a hunting guide camp for his oil company contacts. His skill at hunting got him the name Light Foot. They live in Norman Wells the rest of the year. We can get to Shehanni by canoe. Are you up to a 20 km canoe trip?"

"That sounds exciting and is well within my ability."

"From there we go back to Norman Wells, then fly to Inuvik the following day. After that, it's down to Tuktoyaktuk. I left our departure for Fort Liard open, because you'll likely make more contacts in Inuvik whom you'll want to speak with, including our mutual friend Great Bear Jackson. We could, for example, visit First Nations people in Aklavik or Fort McPherson, both fairly accessible."

On Tuesday, Julia and Nancy completed most of their itinerary and reservations for Fort Simpson, Norman Wells, Fort Good Hope, and Inuvik. Julia met once more with Hollsworth and other members of NAPI staff.

* * *

As they left NAPI offices that afternoon, Julia had no reason to suspect anything strange about a vehicle across the street, with Todd Barton and his accomplice, Nick Savage, observing their moves. Barton had already obtained Julia's itinerary for Yellowknife to Inuvik through Ted O'Brien, who had described his hack into airline security as a piece of cake. He had also made a few well-placed enquiries at NAPI.

Barton told Savage, "You know who you're tracking. Pick the right time and place to shock this young brat out of her mission."

"Don't worry," replied Savage, "once I'm done, she'll head back to Vancouver with her tail between her pretty legs."

"Here's their itinerary for Fort Simpson, Norman Wells, and Fort Good Hope, from where they'll most certainly be taking a canoe trip up Jackfish Creek to the Dene Shehanni settlement where Nancy's uncle runs a guiding service. After that, they head to Inuvik, where I'll handle things. Then they have an open reservation to Fort Liard, later to Watson Lake in the Yukon. I want no direct contact between the two of us, unless I call you. Use your Nolan Smith alias up here from now on. You'll send your information to Ted O'Brien, coded that is, and he'll pass it on to me. Here are our codes for movement: S for you, 1-6 for each of the towns, 1 for Simpson, 2 for Wells and so on to 6 for Watson Lake. Any changes in between, we use letters. If they take a diversion between Inuvik, which is 4, and Fort Liard, 5, for example, then that would be 4a, 4b and so on. And refer to the two girls as birds, B1 for Julia and B2 for Nancy. Memorize these few codes and then destroy them. Got it?"

"No sweat," replied Savage.

"Just remember, we don't want anyone killed, but we need to prevent or at least delay this legal report that NAPI thinks will help them. I'm headed directly to Inuvik. I'll likely contact you there, but don't approach me directly. Keep me up to date by text through O'Brien as to what's going on. Always clear your texts immediately from your phone as a precaution. One more thing: if I get a message to you to 'close the web,' it will mean you have to kidnap Ms. Julia. It may become necessary to use her as a bargaining chip with her daddy."

* * *

Julia and Nancy spent the evening discussing possible contacts they should meet, while packing for the next day. Julia called her mom just as she was preparing to dash off for the start of several night shifts at the forecast office. They took a few minutes to update each other. Carol was relieved to learn that Julia had a good partner to accompany her on the rest of her northern trip and that they just might be able to link up with John for a couple of days. Julia heard a few details about her dad's trip to Africa and that he would be back in Vancouver in two days' time.

"Tell Dad that I've been getting some really high readings of methane concentrations all around here. I'd like to know if it's normal or whether my sensor is out of calibration."

"I'll be sure to tell him," said Carol.

Julia agreed to call her mother again from Fort Simpson the following evening.

13. Nightmares and Storm of the Century

Later that evening, Carol had ended a week off to start a night shift at Vancouver Weather Office. During her first shift-change briefing, she noted that a large, rapidly-deepening storm was forming over the eastern Pacific at latitude 45N. Cold air was streaming southward from the Aleutians into the storm, allowing it to pick up moisture from the relatively warmer waters and energizing it. The storm was moving northeast toward northern BC.

While it was outside the responsibility of the Vancouver office, she also noted that a low off the east coast of Florida was expected to deepen rapidly over the increasingly warm Atlantic waters there. Unusually high sea surface temperatures (SSTs) exceeding 25°C were a major factor. The east coast situation was complicated by the earliest development ever of a tropical storm in the Caribbean southeast of Haiti, in mid-May, already given the name *Aletta*. The storms on both the west and east coasts were associated with major high amplitude upper troughs extending north-south from Arctic regions to the subtropics. As if that was not enough, a major Pacific El Niño off the coast of Central America and Mexico had intensified, with SST temperature anomalies 5°C higher than normal, even stronger than the record 2015 El Niño.

"Looks like an interesting shift," quipped Carol.

"Yes," agreed the outgoing shift supervisor, "and the numerical guidance from both Washington and Montreal agree that the Pacific and Atlantic SST anomalies appear to be in synchronization. Something really drastic is going on in the northern hemisphere atmosphere. Temperatures throughout the hemisphere are already well above normal for this year. With this strong El Niño, a record warm year is in the offing again. Something to bear in mind, with the numerical guidance suggesting record high temperatures and precipitation amounts. Despite that, the ridge separating these two upper troughs has brought relatively cooler air down across the eastern US. That cool air is about to move out over much warmer SSTs, and you know what that will do to the Florida low And to top it off, Tropical Storm *Aletta* in the Caribbean, has now reached hurricane strength, and will create an interesting mix when it recurves northward.

"Here's something else," he continued. "The models predict that both the eastern Pacific and Florida lows will bottom out at 900-910 hPa—I know, I find that hard to believe myself. I've never seen lows deepen this much before, especially not two lows simultaneously on either side of the continent. And both are sucking in plenty of tropical air to boot, so precipitation potential is extreme. Much of the east coast will experience hurricane-force winds and torrential rainfall. Peak rainfall amounts are expected in both Washington and Montreal, which might impact on our numerical guidance friends at both. So stand by for some extra work if something untoward happens there.!"

"Gottcha," replied Carol.

"Good luck."

"Thanks, see you at tomorrow evening shift change. I hope."

Carol studied the latest charts, already over five hours old. New numerical guidance would start arriving in a little over an hour, giving her time to get familiar with the older information first. Central pressure for the Aleutian low was already down to 945 hPa, while the east coast low had moved offshore South Carolina and was still at 990 hPa. Hurricane *Aletta* was predicted to reach at least Category 4 by the time it hit the warmer waters off Florida, following on the heels of the extra-tropical low already deepening there. *But what will happen then? Will the two merge early? Oh well, let Montreal and Washington computers worry about that one,* Carol thought. *We have this Aleutian low to be concerned about first.*

An hour later, she looked over the shoulder of the local surface analyst, pursing her lips as she noted the Pacific low had already deepened by another 15 hPa to 930 hPa. "That's a phenomenal rate of deepening," she commented to the analyst.

"Some West Coast stations are reporting 3-hour pressure falls of almost 10 hPa; I've never seen anything like this!"

"How far has it moved since 0000 UTC," she asked?

"It's moved more than 200 km in the last six hours. Still continuing northeast, maybe slowed a little while deepening, but still tracking at about 40 kph."

"We'd better update the weather warnings for the BC West Coast and coastal waters. This is not looking pretty." After seeing to the warnings, Carol went off to the lunchroom for coffee. Out of habit, she picked up the evening copy of the Vancouver Sun. The front page headline read, "CUUON going for Black Gold in the Beaufort and Barents Seas." *Oh Lord*, she thought, *just what Eric wants to read. What blinders they have! Have they run out of brains, or are they simply selling their souls?* Another headline read, "Mackenzie Pipeline on Hold Pending Review." *At least that shows some wisdom*, she thought.

After scanning the rest of the paper, she went back to the operations office. Her analyst immediately caught her attention, "Our phenomenal low has gone impossible! The pressure tendency has fallen 12 hPa in three hours! At that rate it could hit 900 hPa shortly after 1200 UTC.

"You've got to be kidding," said Carol.

"That's not even the worst of it. The east coast low is deepening at about the same rate, down to 960 hPa already. It's accelerated northward to just south of Hatteras. And get this, it's snowing heavily in the Blue Ridge Mountains of Carolina and Virginia, in late-May for Pete's sake! It doesn't end there. According to NOAA, Hurricane *Aletta* is already a Category 5. It's expanded to record size, 2000 km across, with maximum sustained winds of 180 kph; and it's pounding Haiti. Man, Haiti is taking a beating these days! I checked and the earliest ever for a Category 5 before this was *Emily* in mid-July 2005. They're calling it the largest hurricane ever recorded over the Atlantic and it's likely more dangerous than either *Katrina* in 2005 or *Haiyan* in 2013. There are no communications or weather data out of Haiti or eastern Cuba at the moment. There is also a super-typhoon forming east of the Philippines headed north toward Japan. Our weather is completely unraveling right around the globe."

"Maybe we're seeing storms being initiated directly by global warming for the first time," Carol opined. "There just can't be any other rational explanation for this mess."

As she sat to contemplate the area forecasts, including wind and precipitation warnings, she wondered how the storm brewing offshore might affect John in northern BC later that day, or even Julia somewhere in the Northwest Territories.

* * *

Meanwhile, in the course of John's survey work near Dease Lake, he had been speaking with many of the locals. He kept hearing stories of how the warming climate was affecting northern communities. He was discussing these stories with Tony and his supervisor over coffee. The supervisor suggested that such stories were greatly embellished and they probably should pay little attention to them. Still, John and Tony had been making regular field measurements of atmospheric methane in the Dease Lake area and were seeing values all above 2000 ppb. John was redesigning the sensor's electronics, adding a transmitter so that it could transfer data through a satellite back to UVan, where his dad and Professor Pearce could access the archive. Tony was writing software to process the data on-site and to handle the data communications.

On the same night that his mother started her night shift in Vancouver, John had gone to bed early, as he had a long drive to a new site the following day. Bothered by the stories he'd heard from locals that day, he had a very restless night of nightmares. At one point, he woke with a start. It was already light outside and Tony was at the door.

"John, you'd better come out, someone is here from some Narc Squad, he calls it. He wants to ask you about drugs or something,"

"What the heck is a narc squad?" John mumbled as he pulled on his pants. When he opened the door, he saw two men standing there, one tall and muscular, the other somewhat short and stubby. Neither looked too friendly. Both wore dark navy blue trench coats with hats from out of the 1940s. Despite their unfriendly-looking nature, John almost broke out laughing, for they looked rather ridiculous. "What can I do for you gentlemen?" he asked.

The tall one said, "We're with the BC Climate Narc Squad. We're investigating a drug cartel up here. We'd like to question you."

"You won't find any drugs around here," said John. "And what do you mean by Climate Narc Squad? There's no such thing. Try the local pub, I guess."

"This is not fun and games, young man. We're serious."

You sure look funny and very unserious, John thought without saying so out loud. Then he could not control himself and burst out with a laugh.

"Do you know somebody called Eric Nicholson?" the tall character asked. "The heck with it, I think we'll take you in, anyway. Carl, cuff this guy. And then let's get his sister."

On his guard now, John replied, "Okay, okay, cool it. On what basis are you arresting me and could I ask if you have a search warrant?"

"We don't need one with the Narc Squad."

Noticing his company truck was idling, though he could not remember why, John played for time and said, "All right, I'll go with you quietly, but just a minute; I have to turn off my truck." As he went by the two, he noticed them looking at each other smiling. *There's no way these two clowns are legit,* he thought. *I've got to get out of here, fast.*

He opened the truck door, leaning in as if to turn the key off, then jumped in while slamming the door shut. He shoved the gear into reverse, spraying gravel over the two toughs as he hit the accelerator, then shifted into forward and raced away. Looking in his rear view mirror, he saw Tony in the rear cab, then the Narc Squad gaining on them in what looked like a Corvette. John pushed the accelerator pedal harder, glancing at his gauge and realizing he was already doing over 110, and on a gravel road. Just as he reached a sharp turn the Corvette came alongside. John glanced left, staring into a rather large revolver pointed at him. He saw the flash, then heard a bang. He screamed, blacked out, then heard another bang-bang-bang.

Suddenly John woke up in his bed, drenched in sweat. He heard the same banging, then realized someone was at the door. "Who's there?" he said rather nervously.

"It's me—Tony! What's going on, I heard you screaming."

"Oh gosh, I think I was having an awful nightmare, at least I hope it was. Hang on, let me unlock the door. I need to talk to someone."

After relating his dumb nightmare, John said, "That's two nights in a row that I've had nightmares. Both times they involved Dad and Julia. I wonder why?"

"Probably because of the threats your family has had lately," Tony answered, "and you're naturally worried about them."

"Yeah, I suppose that's it. But you know, I think I'm going to call Julia right now. Mom asked me to call her last evening but it was too late. All this stuff feels like a terrible premonition."

"Wouldn't hurt. Why don't you do that? It's only 6:30, but the cafeteria should be open by now. I'll head over for breakfast and you can join me there, after."

"Okay." *Climate Narc Squad? How ridiculous can you get?*

He dialed Julia's cell number. After three rings, recognizing the caller-ID, she answered, "Hello, John-boy, how are you. How's the job in Dease Lake?"

"Pretty darn good," he replied. "How about you? How are your northern interviews going?

They're going really well." I had no idea this pipeline business was so complex, so many different angles. And I guess I'm really learning just what Dad's work on climate change is all about. I had no idea how important this really is and just how threatening global warming impacts really are. Have you taken any readings with your methane sensor?"

"Yeah, I did, but my sensor seems to be out of calibration, because all the values are way over the global averages."

"Like, how much?"

"I took a few readings at different locations around Dease and they were all around 2200 ppb."

"Then they may very well be reading okay, because I've been getting values of 2500 to 3000 ppb around Yellowknife. You should keep a record, GPS locations, date, time, and so on. Dad and Dr. Pearce will be very interested, because apparently his grad student got values up to 2400 ppb last summer up here."

"No kidding! I'll start keeping a record like you suggest. By the way, I'm sure hearing a lot about local climate impacts around northern BC. We'll have to compare notes sometime."

"For sure. I'm leaving Yellowknife tomorrow for Fort Simpson with a fantastic new friend, Nancy Wedzin—she's First Nations Dene. Nancy has made up our itinerary, including all our travel and accommodations. We're meeting with First Nations people in Simpson, Norman Wells, and a Shehanni settlement near Fort Good Hope. We'll go to Inuvik, Tuktoyaktuk, and Aklavik the next week. After that, we'll be headed to Fort Liard, and from there, Watson Lake, Yukon. We should be there in about two weeks. Perhaps I can visit you in Dease Lake after that, before heading back to Vancouver."

"Why don't I meet you in Watson instead? You know Tony is working with me here. Our work is flexible enough that we can both take a few days off later this month and meet you and Nancy there."

"That's too cool," said Julia. "I think I'll be ready for a break then too. Why don't the four of us take a couple of days and drive up to Whitehorse? I'd like to visit the archives at Yukon College and see what local information there might be on northern pipelines."

"It's a plan, then."

John then described to Julia his strange nightmare and how it caused him to worry about her. "Almost like a premonition or warning of danger," he added at the end. "Have you heard from Dad? Is he back from Africa yet?"

"Mom said he was leaving Durban today, in fact," replied Julia, "and he should be back in two days, following a stopover in London. Mom said he sounded pretty pleased with the trip, except that he was shocked by what he saw on a two-day trip to the Sahel region, something that a PhD student is working on. It's the student whose defence he is going back for in August."

"He sounds as busy as always. Well, Sis, you look after yourself. I only have one sister ya know. And I'll see you in about two weeks' time. Email your itinerary to me, would you, so that we can plan our shorter trip?"

"Okay, Little Bro, will do; and I'll see you soon. Don't forget to take those methane readings. Luv ya. Bye!"

Tony was excited about the change in plans and readily agreed. It was a scenic 250-km drive to Watson Lake over a paved highway.

* * *

Meanwhile, back at the weather centre in Vancouver, Carol was reviewing the 1200 UTC analyses and latest numerical guidance from Montreal. She had never known such erratic weather patterns in her 20 years of forecasting experience. The Pacific low had moved into the Gulf of Alaska and deepened to 905 hPa, a record low sea level pressure. Most of the precipitation appeared to be in the Yukon and Alaska, but south coastal BC was experiencing hurricane-force southwest winds gusting in excess of 100 kph. Meanwhile, the east coast low was just south of New Jersey, deepening very rapidly with its central pressure down to 930 hPa. *Aletta* was being described as a super-hurricane, likely the most severe ever. It had virtually destroyed Haiti, skirted just north of Cuba and the eye would pass over the eastern Bahamas in two or three hours. There were no communications with Haiti at all. Nassau had apparently been devastated. The predicted track virtually followed the low pressure centre up the coast. It appeared that what the record low pressure system did not destroy along the east coast, *Aletta* would finish in a day or so. Carol sighed as she completed her latest warning updates for the BC coast and adjacent waters.

Her thoughts turned to Julia and John in Northern BC, which was expected to experience heavy rains as the Aleutian low continued northeast, but it would then track more easterly as it crossed the mountains into northern BC and the Yukon, with heavy snow likely over the Yukon. "I should give those two another call and warn them not to get caught out," she thought.

Going to the lunchroom for a short break, she managed to reach John by phone and quickly gave him the lowdown on expected weather. Julia was enroute to Fort Simpson, John told his mom, and would arrive well before any storm hit. Carol was delighted that he and Tony planned to meet up with Julia and Nancy in Watson Lake. John promised his mother that he would call Julia again to warn her of possible weather problems.

Before heading back to her desk, she briefly viewed early CBC television news. Damage and flooding in Puerto Rico, Dominican Republic, Haiti, eastern Cuba, and the Bahamas were catastrophic. Early indications were that the number of deaths would collectively exceed the 2010 Haiti earthquake disaster toll of 200,000. News from the eastern seaboard was certain to report increased damage and death toll. Heavy wet snow and freezing rain were already falling in Montreal, while winds with heavy rain and flooding were widespread from Washington up through New England, even before *Aletta* could strike.

Back at her desk, she noted that wind damage was being reported all along the BC coast. Power was out through much of Vancouver Island. At that moment, lights flickered in the weather office and emergency power immediately kicked in. "Oh Lord, I hope our computers survived that surge," she thought.

Luckily they did. Shortly after, Carol learned that there was an electrical blackout from Seattle to north of Vancouver and through most of Vancouver Island. Major outages were occurring throughout eastern North America as well. Canadian Meteorological Centre computers in Montreal were down completely, with no indication when they would be back on-line. Apparently, even emergency power was down there. Thankfully, Washington numerical guidance was still operational. A few hours later, Carol headed home completely exhausted.

She slept until mid-afternoon, then sat up to listen to the grim news on a battery-powered radio she had, since power was still down through most of Vancouver. The BC premier had declared a state of emergency throughout most of Vancouver Island and the Sunshine Coast. Many homes had damaged or destroyed roofs, securely-docked fishing boats and yachts had been destroyed in many coastal towns from Victoria to Campbell River. One of the BC ferries had broken its moorings, and before it could be brought under control it had destroyed some sailboats and yachts in the basin. As the low crossed the Saint Elias Mountains separating Alaska and the Yukon, a late-spring snow was already falling in Whitehorse, with local amounts up to 50 cm forecast.

However, this was mild compared to events in eastern North America. Emergency teams throughout the northern Caribbean and Florida were estimating deaths approaching 250,000, while many cities and towns were virtually destroyed by onshore storm surges, spawned tornadoes, and winds gusting in excess of 300 kph as *Aletta* barged through, maintaining Category 5 intensity. The earlier low pressure centre had stalled near Boston, pummeling all of New England and the southern Maritimes with winds in excess of 100 kph and rainfall amounts of 5-10 cm, while southern Quebec had received 50 cm of wet snow, mixed with freezing rain. But the worst might be yet to come, for *Aletta* was about to merge with the low, combining its tropical moisture mass with copious moisture which that low still contained.

Carol thought, *It can't really get much worse. Or can it? Maybe Eric should have stayed in Africa for a while. This will take weeks to sort out, I'm sure! Groan, and I still have two more nightshifts to work!*

* * *

Back in Dease Lake in northern BC, a cool easterly wind was picking up. John and Tony checked the local news while eating breakfast and were dismayed by the weather forecast—increasing winds with rain as a low crossed the mountains into northern BC, and winds veering into the southeast later in the day—but, heavy wet snow was predicted for the Yukon and south to within 100 km of Dease Lake.

"Wow, better now than when we travel to Watson," commented John. "I sure hope the snow doesn't reach as far as Julia. Hmm, she should be in Fort Simpson later today."

Tony added, "I'm sure she'll check the forecast before heading further north."

In fact, the low was dissipating rapidly and veering southeastward as it crossed into BC, although this made for a cooler day in the Northwest Territories. Whitehorse received 20 cm of wet snow, which quickly melted over the next two days, while the storm only brushed the Northwest Territories after crossing the Mackenzie Mountains separating the Yukon and the Northwest Territories.

* * *

The results of the east coast storms were appalling. *Aletta*, which had already caused hundreds of thousands of deaths in the Caribbean, had merged with the deep low that had stalled over New England. Rainfall amounts exceeded five inches throughout New England causing widespread flooding. Winds exceeding 150 kph took roofs off of houses and businesses alike, brought down power lines, and destroyed whole forests of trees. But the most severe impact was felt later as rain turned to snow with amounts of 60-120 cm from Washington to Toronto, Ottawa, Montreal, and Quebec City. This was further complicated in southern Quebec and Maine by freezing rain. The combination took down power lines all through the northeast, with widespread blackouts and brownouts. Although adequate warnings had been disseminated in time, highway accidents were still horrific. In many cases, rescue operations could not be carried out due to high winds and blocked roadways. Several thousand people died in vehicle accidents, from downed high voltage electrical lines and fires, and from exposure to the brutally cold elements. *Aletta* was clearly the storm of the century.

The amount of energy output by this storm combination was beyond anything of record. Its root cause, a more energetic atmosphere resulting from anthropogenic global warming, could no longer be ignored by western governments. The economic damages alone would flatten the insurance industry and it would take literally months to restore order in eastern cities.

Clean-up and power restoration was accomplished rapidly in Vancouver. Eric's flight from Europe managed to land the following afternoon.

Within 24 hours of Eric's return from Africa, he and David were called to Ottawa to brief Prime Minister Mulligan Thomas and his Environment Minister, Webb Andrews. The prime minister quickly followed up with a call to US President Illyana Dinton, requesting an emergency meeting on the climate crisis. However, the President, under great pressure from the petroleum industry, notably CUUON, suggested a delay while the impacts of the storm were evaluated. Eric suspected this would take weeks, but at least he and David had finally convinced the Canadian government to pay more attention to what was going on in northern Canada, particularly with respect to permafrost melt, fracking, offshore drilling, and methane emissions.

14. Sub-Arctic Pipelines, Permafrost, and Methane

While Eric was in London on his way home, Julia and Nancy had left Yellowknife on their way to Fort Simpson. They were to meet a local chief of the DehCho First Nations the following day. There were several dozen people on the same flight, but few strangers stood out, except one chap in blue jeans. As he walked down the aisle to his seat one row forward of Julia on the opposite side, she noticed a distinct scar crossing his right cheek and a rather prominent nose. *Probably a pipeline crew member*, Julia thought. Several times during the flight, Julia could not help notice as the stranger subconsciously rubbed his forefinger across the bottom of his large nose, but apart from his facial scar there was nothing else about him to take her attention. She promptly ignored his presence.

They arrived at Fort Simpson Airport and took a taxi into the town. With over 18 hours of daylight in late-May, they had plenty of time to take in a few sights. Most impressive of all was seeing the mighty Mackenzie River near the end of spring breakup. Looking out over the river, Julia commented about the power of nature evident in the river.

"The discharge you're seeing will almost double in the next few days, now that we've had spring breakup," said Nancy. She continued explaining to Julia, "Sometimes the ice jams flood the town because the ice breaks earlier upstream. That ice will then dam at different locations along the Mackenzie, causing local flooding. If you get a lot of water coming out of the tributary rivers early, especially the Athabasca and Peace rivers, while the Mackenzie is still frozen downstream, then you can have some really big jamming as the ice is carried down-river. And Fort Simpson is particularly vulnerable because the Liard River joins the Mackenzie right here."

"So, will that 20-foot high ice jam over there cause flooding tonight?" Julia questioned.

"Oh, that's a minor inconvenience for locals, since the main ice breakup is finished with here. What you see there is mostly slush, with some freezing build-ups overnight. That will probably be all gone by tomorrow, because breakup proceeds rapidly once it starts. The ice breakup should be through Fort

Good Hope by the time we get there later this week, so we should be able to travel inland by canoe."

While Julia and Nancy were taking in the views of the Mackenzie, unbeknownst to them, Nick Savage, now using the alias, Nolan Smith, had taken another flight to Norman Wells, then a quick hop to Fort Good Hope that same day with a small single-aircraft service provided by a local pilot. Because Nancy had written a brief summary of their itinerary for her boss at NAPI in Yellowknife, a few discrete enquiries at NAPI had revealed the girls' further plans to take a canoe up the Jackfish Creek north of Fort Good Hope. Smith rented a quad and spent the next day surveying the land northeast of town along Jackfish Creek. He had been careful to mention to the quad owner that he intended to go fishing around Ontadek Lake east of the town. *Fishing all right,* he chuckled to himself, *fishing for a large canoe.*

The next morning in Fort Simpson, Julia and Nancy met with Chief Margaret Roche of the DehCho. The chief's view of a Mackenzie pipeline did not resonate well with Malcolm Keller's view of the benefits. Her fears echoed the same concerns of First Nations that Julia had read about prior to her trip, with the risk of pipeline breaks and what that might do to the land, wildlife, the Mackenzie, and northern people, being her foremost concern.

"Since the Norman Wells to Alberta pipeline was completed in 1985, we've seen many breaks and leaks, albeit mostly minor, and all hush-hush. But if a break should occur in the wrong place at the wrong time of year, we would be in serious trouble," Chief Roche commented.

"What would be the wrong place at the wrong time of year?" asked Julia.

"Suppose the break occurred over tundra during summertime. Most sections of pipeline away from towns in the Northwest Territories can only be serviced during winter when we have winter roads. During summer, you can't get heavy equipment in to those locations over tundra, so a break then could go unrepaired for many hours after it was detected. Once they know there is a break, they would turn off the oil, but how much might leak into the Mackenzie before they reacted? And how would they service the break without heavy equipment?"

"Ah, yes, I see that," replied Julia.

"Short-term gain for long-term disaster is how I would sum up my feelings about these northern pipelines. There are jobs available for First Nations and others during the construction phase, but little afterward unless one has very special training."

Chief Roche was also quite knowledgeable about the cause and impacts of global warming in the north. In the longer term, melting permafrost and all the related impacts on wildlife and humans, as well as the subsequent release of methane, were high on her list of concerns. Julia mentioned that she had already detected methane readings of 2500-3000 ppb in and around Fort Simpson, well above the 2000 ppb average global values.

That evening at dinner, Julia remarked to Nancy, "I'm pleasantly surprised at how knowledgeable Chief Roche is on climate impacts."

"I'm not really surprised at all, Julia," replied Nancy. "You see, we are living out global warming impacts in near real-time in the north. While southern Canada may expect 2°C warming in this century, we're experiencing that degree of warming in a single decade. You hardly ever notice impacts in southern Canada because they haven't really hit home there yet, but we see changes year-to-year. Our environmental impacts are 5-10 times what you experience in the south."

"That's certainly true. We haven't really observed any *obvious* changes to the climate or its impacts in a large city like Vancouver, at least not just yet. Although we certainly have been experiencing wetter winters and drier summers the last decade, just as the models predicted. But you're also much closer to your environment here than anyone in a large city. Dad tells me that it's not just the global temperature increase that is a major concern, although that directly translates to the melting of permafrost, sea ice, and the great ice sheets in the Arctic. The real concern is the amount of heat energy that we're adding to the atmosphere, oceans, and land areas. Some of that energy is converted to kinetic energy, which directly feeds stronger winds and storm systems, heavy precipitation events, floods, and radical changes to ocean currents. Some of the excess heat energy translates to longer, more severe droughts, failed crops, and famines, particularly in the subtropics. It's an endless list of unsavoury impacts.

"I would really like to hear your dad give a talk on this here in the north. I've heard that he's able to explain science at a level that a lay person can understand."

"Yes, he does lots of that. Listen, I promised my supervisor, Professor Samson, that I would call him again this evening in Fort Simpson. I must go do that now; then we can continue talking.

After checking in with Professor Samson, Julia and Nancy talked on well past midnight, discussing their plans for the next week as they continued northward.

The next morning they took the 500-km flight to Norman Wells. As they were descending to the small airport, Julia noticed some strange islands in the middle of the Mackenzie with some obvious activity on them. "What are those islands," she asked Nancy?

"Those are artificial islands," replied Nancy. "They constructed five or six of those for oil drilling beneath the Mackenzie River. They transport the oil to northern Alberta through the existing pipeline. The proposed new pipeline would be much larger and would replace all of this, although Norman Wells continues to be the oil centre for the Northwest Territories. The petroleum industry and our government claim that the Northwest Territories might have over 35% each of Canada's marketable light crude oil and natural gas. Esso still operates a small oil refinery at the west end of town too. It supplies the energy needs of the general area."

"Wow, this is totally new to me," said Julia. "I gather we stay at the Heritage Hotel tonight. How do we get to Fort Good Hope tomorrow?"

"There's a small operator at the airport who runs a twin Cessna to there," said Nancy. "I've already made a reservation with the pilot."

"Perfect," replied Julia. "Boy, am I glad you came along. I wouldn't know the first thing about getting around these smaller settlements up here."

That afternoon they were given a tour of the town and of the old Esso refinery, which Nancy had arranged for them before they left Yellowknife. They then met with Dene Chief Daniel McKenzie, who reiterated similar concerns that Chief Roche in Fort Simpson had expressed. Julia continued to take methane readings, with values of 2800-3000 ppb around Normal Wells.

That evening during dinner, Julia asked Nancy about plans for the next day, "How will we get to the Shehanni settlement from Fort Good Hope?"

"Glad you asked. Remember I asked you back in Yellowknife about your canoeing experience?"

"Yeahhh," Julia replied with a little trepidation.

"You get to use that experience. I have cousins we'll visit in the Shehanni settlement up Jackfish Creek. They're Dene like me."

"How far do we canoe," asked Julia.

"No more than 20 km. But, if you'd rather, we can always rent quads. There are some well-worn trails."

"No way. Canoe sounds great, and I'm not afraid of a mere 20 km. I take it that spring breakup will be over?"

"Jackfish will be at maximum flow, but the ice will be gone. It's a slow meandering river otherwise and really is not much more than a creek by early-September. Great for canoeing.

"This is going to be fun," said Julia. "I can't wait!"

"I kind of thought that. You're obviously in good physical condition."

* * *

The next morning, Julia and Nancy took the Cessna service to Fort Good Hope, with a short taxi ride north from the town to the confluence of Jackfish Creek with the Mackenzie. There they met Nancy's uncle, Tim Wedzin and his wife, Betty, with two 17-foot fibreglass Clipper canoes ready for the run upriver.

Meanwhile, Nick Savage (alias Nolan Smith) was 10 km northeast, hidden behind a hill 500 m from the east bank of the river. He carried a 450-caliber rifle with high-powered scope, which was capable of dropping a charging rhinoceros in Africa or a polar bear in the Northwest Territories. It included the very latest silencer, so that its discharge could not be heard at 200 metres. It was also easily dismantled into various components for transportation. Nick had been a sharpshooter with the US Marines during the Iraq war, where he had also earned his scar in a knife fight in a Baghdad bar. His objective this time, at least, was not to kill anyone, just to leave a very clear warning message.

* * *

Julia and Nancy were thoroughly enjoying their paddle up Jackfish Creek and easily kept up with Tim and Betty. "Not bad for two city dwellers," commented Tim, realizing that he and Betty held no advantage in paddling over the two girls.

As they rounded a westerly bend in the river, Julia and Nancy heard a crack. Suddenly water was pouring in through a rather large hole in the bow of their canoe. Tim, just behind them, quickly pulled alongside, "Transfer over to our canoe. We'll take it in to shore where I can make a temporary repair. There's a narrow beach on the north side just ahead. We may as well stop for lunch. But I don't understand how that happened."

They pulled in to the shore, dragged the leaking canoe out of the water and unloaded it. Tim immediately recognized the problem. "That's a gunshot hole for certain. It had to be from a high-powered rifle to make a 4-inch diameter hole like that," he said and warned the girls to take cover immediately behind some rocks.

They all took cover. The girls were calm but terrified. "It must have been an accident, but by who," said Nancy. "Where is he?"

"Listen," said Tim, "I believe I hear a quad over that hill across the river. I don't think this was an accident. But I can't understand why. Have you girls had any trouble with others, perhaps someone opposed to this work that Nancy told me about, Julia?"

"None that I know of," said Julia.

"Who would do this, here in the north," added Nancy? "Tim, are you certain that hole is from a rifle bullet? I mean, we didn't hear any shot. Surely we would hear a rifle shot."

"Whoever it is must be using one of those new silencers I've read about," replied Tim, "because I sure heard no gunshot either. And the way that quad was tearing out of here; that makes it pretty certain that it was not accidental. Let's wait a while, just to be certain there is no one else around shooting. We'll plug that hole up, then I'd like to have a look over beyond that ridge. Maybe we can find where he holed up and check for empty shells, anything to give us a clue."

An hour later they rowed across the river, checked out the ridge, and found an obvious location for the shooter, along with a single shell plus some trash left behind. Tim noticed right away, "That shell is definitely from a high-powered rifle, and the shooter is very experienced. I think his shot did exactly what he wanted. It was intended to scare us, or at least you two girls. We'll nudge all this stuff into this bag, because I'm sure the RCMP will be quite interested. Perhaps they can find fingerprints to match up. So don't touch anything with your fingers. I think they may also be interested in talking with anyone who's rented a quad in town. We'll call them on my satellite phone at our Shehanni camp."

* * *

By then, Savage had already reached town and was winging his way southwest into the Yukon. He had no intention of returning to Norman Wells. Realizing that he could be easily traced, he paid the pilot to fly him the 700 km to Whitehorse. At Whitehorse Airport, Savage rented a truck, this time using a new alias of Nadair Sciarra. The pilot, Tony, who only knew him as Nolan Smith, joined him on a drinking spree in town, except Savage drank very little on the pretense of being the designated driver. After dinner, Savage loaded the pilot, only semi-conscious, into the truck. They headed southeast toward Watson Lake. Around 20 kilometres outside of Whitehorse, he turned off into a deserted gravel pit, dragged the pilot from the truck, garrotted him with a length of wire, buried him in a ditch and then departed for Watson Lake. There he would meet up with an old pal, who had been with him in the Iraqi war.

* * *

The four canoeists arrived at the Shehanni settlement during late afternoon, still a bit shaken up, but otherwise unscathed. Tim immediately reported in to Norman Wells RCMP detachment by satellite phone, agreeing to meet them late the following afternoon in Fort Good Hope. Julia and Nancy were treated to a dinner of smoked caribou and Arctic char that both swore was even better than their dinners at the Hub restaurant in Yellowknife.

After dinner, the four new friends sat around a campfire and talked over the events, without coming to any conclusion. The talk returned to pipelines and climate change in the Northwest Territories. Tim told of many incidents with the

119

pipeline between Norman Wells and Zama, Alberta. There had been more than 100 leaks and spills. Accident rates had more than tripled since 2000. "Safety issues got so bad that I decided to get out 10 or 12 years ago and started this camp. I still have lots of friends and contacts within the industry, so we have more than enough business to keep me out of trouble," Tim said.

"What kind of incidents and safety issues are you talking about?" Julia queried.

"You're always under pressure in these jobs involving pipelines, and CUUON, who own most of the Norman Wells facilities, has one of the worst records for this. At first it was little things, like taking a fall, cracking a safety helmet, and requesting a new one. The incident would go unreported in the records, and good luck getting a new helmet. But then they cut back on staff. Often as not you found yourself out in the field without a buddy. They did provide a satellite phone, but when solar activity was high, you often lost all phone contact because of the magnetic anomalies. Plus, field activity was always rush, rush, rush, lots of pressure to get things done in a hurry and hang safety issues."

"Did you complain to management?" Nancy threw in.

"Sure, but they were under pressure too, from head office, so complaints rarely got higher than the next person up in their Canadian office in Calgary. And *they* usually did nothing. But the straw that broke the camel's back was a pipeline rupture north of Camsell Bend; that was, oh, July 2009, I think, about 120 km northwest from Fort Simpson. That area has no road near it. Because the rupture occurred during summer, it was 24 hours before we even suspected it. We shut the line down immediately, but then the problem was to find where it was leaking. I wanted to call in a helicopter and take a crew upriver to find it, but after our local management consulted the Calgary office, they were told to send one man up in a swamp boat, my old buddy Joe Gilday. Joe headed out that morning and by early afternoon, he reported back that he had come across oil coming downriver and that he would go and locate the source. That's the last I heard from him."

"Why? What happened?"

"We're not sure, but he discovered the rupture several hundred metres from the river. Something happened to cause a fire and Joe was immolated, burnt alive. It must have been a horrible way to go, because his body, what was left of it, was halfway to the river. He must have run toward it trying to reach water. That never should have happened. He should not have been alone for one thing."

"But surely things would have changed after that," Julia interrupted. "The National Energy Board should have come down hard on them?"

"That's just it. It bloody well never got reported! I kept complaining for days afterward, demanding an investigation, but it never got beyond our office. Eventually I quit and I guess they were glad to see me go. There were lots of incidents that went unreported, but that was about the worst. Joe and I had grown up together and got jobs together. I still miss him, and to lose him that way." Tim's voice cracked. There was silence for a few moments.

Julia broke the silence, "Tim, you tried your best and maybe your telling this story will help in the end. Nancy told you why I came here, I believe?"

"Yes. I can tell you whatever you want to know. I have to say this, I can't help feeling that this incident was somehow connected, though maybe not directly, to CUUON operations around here. It seems to me that somebody does not want you reporting these things."

"If that's the case, then my being up here may be endangering everybody I speak to, you and Betty, Nancy. Perhaps I should drop this project. I can't …."

"NO, you will not drop out of this, not because of us," Betty interrupted Julia,

Nancy added, "And neither will I. I just know that what you are doing is right, Julia." She put her arm around Julia's shoulder.

"I agree," added Tim. "Just say the word and all of us are here to help you."

"You know," Julia said thoughtfully, "whatever happens, I'm making the very best friends anyone could ever have. You guys are just too much," Julia's voice cracked a little. "Do you really think the gunshot is related to all this?"

"It's related all right, but I'm also certain that it was not an assassination attempt. That gun our 'friend' had was very high powered, and I'm sure he knew how to use it. You would not be alive right now if he'd intended to kill you. I think it was a warning, however. He was trying to scare you off the trail, so I do think you need to increase your security measures. And we do need to speak to the RCMP and follow whatever they say."

"Amen to that! Changing the topic a little, Tim, what do you know about permafrost melt around here?" asked Julia,

"We have plenty of tundra and plenty of permafrost. Although it's disappearing fast and with it our ponds that are so important to wildlife and our way of life. We're just about at the Arctic Circle here, at 66.5° north latitude, so if you're up to a little more canoeing before you take to bed, I can show you a whole bunch of small ponds near here that have drained recently from melt. It won't be dusk until after 1 AM and never gets totally dark at this time of year. These ponds, now dry, used to have lots of nesting Canada Geese in the summertime, but most of the ponds remaining are too small for geese to nest on."

"Hey, you're on. Let's go see it."

They canoed east a few miles, then Tim stopped on the south side of the river. They climbed a small ridge and looked out toward the south at numerous empty pond beds. "All the water simply disappears into Jackfish Creek," Tim stated. "It really changes the landscape for wildlife. It will sure change my life too."

It was a sobering revelation to Julia and kept her awake for a while when she finally bedded down. The next morning, Julia took the time to take more methane readings in and around the settlement. All readings were above 2500 ppb. After lunch they loaded the canoes again, then said goodbye to Betty. Julia, Nancy, and Tim squeezed into the one canoe for the return trip to Fort Good Hope. Going down-river was considerably more relaxing.

On arrival at Fort Good Hope late in the afternoon, they met Constable George Bergman who had come down by swamp boat from Norman Wells that morning. They described the shooting incident that had occurred on Jackfish Creek the previous day. Julia briefly explained her project and Nancy's role in it. She listed locations she had already visited and people she had interviewed. When questioned, Tim added his suspicions that the shooting did not seem to be an accident. He explained that he thought it might be related to Julia's work and that someone did not want her carrying it out.

"Why would you think that?" Cst Bergman asked.

"For one thing," Tim answered, "this guy was using a non-standard, high-powered rifle, unusual for the north. It would make a mess of even a polar bear. He obviously knows how to use it. At the distance he shot, about 300 metres, an experienced marksman would not miss his target. Besides, he had plenty of time to shoot more than once. He deliberately missed us, just shot up the canoe, not only to scare this brave lady, which didn't work, but also to delay us, presumably so he could make his getaway."

"Hmm," said Cst Bergman, "then he should be easy to find. There is only one quick way out of here and that is using Tony's Northern Service. Glancing at Julia he added, "Which I presume you and Nancy also used to get here from Norman Wells."

"Yes," said Nancy, "so we should go talk to Tony and find out if he flew a stranger out from here yesterday. Otherwise," she looked around nervously, "he is either still here, or else had to go up- or downriver by boat somehow."

"He sure didn't get to Norman Wells by boat. I arrived here by swamp boat from Norman Wells a short while ago. There was no sign of any other boat, and I know no one arrived at Wells from here before I left. I think we'll check at the airport just south of here, where Tony has his office."

They headed to the airport a few kilometres away by taxi. On arrival they discovered Tony's office was closed and his Cessna was gone.

"Funny," Julia said, "he assured us yesterday that he would be here this morning to fly us back to Norman Wells." The constable hailed a mechanic working nearby and asked him about Tony.

"He flew out of here yesterday afternoon with a passenger," the mechanic said. "He told me they were headed to Wells and he'd be back by late-evening. But when he got off the ground, I noticed that he headed southwest across the Mackenzie Mountains instead of southeast. He hasn't been back since, so I assume they changed their mind and headed into the Yukon."

The constable related this to Tim, Julia, and Nancy, then suggested, "I think your marksman headed to the Yukon yesterday. I'll call for a check on their destination."

Back in the village half an hour later, Cst Bergman informed the three that Tony had flown his passenger to Whitehorse the previous day, had filed a return flight plan for last evening, but his Cessna was still parked at Whitehorse Airport. "We have to consider his passenger as armed and dangerous, so Whitehorse RCMP are conducting a search for him, but no one with the name Nolan Smith has turned up. Meanwhile, I suspect you two ladies are stranded here, unless you'd like to accompany me back to Norman Wells by swamp boat. It's too late to leave today, but we can set out tomorrow morning about 8 AM if you're game."

"That would be great," replied Julia.

"I have to warn you that there are a few rapids about 15 km southwest of here, but otherwise it's pretty smooth boating. I can make room for you two and your luggage."

"How far is it to Norman Wells this way, and how long will it take?"

"Oh, 180-190 km. It will take a good five to six hours. Are you sure you want to risk it? There are several independent pilots operating out of Wells that you could hire to pick you up here."

"Heck, no. We would feel very safe with our own RCMP officer, wouldn't we, Nancy?"

"No kidding."

They left the following morning sharp at 8:00. It was a long but fun trip, as they were able to pull in to shore several times for lunch and coffee breaks. Both girls thoroughly enjoyed the spectacular scenery during the boat trip. They docked in Norman Wells during mid-afternoon, in time to check in to their hotel and wash up before dinner. Cst Bergman dropped by an hour later and informed them that there was no news about Tony or the marksman up to that time.

Over dinner, Julia confided to Nancy, "I feel guilty about dragging you into something that is potentially dangerous. You know I won't feel bad if you decide to head back to Yellowknife."

"You don't really think I'm going to let you go on alone, do you? I haven't had this much fun in months. No way you're getting rid of me now! Besides, you need my help."

"I don't know about the fun part, but I sure do appreciate your help. But if we have another incident, then you have to promise me that we give up the project."

"No promises. Sorry!

"You are about as stubborn as my mom and dad, you know."

"Humph, like you can talk."

Julia gave in, "Okay. What's the next step on our agenda, Lady?"

"We head to Inuvik first thing in the morning, where we'll meet my friend and yours, Great Bear Jackson, and your brother's friend, Anawak. There are others we can talk to in Inuvik. We probably should go on to Tuktoyaktuk from there, at least to see the proposed pipeline terminus. Then you need to decide whether we take diversions to Aklavik or Ft. McPherson.

Late that evening, Julia called her mother back in Vancouver and described her trip to date, attempting, unsuccessfully, to pass off the shooting incident as a minor event. Carol did not see it as minor. She reminded Julia about the trashing of her father's office and the murder in Bonn. Julia then spoke with her dad.

Eric asked Julia whether the shooter had been located and arrested. She described as much detail as she knew to her father. She also mentioned her day with Keller's son, Malcolm, that he was estranged from his father ever since the marriage breakup. Then she mentioned the high values of atmospheric methane that they were encountering.

"All my readings have been above 2800 ppb, except east of Yellowknife where they fell just below that," Julia related. "And John is getting high values around Dease Lake as well."

"That is somewhat disturbing," said her father. "David's student reported values in the 2200-2500 ppb range last summer. We'll check the calibration of your sensor when you get back, although it's the same model that David has used up north for the last two years. They check calibrations all the time. He will be very interested in this. I presume you are taking notes of location, date, and time of each reading?"

"You bet. I'm checking values at each location every day, and recording them in a spreadsheet that I could email to you at each stop if you wish."

Given the gravity of all these incidents, Julia agreed to call home at every new location on her travels, including the next evening in Inuvik. Her parents were extremely worried about Julia, yet they hid their concerns as much as possible because they were not going to interfere in what she wanted to do.

* * *

Minutes after the call from Julia, Eric received a call from Hans in Washington.

"Hello, Eric," said Hans, "how are things going there?"

"Just fine, except for concerns we have for our daughter, Julia, working up north," replied Eric. "Anything new in the investigation?"

"Yes and no," said Hans. "Yes, we have some new leads, but no, nothing definite just yet. However, I do want to warn you that we have reason to believe that this Nils Scheer, using another alias, is in Canada. Also, now that you mention your daughter, Julia is doing a legal investigation on pipelines in the Northwest Territories, right?"

"Yes, that's so. In fact, we talked with her just minutes ago. She's been visiting several towns along the Mackenzie River and is now back in Norman Wells, heading to Inuvik in the far north tomorrow morning. There was a shooting incident while she was near a place called Fort Good Hope. They were canoeing to a Dene settlement on a tributary of the Mackenzie out of there."

"Shooting incident? That doesn't sound good. Look, this may not be related, but your Keller friend headed north to Fort McMurray 10 days ago, along with Todd Barton and one other chap. I checked on the third individual. His name is Nick Savage, and he works for Barton, who works for Keller within CUUON. Savage had previously been a sharpshooter with the US Marines during the Iraq war; in other words, a sniper. He underwent a long recovery from post-traumatic stress disorder (PTSD) after the war. We checked with his last commanding officer. While Savage received an honourable discharge because of the PTSD, the officer indicated that Savage had been enjoying his sniper duties a little too much in Iraq. Keller stayed at Fort

McMurray, while Barton and Savage both headed on to Yellowknife. Barton continued on to Inuvik a few days later, but Savage seems to have disappeared, or at least we have no information about his further whereabouts. He may be using an alias now and then. But, here's the interesting point, one which really concerns me because of Julia's work. This guy Savage has an obvious scar on his right cheek. And you'll remember what Dr. Mazurenko told me about one of his attackers?"

"Good Lord, you don't suppose this is the same guy, do you?"

"We have no evidence to say for sure, but I have to be suspicious, if only because of the Keller connection. I just don't like the fact that these characters are visiting the same places as Julia—and possibly not coincidentally."

"I don't like it either, needless to say," replied Eric. "I think it's time I took some leave and met Julia."

"Actually, I'd rather you didn't. The two of you together would be an explosive combination and very tempting targets, if these suspicions are right. Let me speak with our RCMP friends first. Surely they can provide better security than you for Julia at this stage?"

"Perhaps you're right, but you're not her dad. If you were, I'll bet you would be thinking exactly what I just suggested."

"I'm sure you're right, and I would be equally wrong. However, my training and experience does give me a decided advantage in that respect. Despite our suspicions, we absolutely cannot make any arrests yet. We need to gather clear undeniable evidence to ensure that these guys get convicted. You have an added incentive there yourself, because if we could remove at least some of the denialist arguments once and for all, it would make your job easier, would it not?"

"You're perfectly correct again, so yes, it certainly would make my professional life less stressful."

"Oh, what I didn't mention yet is that I have a flight to Vancouver early tomorrow morning. I thought we might get together as soon as I arrive. Could you hold off doing anything drastic until then? We want to first ensure Julia's safety and then set a trap for this trio. I was planning to be there two days ago, but we have had absolutely horrific weather all along the east coast, from Florida all the way to your Maritime Provinces. And I suppose you've heard about that early hurricane and what it's done in the Caribbean? Is this getting to the tipping point that you climate scientists talk about?"

"It may very well be, but it's too early to say for sure. We hope not. Anyway, give me your flight number and arrival time for Vancouver, and I'll meet you at the airport.

"It's Delta 555, arriving at 10:55 Vancouver time. I'll see you then."

"Right. Bye for now."

* * *

The next morning, after checking in for their 8 AM flight from Norman Wells to Inuvik, Cst Bergman met Julia and Nancy before boarding. "Good morning Julia, Nancy. I just thought I would pass on the latest on our investigation of your mystery shooter. Assuming he had to have arrived by air sometime in the past week, we have narrowed down possible suspects to one individual who arrived the same day as you. Have you ever heard the name Nolan Smith before?"

"Not at all," said Julia."

"Someone by that name rented a quad that day and indicated he was going fishing on Ontadek Lake east of Fort Good Hope, but we think he headed northeast, because that was the only rental this week. "Did you notice any odd character on either of your flights who might have been tailing you?"

"Not really," said Julia. "Although there was one man on the flight from Yellowknife who kind of stood out for me, but only because he had this obvious scar on his face, on his right side. I remember thinking that he was probably a pipeline crew member, but I doubt that this was significant."

"Maybe, maybe not," replied Cst Bergman. "I'll check back with the quad rental agency this morning. If they mention that scar, then we could be on to something. We have a good graphics artist on site in Inuvik. If this turns out to be a lead, we'll contact you there to give a more detailed description and see if he can come up with a possible face."

"We have already arranged to meet with Cpl Bob Jackson there, so we'll be easy to locate."

"Ah, Great Bear, he and I have fished together. A good man. … I think that's your boarding call. Have a good flight, and I hope we can come up with something today. Bob will let you know what we find out."

"We sure hope so too," said Julia. "Thank you for everything, especially that delightful swamp boat trip upriver yesterday. I really enjoyed that."

"Me too," added Nancy. "Thanks so much for all your help."

"All part of the service. You'll hear from me again through Great Bear in Inuvik. Meanwhile, you girls be on your guard from here on, and stay safe."

As they boarded their flight, Nancy remarked to Julia, "He's kind of cute, isn't he?"

"Who? Oh, you mean Cst Bergman. I didn't really notice."

"Heck you didn't! I saw you smile to him, and he smiled back".

"You notice too much sometimes", and they both laughed.

15. Offshore Methane

The 1½-hour flight to Inuvik was uneventful. Both Julia and Nancy were on their guard for any suspicious looking individuals. They had just picked up their baggage when an RCMP officer, Cpl Bob Jackson in the flesh, walked up to them.

"Great Bear," called out Nancy and grabbed him in a huge bear hug. "So good to see you again."

"You too," said Great Bear, "and I'm pleased to see you this morning, both personally and professionally."

"Professionally, eh, but first let me introduce you to my friend Julia. Julia, I'm sure you already know that this is the great Cpl Bob Jackson."

"Pleased to meet you, Cpl Jackson. Nancy has told me about you."

"Only the good parts, I hope," replied Great Bear.

"There are no bad parts about you Great Bear," added Nancy quickly.

"She certainly didn't tell me any bad things," said Julia.

"So," said Nancy, "what is there professionally to report which you just alluded to?"

"I heard about your adventure out of Fort Good Hope. Cst Bergman called me just an hour ago with an update and asked me to meet you here. We think we have identified your culprit. You mentioned a chap on your Yellowknife flight with a scar on the right side of his face. The quad rental agency identified their only renter this week as having a similar scar. That was the chap who rented the quad the day before you set off. We have already had our graphics artist draw up a composite face from their description. We would like to do likewise with your description and compare the two."

"I'll do anything that might help nail this guy, but I'm not sure I can really recall much else about him," said Nancy.

"You'll be surprised what our artists can draw from your memory. They have considerable training in this, besides their artistic talents.

"Would you like us to come down to your offices right away?"

"If you wouldn't mind; that would facilitate things. We're also trying to track down the pilot who may have taken Smith to the Yukon."

Driving into town, the first thing Julia noted was all the pipelines criss-crossing through Inuvik. "Those are no doubt mostly water and sewer pipes, aren't they," she remarked to Great Bear.

"Yes, since the ground is frozen most of the year round, they have to be above ground. However, the melting permafrost is creating havoc with them, not to mention with building foundations and just about everything else that humans have built around here."

Arriving at the RCMP offices, Julia decided to first take a methane reading.

"Wow!" she exclaimed, "Just over 3100 ppb! That's the highest reading I've recorded yet."

"What did you expect?" asked Great Bear.

"Global methane concentrations have apparently been rising for the past decade, to 1800 ppb. But we detected values more between 2500 to 3000 ppb. This is our highest measure yet."

Later at RCMP Inuvik HQ, after half an hour with the graphics artist that included considerable questioning, Great Bear showed Julia the composite drawing from her description, along with the composite made from the quad rental agency description. They looked very similar.

"That's him, I'm pretty sure," said Julia. "Also, this may seem trivial, but I noticed several times during our flight to Fort Simpson that this guy seemed to have a compulsive habit of rubbing his forefinger across the bottom of his rather large nose."

"The fact that it's a personal habit may turn out useful in locating him later, especially if he uses other aliases. We'll be getting an all-points bulletin out on this guy, armed and dangerous. Julia, let me drop you and Nancy off at the Mackenzie Hotel where I'm told you have reservations. When you're ready, we can talk about your investigation. I'm not sure I can provide much that you haven't already heard, but we'll see."

"Nancy and I are pretty much ready to go. We'll just drop our bags in our room. Why don't you have a coffee with us at the hotel?"

"I'll do just that. I'll let our secretary know where I'll be on our way out."

Five minutes later, Julia and Nancy were checking in at registration. Great Bear said, "I'll be in the restaurant when you're ready. But before we discuss pipelines and the impacts on the north, I want you both to think really hard about this. Do you have any reasons at all to think there may be another attempt at stopping your interviews and reporting? We need to determine if there is an organization involved in this, or whether this guy Smith was acting alone. Let's talk about that first in a few minutes. Okay?"

"You bet," replied Julia.

Todd Barton, sitting in the lounge near the door, observed Julia and Nancy checking in and was curious why the RCMP constable was so attentive to the young ladies. *Hmm, I need to stay undercover*, he thought to himself.

* * *

Back in Vancouver, Eric met Hans at the airport shortly after 11:00 that same morning. They went over all the events to date. Hans then headed to RCMP headquarters to get filled in on information from the Northwest Territories detachments.

"You just dodged a bullet getting in here. Carol called me just now to say she was called in to work overtime at Environment Canada. Apparently there is another pretty severe storm with high winds headed our way. This time it's making a beeline for Vancouver rather than heading northeast as the last one did. In fact, storms have been a bit unusual here lately."

"Another global warming influence perhaps?" asked Hans.

"Possibly," replied Eric, "because in May we're usually under more influence of the subtropical Pacific high pressure system. Those are expected to expand northward with global warming. On the other hand, the Earth's atmospheric and oceanic systems are so confused right now that anything is possible I suppose. We could have southerly winds in excess of 100 kph by late afternoon. That would close air traffic with the runways running generally west-east."

"You know, I've almost learned enough about weather since last winter to write a thesis on it," Hans joked.

"And I might make a Sherlock Holmes yet," Eric quipped back.

"Would you care to join me at RCMP headquarters right after lunch and we'll run anything new you have by them."

"Given the involvement of my daughter, I think that's an excellent idea. Why don't we take an early lunch together? I'll call my postdoc back at the office to delay a meeting we had with David Pearce and his grad student. You recall David from the Bonn meeting and also the barbeque at our place a few months ago? There may be a link between David's permafrost data and the new analysis results we have from Mazurenko's data, as well as some methane data that Julia and John have been sending back to me. They were both interested enough to take methane detectors with them."

"I can't say that I understand the science, but I'm beginning to grasp the significance of your results. Let's head for lunch then. My breakfast in Washington was four hours earlier than yours, and I'm starting to feel like a very growly Kraut!"

* * *

Julia and Nancy rejoined Great Bear in the hotel restaurant.

After ordering coffee, Julia opened with, "You know my dad, so you know he's a climate scientist. You also know what my mission is in the north. That's the only possible connection I can think of for why some person or persons might not want me carrying out this study. If that's the reason, then they would also know that NAPI are funding this study through the University of Vancouver Law Department."

"Do you find that a conflict of interest? I mean, your department taking funds from the petroleum industry."

"No. My supervisor made that very clear, and NAPI agreed, that not only would they accept our report without interference, but that we would be free to publish our results. We have that in writing. Also, I detected some discomfort from their middle management in Yellowknife over the whole issue of pipelines. I certainly believe that NAPI will honour their agreement. I felt that level of trust while in Yellowknife, and their future operations may even depend on the results."

"I'm going to check with headquarters in Vancouver to see what plans they have. You may need an escort the rest of the way, so please keep me informed about all your movements. How long do you plan to be here?"asked Great Bear.

"We'll likely be in Inuvik through tomorrow. We're meeting with my brother's UVan friend, Paul Anawak, this afternoon. Paul is from Inuvik and working here for the summer with the Northwest Territories Environment & Natural Resources Department. He'll introduce us to his Inuvialuit people tomorrow. Do you happen to know Paul?"

"Of course. He and I are from the same band. I grew up with his older brother and I'm in and out of his department several times a week. Tell you what, call me after lunch, or whenever you're meeting. I'll drive you down there; it's only 2 km north on the other side of Inuvik."

"That would be great. I'm going to call my parents first to avoid one of them having a heart attack."

Julia went to her room to call home, while Nancy chatted briefly with her friend, Great Bear. There was no answer at home. *Of course,* Julia thought. *Dad will still be at the university, and likely Mom is also at work. I'll try later this evening.*

* * *

At that moment, Carol was indeed at work, puzzling over the latest weather developments in the eastern Pacific. According to the latest numerical guidance from both Montreal and Washington, the storm bearing down on southern BC had the potential for 100 mm of rain. A quick check of climate records indicated Vancouver's normal May rainfall was only 54 mm, while the extreme daily record was 48 mm. This event was a quite unusual event. The wind gradient preceding the storm still promised winds exceeding 100 kph, starting soon. She quickly checked wind records—the maximum wind gust ever recorded at Vancouver Airport in May was 70 kph, and the guidance was indicating steady winds close to 100 kph. They had already issued weather warnings; it was simply a matter of details at this point. It required exceptional circumstances to forecast parameters above or below record values. *Oh well, it is what it is,* she thought.

* * *

Following lunch, Hans and Eric met with the area inspector at Vancouver RCMP headquarters and discovered some new links from the information provided by the Norman Wells, Inuvik, and Whitehorse detachments. No one by the name of Savage had turned up. They also had a missing pilot, the one who flew Julia and Nancy to Fort Good Hope and later flew Nolan Smith to Whitehorse. His aircraft remained parked at Whitehorse Airport. Eric and Hans were shown the composite drawings of Nolan Smith, who had also disappeared.

"Given the gravity of the situation with your daughter, Dr. Nicholson," said the inspector, "we are assigning Cpl Jackson, whom I believe you know, to accompany your daughter and Nancy while they remain in the Northwest Territories or the Yukon. He will accompany them in plain clothes so as not to draw too much attention. I trust you have no problem with that?"

"Absolutely none; in fact, I'm greatly relieved, because otherwise I would be tempted to ask her to return immediately. However, knowing my daughter, she might just delay her departure despite our wishes. She is doing important work up there and is fairly headstrong about completing it." He winked at Hans.

"Ah yes, I know about daughters," replied the inspector, "having two of my own in university right now."

"Then you have my sympathy, sir, but I'm also happy for you."

"Indeed."

"There is one other possible clue I'll add," said Hans, "that I discussed with the inspector earlier but I haven't mentioned to you yet, Eric."

"Oh?"

"My colleagues back in Germany eventually traced the rented truck, the one that struck Dr. Mazurenko, to a Nils Scheer, except this Nils Scheer does not seem to exist."

"How does that bear on activities here?" asked Eric.

"It so happens that the person who rented the truck to Scheer indicated that he had a scar on his right cheek!"

"Good Lord, then do you suppose that Scheer, Savage, and Smith are the same?"

"That's my suspicion, especially given that all three have the same initials, NS."

"I see," said Eric. "Then the missing pilot is in serious danger since he can identify this scarface, if indeed he's still alive? And that also means that I need to keep Julia from being in any contact with him. Once is enough!"

"Yes," said the inspector, "and that's why we assigned Cpl Jackson to your daughter and dispatched forensic experts to Whitehorse to search down the pilot and possibly Mr. Smith, alias whatever."

Eric was agitated by these revelations; yet, he had the utmost confidence in Hans, as well as Cpl Jackson, whom he'd met several times. Hans needed to stay at RCMP headquarters to coordinate all the facts in the case thus far. He agreed to meet with Eric again the following afternoon, after Eric's classes.

Later that afternoon, Eric sat down with Chi-Min and David to discuss their joint methane results. Eric mentioned that Julia had been measuring methane concentrations in the 2500-3000 ppb range at Simpson and Norman Wells, but he was uncertain of the calibration.

"What sensor is she using?" asked David.

"It's a Figaro TG5000 series," replied Eric, "and John is using the same instrument in Dease Lake. He called his mother this morning and mentioned that he's getting values around 2200 ppb."

"Same instrument series that my student installed last summer, when he had readings as high as 2300 near Inuvik. That sensor is accurate to within 50 ppb and its sensitivity to +5 ppb, even without recalibration, unless it's been dropped or otherwise damaged. That's not good news, Eric."

"We should hear from Julia again this evening. She was headed to Inuvik. Let's hope the values there are no higher than 2300."

* * *

"Ok, boss, what's next?" Nancy asked.

"It's almost lunchtime, and we're meeting Paul at 2 PM. How about we roam about for the next hour and take some more reading."

"Sounds about right to me," replied Nancy.

Shortly after, with five methane readings all around 3100 ppb, Nancy said, "Munchie time?"

"For sure," replied Julia, "and then we can call Cpl Jackson, since he kindly offered to drive us. I wonder what these methane readings mean in the overall scheme. Dad is meeting with Professor Pearce today. They'll be discussing our data and whether they mean anything significant."

* * *

An hour later, Great Bear turned up in plain jeans, shirt, jacket, and boots.

"Hello," said Nancy jokingly, "are you off work or on holidays?"

"Neither," said Great Bear. "I'm on duty to accompany you girls wherever you go for the rest of this trip, believe it or not. Orders from Vancouver, no less."

"Somebody's getting serious about all this," said Julia.

"Without divulging all the details, your dad and some German detective called Hans Stahl have uncovered new evidence, and the chief inspector is taking no chances. You're in my charge now ladies, or, maybe I'm in your charge, I'm not quite sure."

"We'll take it either way," said Julia, "and glad to have you on board. Besides, apparently the Mounties always get their man, so we must be safe."

"Don't get carried away with that saying, but I promise to do my best."

"That will do for us," said Nancy.

The three headed to the Environment & Natural Resources Department in a new GMC Yukon truck with all the bells and whistles. "Headquarters approved this rental just because of you two," said Great Bear.

"I'm impressed," said Julia.

"So they should, for someone as important as Julia," added Nancy. Julia blushed.

* * *

The three met Paul Anawak 10 minutes later. "Good to see you here, Julia. Hi, Great Bear," said Paul. "Julia, how's little brother, John?"

"He's fine, in fact, he's not so far off. He's working in Dease Lake in northern BC. By the way, have you met Nancy before? She's become my dear friend and workmate on this tour."

Paul, turning to Nancy, commented, "I recall meeting you a few years back when you were at Aurora College with Great Bear here. Good to see you again, Nancy."

"And you," replied Nancy.

Turning to Julia he continued, "I knew about John's co-op position. He was pretty excited about getting that job for the summer. Our mutual friend, Tony, has a job with the same company. We're hoping the three of us will get together up here yet this summer. So, what can I help you with?"

"As I explained to you earlier, I'm basically interviewing the Northwest Territories people to get their concerns and feedback on the pipeline debate, as well as the opinions of the various industries involved. My report will form part of my PhD thesis in law, so I'm summarizing various legal aspects. Apparently, this has attracted the attention of others, particularly those in the climate denialist community, funded no doubt by big money."

"What makes you suspect that?"

"We've run into a problem or two. We've been shot at once, and you'll note that Great Bear is with us?"

"Hard not to notice him. I must say that I did wonder why he was with you today."

"Paul," interjected Great Bear, "this is in strict confidence, but I've been assigned to Julia and Nancy for the duration of their travels in the Northwest Territories and the Yukon. That's why I'm in plain clothes, not to attract attention."

"Mum's the word," replied Paul.

Julia asked Paul, "Working with the Northwest Territories Environment Department, you likely hear a few things about climate change, carbon dioxide, permafrost melt, methane, Arctic sea ice melt, polar bears and even more, right?"

"Certainly do," replied Paul. "Where do you want to start?"

"How about methane, since I've been getting very high readings ever since we started out on this trek. Has methane always been high in this area?"

"No, just this past year, in fact. Apparently some grad student last summer was getting readings as high as 2300 ppb. What sort of values are you seeing?"

"That would have been Professor Pearce's student, but right now we're getting values around 3100 ppb. Doesn't sound good."

"Wow, it sure doesn't! Maybe you should report back to your Professor Pearce or your dad."

"I'll be calling dad this evening. He's sure to be very interested in this."

"In the meantime, since you mentioned permafrost melt, I'd like to show you some drained ponds just north of here. Last January, my dad broke though the ice, dropped a match, and just about lost all his hair. It just exploded from methane ignition. Much of the permafrost around here is melting. In fact, it's causing havoc with water and sewer lines in Inuvik. I'll show you some breaks on the way out of town. I see you all have boots on. That's good, because I want to take you hiking a couple of kilometres off the road."

As they buckled up in Paul's truck, Julia asked him what other changes were being noted that might be attributed to the changing climate.

"Spending most of my time at school in Vancouver the last few years, I'm not totally informed about that, but if you have time this evening, I'd like you to meet my dad. I guess he knows just about everything around here that's changing in any way."

"I'd like that," said Julia.

Paul added, "Just up ahead at the intersection of Navy and Marine Bypass Roads, we had breaks in both the water and sewer lines that are just being repaired now. The lines were only put in last summer." He stopped next to a restaurant, and they all got out.

"Wow, the ground's really soft here," Julia commented.

"Yeah, and they're having to bring in a lot of fill. The pipeline bed sank about 10 feet here."

After a few photos, and a methane reading of 3200 ppb, they drove on north.

"That was our highest reading so far."

"You'll likely get equally high values north of here, the closer we get to the Arctic Ocean … oh, just a minute. I'm going to pull off here and let this guy go by. He seems to have been following us. When we stopped back there, he stopped a hundred metres further back."

Great Bear turned and watched intently as the black 4x4 roared by them. He glanced at Julia, who nodded slightly.

Nancy commented, "I hate sounding paranoid, but I wonder who that is."

"Not to worry," said Great Bear, "there's only one guy in the truck and there are four of us."

"I take it you may be expecting someone," said Paul.

"Hopefully not," replied Great Bear. "But we'll be ready."

Paul drove on for about 15 km, then pulled off to the side of the road. "It's about a kilometre east of here, but the trail should be pretty good right now, not too much bog." Julia took a methane reading, still 3200 ppb. Forty-five minutes later, they reached what used to be a small pond about 200 by 500 metres.

"It drained completely last summer when I was here last," said Paul. My dad said that last winter he had to be careful to put out his pipe, because the methane was so volatile."

"Wow," said Julia, "I'm reading over 3400 ppb." That's getting close to double the global average of 1800 these days."

"Maybe we need a new global standard," said Paul. "I've heard of values that high in Tuktoyaktuk recently. You'll notice how the water all drained out from the north end of this pond."

"Where does it go?" asked Nancy.

"On to the next pond down. Then, presumably that one melts at one end and drains on to the next, eventually on to the Arctic Ocean. It plays real havoc with waterfowl, who migrate up here just to breed. They need these small ponds."

They visited one other pond on the way back into Inuvik, with similar methane readings. Paul suggested picking the girls up after dinner to visit his dad. They headed back to the Environment Building. Great Bear then drove the girls to their hotel and went as far as the desk with them.

* * *

The desk clerk caught Great Bear's attention and said, "Bob, I happened to notice some guy at the ladies' door. I interrupted him because he looked suspicious, not any guest of ours. Struck me that he might have been trying to break into their room, and I kind of surprised him. When I asked him what he was about, he said he was just placing a note under their door—said he knew both of you. Then he kind of disappeared in a rush. Thought I should let you know."

"Thanks, I'll look into that." said Great Bear.

Motioning the girls to one side, Great Bear said, "I think this means we tighten up security, okay?"

"We would feel much better if you did," said Nancy.

"Check to see if that guy really did leave a note under your door."

Opening their door, Julia confirmed, "Nothing here."

"I'm not surprised. I'd suggest you two not leave anything at all sensitive in your room, like your laptop, any notes you've been taking. Bring them with you at all times."

"Sounds like a good idea," said Julia.

Great Bear gave Julia and Nancy his cell number and said, "Call me at any time on the slightest inclination. I won't be far off, since I'm taking a room here tonight too."

That evening they had a long discussion with Paul and his dad, Brian Anawak, of the Dene Nation. Brian spoke about changes in caribou herds, especially in their migration habits.

"Most caribou herds are in decline," he said, "but not so much as was expected. Winters are not as harsh, so perhaps their survivability is up because of that, despite their lower numbers. We used to follow the herds into their summer forage areas in Alaska, but it's not as easy to travel anymore with all the tundra thawing out."

"What do you know about polar bears?" asked Julia.

"Hardly see any anymore. I think they all stay further north, now that we don't have much sea ice in the summer. Tell you one thing though—we seem to get lots of salmon in our rivers. Never used to see them before, only char."

"Why is that?"

"The rivers stay open longer and tend to warm up a bit. I suppose that's attracting salmon runs for spawning."

"What other changes have you noticed?"

"Lots of animals and birds these last few years that I never saw before. Guess they're moving further north. Maybe they don't like you white folk anymore. Ha-ha. Sorry, just kidding."

"There may be some truth in that though, the way we're tearing up the country. Paul, I should ask both you and your dad, what are your feelings about the proposed new pipeline from Tuk? I gather it would come through Inuvik, then south along the Mackenzie."

"Bad news," Brian replied immediately. "A few short-term jobs while they build the pipeline, then we have nothing to show for it, just wait around for breaks, which we're convinced will happen."

"That about sums it up," added Paul. "There's little long-term benefit, if any, for the territories, since the oil and gas would just be passing through. And like Dad says, breaks are inevitable."

"The NAPI officials sounded much more optimistic than that."

"And well they might," said Brian. "They get a large share of the profits after all. We're not so worried about the gas line, but once they start piping heavy crude oil down from Fort McMurray or Norman Wells, there'll be hell to pay when those pipes break. As they likely will!"

"What makes you so sure there'll be breaks?" asked Julia.

Paul replied, "Look, it's over 2000 km from McMurray to Tuktoyaktuk, over the most inhospitable terrain there is. They can't possibly monitor the whole pipeline continuously. With the way our permafrost and ground are thawing and moving, pipeline breaks are really unavoidable. And our territorial government is not placing enough conditions on the oil industry. They see too much money coming in."

"What do individuals say about all this, apart from government?"

"Julia, most people in the north, especially our Dene and other First Nations, are here by choice, have been for thousands of years. We like the lifestyle, the hunting and fishing, camaraderie that is rare in southern Canada. I mean, people are somewhat interested in the economy and jobs and all that, but if we had to make a choice between here or a job down south, we'd still be here."

"It's in our blood," added Brian. "Can't take it away. There's no life like this. But if it's destroyed by pollution and climate change, the companies can always move away. What's left for our people then?"

"I understand," said Julia. After a pause, she added, "You've been most helpful, Mr. Anawak. Thank you so much. I think Nancy and I will just walk back to the hotel. It's not very far, and it stays light here all evening this time of year."

"Oh, no you won't," said Paul. "Great Bear called me just now and gave me explicit instructions that you were not to be left alone. We don't want any more *accidents*, accidentally or not."

As they were leaving, Mr. Anawak added, "I hope you'll come back. And bring that brother of yours. Paul never stops talking about him. We'd love to show you folks what real hunting and fishing are all about."

As they drove back, Julia asked Paul about flights to Tuktoyaktuk and Aklavik.

"It's only about 125 km to Tuk and maybe 50 to Aklavik. I have a buddy who operates a twin engine service to both. He'll give you a good deal on flights if I talk to him."

"That would be great. I think we might head to Tuk first, perhaps tomorrow afternoon, stay for a day, then down to Aklavik the next morning for a few hours and back here that evening. Would you mind trying to get us a reservation for that?"

Nancy quickly added, "It would likely have to be the three of us, as Great Bear won't let us out of his sight, which does not bother me one bit, given the circumstances."

"Four, counting myself," Paul replied, "as I need to check in there. But no problem. I'll phone you in the morning and let you know."

They called Great Bear as soon as they arrived at the hotel. He suggested they meet for breakfast and confirmed he would indeed accompany them on the flight. Julia then called home.

Carol answered the phone, obviously relieved to hear from Julia. "Julia, dear, where are you now? We missed your call last evening, as I had to work and your father had to meet with Hans and the RCMP. Have you had any more encounters with these characters?"

"No, nothing we could put our finger on, although we did have a suspicious character who seemed to be tailing us outside of Inuvik today. But we have the RCMP following us around, so we feel quite safe. Is Dad home, because I have some new information on methane to pass on?"

"Yes, he is. From what I've been hearing, he'll be very interested in any news you have there. How are your interviews going, by the way?"

"My gosh, it couldn't be better, Mom. I've met the most wonderful people and I'm getting plenty of feedback on pipelines and climate change. I didn't realize how knowledgeable northern people are about climate change and its cause and effects.

"That's wonderful, dear. I'm sure Professor Samson will be pleased to hear about that too. What are your plans from here? Are you headed back yet?"

"Not yet. Because of the methane results, we're going to Tuktoyaktuk tomorrow, then a side-trip to Aklavik on the way back to Inuvik the following day, then maybe a one-day diversion to Fort McPherson. After that we'll head to Fort Liard—that's almost into northeast BC. There one day. Then it's on to Watson Lake where we plan to meet up with John and Tony. I promise to call you from Tuktoyaktuk tomorrow evening, ok?"

"All right. Your father is anxious to speak with you, so I have to give up the phone. Bye for now."

"Bye Mom. Love ya."

"Hello Julia. How are you?"

"Fine, Dad. I had no idea how much this trip would involve. I've met fantastic people, and also maybe some of the worst. But don't get me wrong. I wouldn't trade this trip for anything."

"Just as long as you stay safe. That's all we worry about."

"Great Bear and Paul are both looking out for Nancy and me. It makes me feel secure knowing that you, Mom, and John are there for me too. But look, you'll be most interested in our methane readings."

"I expect so, given what we're hearing from other sources."

"We started getting readings of 3100-3200 in Inuvik when we arrived. Today, Paul took us about 30 km or so north of Inuvik to a drained pond. We recorded 3400 ppb there. Paul has heard of higher values near the coast at Tuktoyaktuk. So, if for no other reason, we're planning to go there tomorrow. Paul is also getting us in touch with the Inuvialuit band there. I'm getting the same pessimistic opinions back from everyone here, but since Tuktoyaktuk is the end-point of the proposed pipeline, I need to hear from the locals there."

"I must say that I'm very pleased that you had the foresight to collect some methane data while there, although I can't say that I'm pleased with the results. It's very much what Professors Pearce and Mazurenko have been warning us about, but even more serious than we thought. Also, Prof. Pearce doesn't think your sensor calibration is off. It's essentially the same sensor that he uses and they are very reliable. Meanwhile, I gather from overhearing your mother speaking, that you've not had any further serious encounters with our denialist friends."

"No, but, there have been a couple of suspicious incidents."

"Oh? How's that?"

"There seemed to be a truck tailing us north of Inuvik yesterday. Whoever it was stopped further back when we did, then when we stopped a second time, he sped by us. When we got back to the hotel, we learned from the manager that he had caught someone trying to break into our room. The guy disappeared in a hurry. Coincidental incidents, perhaps." In truth she did not feel they were.

"Okay, but keep on your guard, and be careful. Are you flying to Tuk or driving on that new highway they're building?"

"I wasn't aware of the highway, but Paul has a pilot friend who operates a small passenger service between here and Tuktoyaktuk and Aklavik. It's less than an hour flight time to either."

"Just as well, I suppose, since the Mackenzie and tributaries are at their highest flow right now. That new highway might be soft in spots. Look after yourself. It's reassuring to us to know you have Great Bear along, plus Paul. I'm assuming that Great Bear is going with you tomorrow?"

"We couldn't get rid of him if we tried. And we certainly wouldn't try. He's very helpful, knowing all the people and much more." Whispering she added, "Plus I have a feeling that Nancy is quite attracted to him. She knew him before in college. She can't hear me as she's in the washroom."

"I had a chance to speak with Great Bear's Vancouver supervisor today. They are very impressed with him too. I'll let you go. You'll call us tomorrow evening I expect?"

"Yes, from Tuktoyaktuk. Good night, Dad. Give Mom a big hug for me."

"Will do. Bye."

* * *

The next morning, Great Bear was in the restaurant when they came down for breakfast at 8 AM.

"Good morning, ladies. Hope you had a good rest. Could be a busy day."

"Good morning, Great Bear," the girls said in unison.

Breakfast and Paul arrived together.

"Good news, girls," said Paul. "My buddy has an oil exec headed to Tuktoyaktuk today, plus my boss wants me to check out this methane eruption for our own reports. So you'll be getting a pretty special rate for the flight to Tuk, maybe a bit more for the return trip through Aklavik. He says he'll stay overnight himself, so we can leave tomorrow for Aklavik whatever time you wish. He may pick up an extra passenger at either place."

"Wow, personalized service," said Julia.

"However, his oil passenger wishes to leave at 9:00, so we need to get a push-on."

Half an hour later, they were at the airport meeting Paul's friend, Duane Day. They met the oil executive just before boarding the Beechcraft twin prop. He introduced himself as a manager with Esso. He was headed to Tuk to check on offshore facilities being organized there. Julia asked him whether he also represented CUUON. He replied, "No, but they are planning operations in an adjacent region to Esso's lease offshore. What may I ask is your business in Tuktoyaktuk?"

Having to think fast and also be prudent, Julia replied, "Oh, we're carrying out some social research on First Nations along with my partner, Paul, here." Indicating the others, she added, "Nancy and Bob have been assigned to me by First Nations people to help with the study." That was close enough to the truth without raising any suspicions by the oil executive.

"I wish you success. We have found the First Nations people in the north very gracious and willing to help."

Paul took the co-pilot seat next to Duane. The oil exec stepped aside as Nancy and Julia boarded first, followed by Great Bear.

Forty minutes later they were on the ground in Tuktoyaktuk.

Nancy had made reservations at Hunter's B&B the previous evening. Before leaving the airport, Julia pulled out her sensor. "Hmm, 3900 ppb. New record folks."

They checked in at the B&B, then headed down to the shore where new docking facilities were being built. Methane readings varied from 3500 to 3900 ppb around the town. After lunch they headed to the Inuvialuit Land Administration office where they met with Chief Patrick Elias.

Great Bear spoke first, as he already knew Patrick from having given several talks to the Inuvialuit as the area constable. "Hello Patrick. I trust you're not having any new problems with teenage break-ins?"

"Not since you last spoke at the high school as a matter of fact," replied Patrick. "I think you really smartened them up a bit. And hello, Paul. You two brought some new friends, eh?" Patrick also knew Paul from work that the Environment & Natural Resources Department were carrying out in Tuktoyaktuk.

"This is Julia Nicholson from Vancouver," said Paul. "Her brother and I are good friends from the University of Vancouver. And, this is Nancy Wedzin from the Yellowknives Dene, who works for NAPI in Yellowknife, but she is on leave helping Julia with her project. I'll let Julia explain the rest."

Julia introduced herself and summarized the project she was working on. "I'm trying to tie down why we are getting such high values of methane readings. The highest values I've found are right here at Tuktoyaktuk. Can you tell me if there are any oil or gas drilling holdings in the area or offshore, for example?"

Patrick was in charge of administering Inuvialuit-owned lands around Tuktoyaktuk. He indicated that he could not release any information on land leased by the petroleum industry. He then immediately suggested that they should all go over to the local coffee shop for coffee. Thinking something was up, Julia said they would love to.

Once seated for coffee, Patrick started to open up. "As land administrator, I am obligated not to tell you anything about what's going on with the oil industry. However, I'm not the land administrator right now, so what would you like to know?"

Julia took the opportunity. "Are there any gas or oil drilling leases in the area or offshore?" she repeated.

"Plenty offshore," he said. "And I know they have made some big finds, although they are not releasing any details to the Land Administration. Esso has a large holding 150-300 km northwest of here in the Beaufort. But recently, CUUON apparently struck a large field about 500 km north. Then Esso suddenly stopped drilling for some reason, but we know there is a lot of activity out there. One of the CUUON chief executives arrived here a few days ago. He's meeting with their group in their temporary offices down the street."

"And one of the Esso executives flew up with us this morning," Paul interjected.

"You might be wise, young lady, not to tell these people what you are doing here. We may never find out what the oil people are up to if they know outsiders are interested already," Patrick went on. "But then, CUUON is not telling us anything anyway. We certainly know about the increase in methane gas, since it's one of the things we are set up to detect. As you know, methane is odourless, so we need to know if it's getting out of hand, which it certainly seems to be doing. By the way, what sort of values are you reading?"

"We're simply measuring atmospheric concentrations. So far we've seen values of 3500-3900 ppb," Julia offered.

"Hmm, that's higher than the 3400 ppb we measured yesterday. I wonder if that technician of ours is finding higher values today. It would be good to compare."

"It would be helpful to us too. I keep wondering whether our sensor may be off calibration, so a comparison would help us both."

"Let's get back to the office, and we'll look into that right away. This is certainly serious enough that I can break silence in our office after all."

Back at Patrick's office, they found his technician in the small workshop.

"Patrick," he said, without being asked, "These methane readings are still going up. I've measured as high as 3800 ppb today."

"That confirms one thing," Patrick said looking at Julia. "Why don't we compare readings from the two sensors together just outside?"

The Land Administration office was using a different brand of sensor. They placed the two side by side on a picnic table outside and switched them on. Julia's sensor read 3785 ppb, the other was 3780.

"Well within our sensor's stated accuracy," Julia said.

"How long do you plan to stay?" asked Patrick.

"Our flight leaves for Aklavik in the morning. We're staying at Hunter's B&B tonight."

"I'm going to go see this chap from CUUON. That's their offices over there by the way," pointing to a red warehouse about half a kilometre away, "and I also plan to call on the Esso people who are responsible for their field. We need answers and I think we need them fast. Something is up and I intend to find out. Is it okay if I pay you folks a visit this evening?"

"That would be great," said Julia.

Paul added, "you know that my office needs to be informed about this too. If necessary, I'll stay over and see it through. We'll delay our plans until we hear from you this evening."

"And thank you for your cooperation, Patrick," Julia added.

"No problem," replied Patrick. "We're all in this together."

On the way back to Hunter's, they passed by CUUON's warehouse, where someone was just about to enter the building.

"Hmm," muttered Nancy, "that guy looked familiar."

"The chap who just went into CUUON?" Great Bear asked.

"Yeah. Wait, I know, he was in our offices at NAPI the day you went out west with Malcolm, Julia."

"That's not so surprising, I suppose," said Great Bear, "since NAPI is planning the pipeline up to Tuk and CUUON is a major investor. But all the same, given your peculiar events with persons unknown, I think we all need to be on our guard. Nancy, do you recall a name for this guy?"

"No, I wasn't involved in any of the discussions with him. But I bet I can find out with a quick call to our offices."

"Good idea. Do that. You know the old military saying, 'Know thy enemy!'"

Julia, Paul, and Great Bear stopped at the restaurant for lunch, while Nancy went to their room to make the call in private.

Nancy met them in the restaurant twenty minutes later. "His name is Todd Barton, if that means anything to either of you. He was at NAPI discussing the pipeline, then took a flight to Inuvik before coming here. Hmm, Great Bear, you don't suppose that ...."

"You mean that he might be the one we thought was spying on you, perhaps even the one who tried to break into your room at Inuvik? That's a possibility that we need to keep in mind. You girls continue your lunch. I think I'll call our superintendent in Vancouver and see if they have anything on this Barton guy."

Great Bear left for his own room.

"Things might be heating up," offered Julia.

"Yeah, although I think we've had enough suspicious events for this trip."

After lunch, Paul went to visit with leaders to discuss the population of the Tuktoyaktuk Peninsula caribou herd. Julia and Nancy met up with Great Bear again.

"I have some new information," said Great Bear. "Julia, you're aware that your dad had his office trashed and that they found the culprit?"

"Yes, apparently it was one of his students."

"They found a name on the student's hard drive, one Todd Barton. He works for Malcolm Keller, one of your dad's denialist friends. Naturally, our Investigations Division has been following this up. Both Barton and Keller were recently in Fort McMurray. Barton went on to Yellowknife from there. That's when you saw him, Nancy."

"I smell a rat," said Julia.

"And so you should," said Great Bear. "But wait, here's the kicker. Our *Savage* character works for this Todd Barton. And, they have reason to believe that Savage is using several aliases and may even be the one who murdered your dad's Russian colleague, Professor Mazurenko. This really adds more substance to our other suspicions, although we still have some missing links."

"Is this Todd Barton dangerous?"

"They don't think so, but they suspect that Savage is doing their dirty work, so we can't afford to take any chances. However, Headquarters does not want me making any arrests or even any enquiries about Barton, unless he steps out of line. They want to pull the web tight first; otherwise, Savage may get away. They're fairly certain that he's guilty, but it lacks hard evidence still."

"So, we need to be very careful, is what you're saying."

"Absolutely. I've changed rooms so that my room is adjacent to yours, and that's the way it has to stay from now on."

"Works for me, and thanks. Julia and I feel better for that," Nancy said.

* * *

Chief Patrick Elias dropped by that evening. They all met in Great Bear's room.

"The news is not good," he informed them. "Esso has stopped drilling operations because of the methane leaks, at least until they diagnose what's going on. I was informed by the CUUON executive that they don't feel there is any problem or danger to anyone, so they plan to continue operations for now. I asked him about the methane leaks, but he said this was not unusual. I plan to contact the federal Environment Minister tomorrow as the next step. We may need your confirmatory data that you've found at other locations. Can you possibly write me a summary tonight and email it to me?" He passed Julia his business card and Julia reciprocated.

"Certainly I will. I neglected to mention that my dad is a climate scientist at the University of Vancouver and this is of particular interest for him. He was collaborating with a Russian colleague who discovered similar results off the Barents Sea last winter. His colleague was killed in an accident during the climate summit in Bonn in February, although they think it may have been murder."

"Ah yes, I am familiar with your dad's work—like father, like daughter. And I heard about that professor's death, Mazurenko wasn't it?"

"That's right. And chances are very good that Dad may wish to confer with you as well. Perhaps he and his colleague will want to install more methane detectors."

"Excellent. I'll be delighted to hear from your dad, anything at all that may help us here. I will look forward to your report. If you don't mind, I would like to forward a copy to the federal Environment Minister. Will that be okay with you?"

"Absolutely, yes."

They all said good night and Chief Elias departed.

"This gets ever more mysterious. Do you still want to head to Aklavik in the morning?" asked Paul

"I think so, unless something else comes up. We may as well get data and feedback from all major communities and Aklavik will almost complete the north."

"Actually I would like you to meet someone else there — my uncle, my dad's older brother, John Anawak. He is known as an Inuvialuit visionary and is very knowledgeable about the northern environment."

"Okay, then. Is our pilot set to go as well? And could we delay until about 10 AM? I'd like to drop by and say goodbye to Chief Elias after breakfast before we leave."

'Sure thing. I'll give him a call shortly and let him know."

Afterward, Julia called home, updated her dad on the latest methane results and passed on Chief Elias' contact information.

16. Flight Emergency and Climate Storm

The following morning Julia, Nancy, Paul, and Great Bear met Duane at the airstrip at 9:45.

"All set to go," Duane greeted them. "We have one other passenger headed to Aklavik this morning, Chief Merven McLeod, so we have a full load aboard.

"Hi Merven, good to see you again," said Great Bear.

"What brings you up here today," asked Merven, "not enough crime in Inuvik? Ha, ha."

"We like to share it with you folk up here."

"I was out early fueling up and doing my safety check," continued Duane. "Looks like a great day for flying, weather-wise. You guys must have been quite busy. I even had one of your contacts out here this morning asking about you."

"Oh," said Great Bear. "Who was that?"

"Some guy from one of the oil companies, just as I was going for breakfast."

"He didn't say who he was, did he," asked Julia?

"Nope, but he said he was a friend of yours, thin-looking guy with a mustache. You must know him? I told him you were headed back this morning, which is why I was here early. Give me a couple of minutes to warm up my baby and call in my flight plan, and we'll be off. Just a short hop, about 170 km, should be there about 11:30." He climbed up into the cockpit.

The others were quiet for a moment, then Great Bear spoke. "That's suspicious. My guess is that it's this Todd Barton that you mentioned yesterday, Nancy. I'd like to know just why he's so interested in your movements. I've a mind to go interview him, but that might delay us another day, plus I'd rather not raise his guard until we have something definite on him. I think we need to be sharp on this. Paul, why don't you quietly warn Duane, maybe have him do an extra safety check on the aircraft?"

"You bet." Paul went and spoke with Duane, who immediately shut down the engines that were warming up. He got out and made a very careful inspection of his aircraft. Ten minutes later, he declared everything checked out okay and they were ready to leave.

Once in the air, just above 10,000 feet, Duane announced, "Ladies and Gentlemen, this is your captain speaking. Welcome to Inuvik Independent Air. Our heading is south-southwest 220 degrees to Aklavik, about 170 km distance, our airspeed about 200 kph, so our ETA at Aklavik is approximately 11:30 AM. Please buckle up and prepare for take-off."

"The sun is shining, everything seems to be going like clockwork," Julia said to Nancy

"Oh, oh, don't say that, Julia. Let's not forget Murphy."

Being old friends, Great Bear and Chief McLeod were in the back seat having an animated conversation and seemed to be enjoying themselves. Paul was up front with Duane.

About 20 minutes into the flight, they felt a slight lurch, the right engine seemed to stutter, then lost all power. They immediately lost altitude while Duane was rapidly checking his instruments. Shortly he announced, "We're not in any danger even though we've lost one engine; I lost fuel flow to my right engine and I shut it down altogether because I can see fuel leaking from the cowling. I made certain both tanks were full this morning so that I don't have to fuel in Aklavik, but somehow we've sprung a leak—very odd. These Beechcraft Barons can normally fly a few hundred kilometres on one engine, even with this full load. We'll just fly a little lower and save fuel. Most likely it's something I can fix quickly in Aklavik.

However, a few minutes later, the left-hand engine seemed to sputter, a few times, then caught again. Duane looked concerned and said, "I've never had this happen before; it's highly unusual for two engines to give trouble on the same flight … unless?

Great Bear cut in, "Unless our friend tampered with the engine this morning while you were at breakfast?"

"Good Lord, no one would do that, would they? Let's all be cool. If worse comes to worst, we can always glide quite a distance and find someplace to put down." He actually did not feel very confident about that, but he did not want to worry his passengers unduly. Then his left-side engine coughed again.

"Okay everyone, take a look around. If we can find a dry flat spot, I'll simply put down gently before we lose it. I'm confident this is something I can fix myself."

Julia spoke up, "How far are we from that new highway from Inuvik?

"Right," Duane replied, "that's a damn fine idea. It should be off to our left, in fact just to the left of that next big pond coming up. Anyone see it yet?"

"I see it," said Nancy. "Just beyond the pond and a few degrees to the left of it."

"Got it," he said. "Everyone check your seatbelts, there might be a few rough spots on the road. It's still fairly soft gravel and we'll be going straight in."

Everyone was quiet, everyone was tense, and everyone was listening to that sick engine, but it seemed to be running smoothly now. Duane had banked left to take the shortest route to the highway and it had taken five or six tense minutes to reach it. In the meantime, he had radioed his position to Inuvik with a Mayday call. Just as they arrived over the highway, the engine suddenly gave up altogether. He quickly cut the fuel supply and spoke to Nancy who was sitting directly behind him. "Do you see that fire extinguisher behind my seat?"

"I see it."

"As soon as we touch down I want you to unstrap it and be ready to hand it to me when I stop. We just might have an engine fire after that fuel line blew out and I'd like to salvage the engine if possible." Then to everyone, "We're okay folks, this baby has plenty of gliding capability. I just want everyone to stay calm and we'll be okay. As soon as we stop, undo your seatbelt, then I want everyone out and clear of the aircraft A-S-A-P, just in case of fire." He gave them the thumbs up sign. They all replied in kind.

They touched down just two minutes later. It was a bumpy landing, with loose gravel flying everywhere. It took another minute before they came to a full stop. Nancy quickly handed the extinguisher to Duane. He was out on the wing immediately, as the others quickly vacated. A quick check revealed no fire.

"Whew," he said. "I have to admit to a few anxious moments there. Julia, thank you for thinking of that highway. I knew we were close, but I haven't paid much attention to it as I've not driven it, since it's not officially open yet while they still work on some soft spots. It's all built over the permafrost, and some of that is still melting. But thank God for this straight stretch here and not too bad a landing. The main thing is, I believe everyone is okay, except for a few frayed nerves?"

"You did a fantastic job getting us down safely," said Julia. Everyone nodded their heads. "I hope the loose gravel didn't damage the aircraft too much."

"Nothing a little paint work can't fix on the undercarriage. Let's see what the problem is. It's almost certainly a fuel line." He started to remove the left-hand cowling. "And I don't think it was coincidental that both occurred on the same trip."

"And I think Mr. Barton will have to do some fast explaining of his activities this morning," said Great Bear. "I'm sure you can identify the gentleman you spoke with this morning?"

"I certainly can," the pilot replied, "and here's the problem." He indicated a detached fuel line. "Someone backed off the fuel line coupler until it was barely finger-tight. It could not normally work off on its own because of a locknut coupling. It didn't take too much vibration until it worked all the way off. You'd best speak with that saboteur first before I get my hands on his neck."

"Try to minimize your fingers on the cowlings and fuel line," Great Bear said, "perhaps our fingerprint expert in Yellowknife can get the saboteur's prints off it, if indeed our suspicions are confirmed, and just in case he doesn't fess up."

Duane had just removed the right engine cowling when he exclaimed, "Yup, same thing! He could have done this in 10 or 15 minutes max while I was having breakfast. Both engines were able to operate on take-off, but it was only a matter of time before the lines worked free altogether. This was definitely deliberate. But, as luck has it, I'll have this all fixed in 10 minutes." He got into the baggage compartment and brought out a small package of tools.

Paul spoke for the first time, "My gosh! This is attempted murder, isn't it, Great Bear?"

"We might get that to stick. The key thing will be for Duane to positively identify Barton and get either his confession or his prints. There has to be due process, so for now we cannot assume his guilt despite our strong suspicions."

"It shall be my great pleasure to identify him," replied Duane. "Even with getting down safely, this could have destroyed my aircraft and my career. I have three hundred grand sunk into this; a new one costs up around a million."

"I know some officers in Vancouver, including an Interpol detective, who will want to speak with Mr. Barton. This may well be the break they've been looking for."

Just then, they heard a truck coming down the highway from the north. It slowed and came to a stop just behind their aircraft. Two men got out and yelled "Is everybody okay?"

"We're all fine, thanks. Oh, hi Bill, we had a little problem."

"Yeah, we were having lunch a couple of miles north of here where we're repairing soft spots. We noticed your change in flight. It sounded like you were on one engine, then suddenly you were just gliding. We knew you were in trouble, so we got here as soon as possible."

"Thanks. We won't be blocking the road long, as I'll have the problem fixed in a few minutes. I just need to check over my undercarriage to make certain no other damage was done. We had a lot of loose gravel flying up on touchdown."

"If it would help," Bill replied, "we have a grader and roller about 5 km south of us here. I could radio them and have them both up here in 20 minutes or so. They could smooth out that surface ahead of you in less than an hour."

"By gosh, that would save me more stress if you could," said Duane.

"I'll get right on it," Bill said, walking toward his truck.

A few minutes later, he was back and said "They're on their way; shouldn't take more'n 10 minutes to get here."

"That's great," said Duane. Turning to his passengers, he added, "Perhaps some of you could help me look over the undercarriage, just to check for any obvious damage from rocks."

Five minutes later, Duane said, "We're okay, so why don't we break out some snack food. We'll just relax and wait for these guys to turn this gravel road into a proper runway. I'm going to start up my engines while the cowlings are off, just to make certain we're shipshape and no more leaks in the fuel lines."

They could already see dust at the start of the long straight stretch to the south, as the grader preceded the roller. A little over one hour later, Bill came up and spoke to Duane. "Duane, you are clear for take-off." Grinning, he added, "You can file your flight plan with me."

"I owe you buddy. Next time you want a trip down to Yellowknife, you're on free!"

"No problem. All part of the service we provide. I hope you folks will have a good flight the rest of the way."

They all shook hands. Ten minutes later, their takeoff was considerably smoother than the landing. Great Bear had already used his satellite phone to call his office in Inuvik. He had instructed his partner to use regular Aklak Air service to have Todd Barton brought to Inuvik and detained for questioning on suspicion of public mischief, just for starters. A fingerprint expert would be brought in from Yellowknife that afternoon. He also called RCMP headquarters in Vancouver and described the details of the incident.

On the way to Aklavik, Great Bear told the others that they would all need to be present to give testimony in Inuvik over the next two days. "Something else too, Julia. Depending on how things go with our saboteur friend, our Vancouver headquarters wants me to go there for one day after he arrives in Vancouver. That Interpol chap working with your dad needs a full briefing from me in person. You and Nancy may have to be on your own for a day or two. We'll have to discuss how that can work."

* * *

While all this was happening, a new tropical storm was brewing over the Caribbean. Named *Barry*, it was already a Category 4 hurricane, pounding Haiti and Cuba, after the devastating super-Hurricane *Aletta* only 10 days previous. *Barry* was predicted to reach Category 5 status in 48 hours once it arrived over the abnormally warm waters offshore Florida, a large area of 28°C SSTs.

* * *

That same day, Eric was in consultation with David Pearce. The Barents Sea data and David's permafrost data, coupled with what Julia was reporting back on atmospheric methane readings, necessitated some urgent government action to halt drilling. They decided that an immediate meeting with the federal Environment Minister was paramount. After discussing a strategy to get the most attention, they called the minister's office early that afternoon. They were immediately linked through to Minister Webb Andrews. Eric quickly updated him on the most recent developments with methane increases in the Arctic.

"I've actually had some advance warning on this," said Minister Andrews, "from a Chief Patrick Elias in Tuktoyaktuk and, believe it or not, from your own daughter, Julia, as Chief Elias included her written report to him."

"Hmph, my own daughter upstaging me! I'll have to speak with her about that," he joked, while feeling immensely proud of her at the same time.

Andrews continued, "I wonder just how much these additional emissions could be tied in with the latest storms presently developing on both sides of the continent."

"Not directly, but the intensity of the storms and the unprecedented early dates for east coast hurricanes do point to the same problem, our excessive carbon emissions, which is now exacerbated by methane release in the north."

"I sense the seriousness of this. Can you possibly brief the PM and his staff on both the climate and these storms tomorrow morning by video conference?"

"David and I can certainly brief you on climate and current Arctic emissions, but I would prefer that someone senior in Environment Canada's weather service take the initiative on the storms part of the briefing. They have the most up-to-date data and charts."

"Could you recommend someone for doing that?"

"Yes, my wife. She is a senior meteorologist in the Vancouver office and is working on these storms as we speak."

"Good, my aide will call the Chief of the Vancouver office and arrange for her to describe what's happening in the weather. You can coordinate with her for the video conference tomorrow morning."

"Consider it done," replied Eric. "Please have your aide inform us of time and location when it's set up, presumably at the Vancouver Weather Centre?"

"We will. Be sure of it. We'll speak with you tomorrow morning, say 11 AM Eastern time, that's 8 AM Pacific, unless you hear otherwise."

* * *

While Eric was speaking with Minister Andrews, Carol had arrived for her day shift at the Vancouver Weather Office. The high-amplitude longwave trough that had led to the west coast storms two weeks earlier, had finally shifted into mid-continent. This was drawing ("sucking" might have been a better word) very warm and very moist air at upper levels from the subtropical Pacific (where El Niño was still intensifying) into the southeast US. That upper trough had a potent northwest-southeast tilt over Texas, and storm genesis had already begun as a rapidly deepening surface low pressure centred on a front over Georgia. In turn, this was drawing low-level colder surface air down across the central US. The potent mixture of these two air masses was inevitably interacting, and in a violent way. Carol noted the temperature difference between the cool air about to flow out over Cape Hatteras waters and the warm SSTs, 10°C versus 28°C, something to cause her to shudder for east coast residents. Hurricane *Barry* was not yet in the mix, but threatening. *When and where will this all end?* thought Carol. *How many storms of the century can we endure in one year, hell, in one month?*

An hour later, her chief dropped by her desk and quietly told her, "Congratulations, you get to brief the Prime Minister and his staff by video conference tomorrow morning at 8 AM sharp, along with your husband."

'Sure, will Santa Claus be there too?"

"Actually, I'm serious Carol. These storms, and apparently new data that your husband and colleagues are collecting in the Arctic, have the PM, our Environment Minister, and others quite concerned. They want a detailed briefing tomorrow morning. Your husband will take the first half-hour updating on the latest methane emission results in the north, then the show's all yours for the weather situation after that. I already have Bill Thomas coming in to take over your shift shortly, so that you can do some preliminary prep for tomorrow morning. I expect you'll want to be in here by 5 or 6 AM tomorrow to update yourself before the PM's main event."

"Why me?"

"Because you're our expert and you've been on for all these superstorms. You can blame your husband for recommending you too! Ha!"

"I'll deal with him later! Will the briefings be in our board room?"

"Yes, we'll have the facilities you need set up. You just worry about the weather."

"And the way the atmosphere is setting up, I think we all need to worry. I'll leave shortly and rest this evening, then come in earlier, maybe by 4 AM."

"Your choice. Good Luck!"

* * *

That evening at home, Eric received a call from Yellowknife. The caller introduced himself as Calvin Hollsworth, Chief of field operations for NAPI. "Dr. Nicholson, NAPI is the company sponsoring the project that your daughter, Julia, is working on through the University of Vancouver Law Department. I spoke with Julia several times while she was in Yellowknife. I was very impressed with her knowledge and her sincerity about this project, but that's not why I called you."

"Go on," replied Eric.

"I'm also the one who suggested that our employee, Nancy Wedzin, accompany Julia on the rest of her trip. Please believe me that this was not any attempt of ours to monitor what Julia is doing."

"From what Julia tells me about Nancy, I don't think she would be capable of anything like that."

"You're correct in that. I've been monitoring what is going on near the Arctic coast myself. That's my concern and why I'm calling you. Personally I have had misgivings about the pipeline project ever since I came here five years ago. Not the pipeline itself so much, but the offshore drilling that the oil conglomerates are doing. I'm well aware of the methane hydrates offshore, as well as northern permafrost, both of which have huge sealed-in stores of methane. Earlier, oil companies thought that they could drill through the shelf to extract oil without releasing the methane. But extremely high values of local atmospheric methane around the coast cause me, at least, to doubt that assumption."

"I fully agree with you," Eric replied. "What can you do about it?"

"I don't know yet. What I *do* know is that we may have a humongous time bomb on our hands. The reserves of methane beneath the shelf are tremendous. Added to that is the methane release from permafrost melt on land that you scientists are reporting. All I can offer is to keep you informed about whatever I can find out. But in all honesty, my conscience will probably have me resign my position soon. Still, NAPI is not a bad company, our top executives are all concerned about this. The problem is that we have a legal contract with CUUON and the Boreal Oil Corporation in Fort McMurray. If the pipeline is approved, NAPI is obligated to build it. CUUON and the others will continue the drilling until someone stops them. All I can suggest is that you use whatever influence you have to convince the federal government not to approve either the drilling or the pipeline. That effectively removes my position, but there are always other jobs available. I can keep you informed from my end until such time as my position terminates one way or another."

"I appreciate your honesty and integrity on this. Incidentally, my daughter detected your sincerity after meeting you and told me so."

"She is probably a bit psychic I guess. I do know that you have one very intelligent daughter, and she has a magical personality—she must make you proud. I would imagine she is getting plenty of feedback from First Nations people for her project. She is very congenial."

"Yes to all that. I do appreciate you calling. Perhaps we can exchange cell phone numbers?"

"By all means. Mine is …."

17. Federal Briefing

Julia and her friends arrived in Aklavik almost three hours late, at 2 PM. Paul phoned to arrange a meeting with his uncle that afternoon, while Nancy was enquiring about accommodations for the night because of the delay caused by the aircraft sabotage. Julia drew out her methane sensor. It indicated 2500 ppb. "Anything below 3000 is a big improvement," she announced.

Paul joined Julia and Great Bear. "Uncle John can see us at 3:30 if you wish. He's the official keeper of Inuvialuit legends in this area. He claims to have known about the future gas problems 30 years ago. I can't vouch for the truth of this, but he has told me some pretty amazing things in the past, things that have come true. But he is also very knowledgeable about the land and the environment, and how everything is interconnected. You will enjoy listening to him."

"I'm sure I will. Let's grab a coffee and doughnut and then go see your uncle."

Nancy joined them then and informed them that she had two rooms at Aklavik Inn, probably the only accommodations available. They should go there immediately to claim them. The two girls took the smaller room with two beds, while Great Bear, Paul, and Duane had a three-bed room.

An hour later, Julia and Paul walked to his Uncle John's home, while Nancy stayed with Great Bear, who wanted to visit the small two-person RCMP detachment there. Julia had sensed a growing relationship between the two, and she had actively encouraged Nancy.

Julia and Paul sat cross-legged with his Uncle John and listened. He held a leather Shaman's belt with amulets and spoke in a heavily accented voice, which rose and fell like an incantation. "My people are not scientists. But they understand how the ice is supposed to work, how it has worked for centuries, supplied us with food. And they have read its changes. They also knew that the melting ice on the land and the sea would release the strange gas that warms the air, and that warming would cause even more gas to be released. This is not good. We need the ice to hunt on and the frozen land to keep the caribou healthy. Without these, the Inuvialuit cannot survive. This we know." He suddenly went quiet. His eyes took on a faraway look.

Paul nudged Julia and indicated that they should wait and not speak right away.

Five minutes went by, then suddenly John spoke again directly to Julia.

"I sense that you know about this too, and that you would like to help. Is it not so?"

"Yes, that's why I came to the north, but more to listen and hear what your people have to say. The gas you talked about we call methane. It does indeed warm the air. And you are right. It is not good. We would like to try and stop the gas."

"The spirits tell me that you are good and that we should help you. You have an Earth father who works at this too. Is it not so?"

"Yes, that is so. He is in the big city, Vancouver, and even now he is studying this problem."

"I can help him if he comes here."

"He would welcome that. I'll tell him."

John was quiet again for a minute. Then continued, "I see danger for you in Watson Lake, not good to go there."

"But how did you …?" Julia started, then glanced at Paul. Paul simply shook his head, meaning, *I didn't tell him your plans.*

"You have a stick that measures this gas," John went on. "If you go to the dead ponds, it will sense more. But go near the sea. That's where the most gas is. The white men digging holes under the sea are disturbing it. They must stop or we are all in danger. That is the key."

Paul motioned to Julia that it was time to leave.

Outside, Julia asked Paul if he had previously briefed his uncle on what they had discovered, or on the rest of their trip, including Watson Lake."

"No," he replied, "he seems to know these things, almost like he reads people's mind."

"That is quite amazing. But why would he give me that warning about Watson Lake?"

"I have no idea, but it does mean that you have to be careful. He is rarely wrong about these things."

"Spooky," said Nancy, "even for a Shaman."

Paul replied, "But I also think that he is more knowledgeable on environmental impacts than the high tech people doing all the drilling. They seem totally blinded by the oil, gas, and profits. They still haven't realized the full impact of what they are doing."

Julia added, "I had a biology prof who once said, 'In a Darwinian universe, safety is an illusion,' so I'm not going to worry about Watson Lake warnings just now. We'll cross that bridge when we get there."

It was 4:30 and everyone was getting hungry. There was a small pub nearby that could cook a steak and all the trimmings. The bartender even joined them and they enjoyed the evening. With the long daylight hours, they all took a walk around town after dinner. Aklavik, like Tuktoyaktuk, was built on the vast Mackenzie Delta and was less than 10 metres above sea level, even though they were 80 km from the coast. It had first been settled in the early 1900s as a trading post for the Hudson's Bay Company. It had boasted one of the north's first radio stations in the 1920s. It was also known as the home of Albert Johnson, famous as The Mad Trapper of Rat River. He had shot an RCMP officer in 1931. That sparked a 42-day manhunt. Aklavik also served as the regional administrative centre for the territorial government until 1961.

The general consensus of the people they spoke with about the proposed pipeline was that it might provide some short-term benefits, but that in the long run they generally feared pipeline breaks. Methane is odourless, so other than Paul's Uncle John, most were unaware of the methane bomb surrounding them.

Later, when Julia and Nancy were alone in their room, out of the blue, Nancy said, "You know, Paul was right when he talked about tech people being blind to the environmental effects, but I don't think they are all like that."

"I think you're right, but what makes you say that?"

"My boss, Calvin Hollsworth for one. He's said a few things to me recently, even before you arrived in Yellowknife, that make me think he has doubts about what NAPI is doing. He honestly worries about the whole north and the people. Just before we left, he told me to tell you anything you wanted to know and to help you in any way I can to get at the truth. That's pretty impressive for a company management person."

"You're right. I got a similar impression from him in the short time I had to talk with him. I think Malcolm Keller's okay too, you know."

"I guess the truth will all come out in the end. One thing for certain, I'm glad I came along. You're okay in my book."

"You too, and amen to that." The two of them hugged momentarily.

* * *

Meanwhile, Great Bear's partner had arrived in Tuktoyaktuk to arrest Todd Barton on suspicion of attempted murder. Barton managed to send off a text message to Nick Savage, now in Watson Lake, before being brought down to Inuvik for his hearing. His message to Savage read simply, *Close the web on B1 at 6.*

* * *

Carol checked into the weather centre at 4 AM as planned. All weather systems had deteriorated since the previous afternoon. The east coast low had accelerated out of Georgia to offshore Cape Hatteras. As anticipated, the injection of cold air in its wake had stalled the low temporarily as it absorbed a tremendous amount of latent heat energy from the warm water surface. It had deepened by 30 hPa in that time and was already pounding Washington with strong north-easterlies and torrential rain. Hurricane *Barry* had reached Category 5 intensity and was devastating the Bahamas and the east coast of Florida as it turned more northerly, toward the waiting larger-scale low pressure system.

At the same time, a quarter of the way around the globe, over the northeast Pacific, a new storm system had formed. It was deepening rapidly and breaking eastward. It too contained remnants of tropical air and was taking a very rapid track for this time of year—directly toward southern BC and Vancouver. Vancouver would receive a deluge later that day.

The initial briefing started at exactly 8 AM Pacific Time, Prime Minister Mulligan Thomas being a stickler for punctuality.

"Good morning, Dr. Nicholson," the PM greeted Eric.

"Good morning to you sir."

"My aide tells me that you folk are also expecting weather later today, although not likely to rival the east coast system."

"I certainly hope not, from what my good wife tells me is going on down there."

"We'll hear from Mrs. Nicholson later. First, we need to know what all the havoc is about up north."

"Certainly! I believe you are all up-to-date on the status of atmospheric carbon dioxide. And despite the 2015 COP-21 agreement in Paris, where all 196 countries signed the agreement to curb emissions from burning fossil fuels, many of those countries have still failed to ratify the agreement. Atmospheric CO_2 concentrations, which hovered just below 400 ppm at that time, have recently accelerated to 420 ppm. You are likely aware that atmospheric methane, or CH_4, has also been increasing dramatically during the past decade. Much of that increase has resulted from decaying peat moss as the northern permafrost melts. But in the past year or two, we have been measuring a phenomenal and unexpected increase in methane from beneath the Arctic Ocean. This threatens to almost double the overall global warming threat."

Eric displayed a series of photos and drawings of carbon dioxide and methane molecules on his slides as he spoke. "Methane, as you may know, is a more potent greenhouse gas than carbon dioxide. There is potentially enough methane all across the Arctic, in Siberia, the Northwest Territories, and Alaska to cause an additional 1-2°C warming in this century, added to the 2-3°C warming that we expect from carbon dioxide emissions, although that 2-3° appears very conservative by itself, given that emissions have risen all around the industrial world. This raises the ante for global warming impacts, possibly to untenable levels for mankind."

"And this latest threat of escaping methane is resulting from offshore drilling in the Arctic?" the PM interposed.

Eric switched to a slide showing an Arctic Ocean drilling operation. "Methane release is common with any drilling for oil, but it appears that there is a higher ratio of methane sitting over Arctic Ocean oil. Drilling on the continental shelves over the Barents Sea and the Beaufort, and more recently offshore the Northwest Territories near Tuktoyaktuk, is releasing large amounts of methane that sits over the oil deposits." Eric switched to a new slide showing historical increases in atmospheric methane since 1985. "When drilling commenced in earnest in 2015, we didn't really notice any dramatic increase right away.

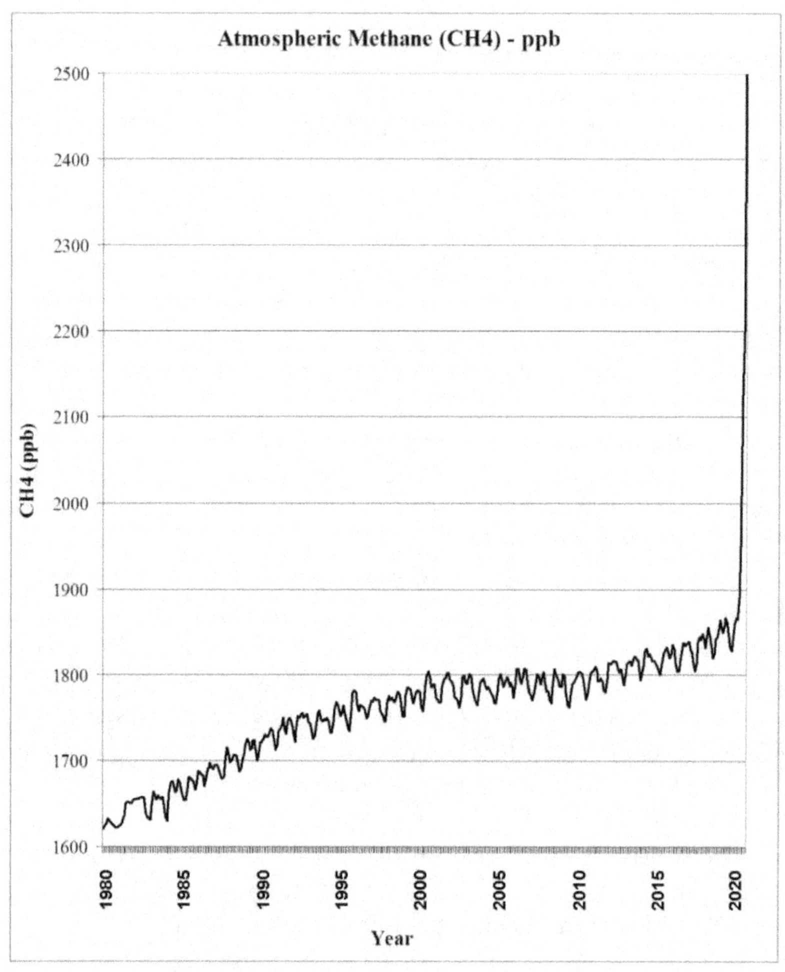

Concentrations of methane since 1985

"But recently, the rate of increase has jumped off the scale, going from 1900 to 2500 ppb in just a few months. We do not know why the sudden increase, but we have a suspicion, and it is critically imperative to verify it. Moreover, the concentrations have continued to rise extremely sharply since then. At Tuktoyaktuk alone, my daughter, who is conducting a survey on legal and social implications of northern pipelines for her

PhD thesis, measured values this past week as high as 3900 ppb. At the current rate of increase, we could have widespread values of 10,000 ppb by the end of this year. If that happens, gentlemen, we run the risk of runaway atmospheric greenhouse warming."

"And what is your suspicion for this?" Mulligan cut in.

"Our suspicion involves methane hydrates or clathrates that sit on the ocean floor on the continental shelf. These are white, ice-like solids that consist of methane and water." (Eric switched to several photographs of methane hydrate). "The methane molecules are enclosed in microscopic cages composed of water molecules. Methane gas is primarily formed by microorganisms that live in the deep sediment layers and slowly convert organic substances to methane. These organic materials are the remains of plankton that lived in the ocean long ago, sank to the ocean floor, and were incorporated into the sediments. Small quantities of methane are continually bubbling off the ocean floor into the atmosphere. Methane hydrates are stable under pressures in excess of 35 bar and at low temperatures. The Arctic Ocean floor, even over the continental shelf, has been in this latent stable condition for hundreds of thousands of years—until recently, that is. As the Arctic waters warm up over the continental shelf, as they certainly are doing, we suspect that just slightly warmer temperatures are allowing methane to be released from the hydrates. Releasing large amounts of natural gas from methane clathrate deposits suddenly could be a cause of past, future, and present climate warming events, and could even trigger a runaway climate warming. It has been suggested that this was a main factor in the global warming of 6°C that happened during the Great Permian Extinction some 250 million years ago. It's complicated by the influx of more saline and warmer Atlantic and Pacific waters into the Arctic Ocean, which creates a layer of water of up to 5°C warmer than the surface water at depths of 100-500 m. Right now, the Arctic Ocean is poised to start releasing more copious amounts of methane. If that happens, the result could be catastrophic."

"Is it possible for this to happen all across the Arctic Ocean?"

"No, methane most likely is only released at the continental margins, somewhere at depths of 100 to 500 metres. Below 1 km, no methane hydrates can be deposited, and no methane release occurs, except from oil drilling. But there is enough of it on the continental shelf to be more than just 'cause for concern.'"

"In layman's terms, what does this mean to the global warming problem?" asked the PM

"Until recently, the atmospheric concentration of CH_4 was just under 2,000 ppb; that is about 2 ppm, compared with CO_2 at 400 ppm. So naturally, CO_2 has been the main focus of climate concerns. However, at the present rates of increase, our best guess is that by sometime next year, atmospheric CH_4 could exceed 10,000 ppb, or 10 ppm. Since CH_4 has 30 times more potential for atmospheric warming than CO_2, CH_4 could almost become the equivalent of CO_2 as a global warmer. In layman's terms, this means that present warming predictions of 2-5°C in this century could be almost doubled. If atmospheric methane continues to increase, we could face a *runaway greenhouse effect*."

"Good Lord, even I know that that would be catastrophic!" exclaimed PM Thomas.

"I'm glad that you recognize the danger here. Previous governments refused to consider it. However, there is one more danger that I have not mentioned yet. This concerns the permafrost question. I would ask that Professor Pearce brief you on that. It has been his specialty most of his illustrious career."

"By all means. Dr. Pearce, please continue," PM Thomas interjected.

"Gentlemen, you may be aware that, we have been concerned about atmospheric methane released from melting permafrost for several decades," David began. "Until now, we have not noticed significant increases in methane from the melting, largely because once the melting takes place, a certain degree of time must pass while the peat bogs start to decompose and release excess CH_4. We had anticipated a couple of decades ago that appreciable increases would take place. That has now occurred. As of a year ago, we were measuring much higher rates of emission over these peatbogs. But recently, something more disturbing was noted, that seems to tie together with the two main sources of methane release in the Arctic; that is, from both permafrost and offshore clathrates. The two sources seem to be connected through weaknesses in the Earth's crust, maximizing the rates of increase in methane."

PM Thomas again interjected, "Are you implying that the methane threat may be even greater than what Dr. Nicholson has mentioned?"

"It is too early to confirm that, but yes, it is entirely possible. Dr. Nicholson and I have been working together on this, ever since the unfortunate death of our Russian colleague, Dr. Ivan Mazurenko."

The PM continued, "I'll ask you both, Drs. Nicholson and Pearce. What are the limits of our expectations on this, that is, the minimum and maximum expectations? What can we do about it? And is there any silver lining at all in this?"

"Go ahead, Eric," said David.

"Without some dramatic turnabout, we are looking at a minimum of 4°C warming in this century; we could actually experience 10°C warming, worse still if that runaway greenhouse actually happens! Warming of 4°C would mean all of the southwest US and much of the subtropics become basically uninhabitable in this century. As well, most land around the Mediterranean would become desert, including much of Spain, Italy, Greece, and Turkey. Drought over the Amazon would increase and much of the Amazon forest would dry up; subsequently, forest fires would start, giving a major positive feedback to the atmosphere from additional CO_2, not to mention the loss of carbon sink from the former tropical rain forest. In terms of people, it means that several *billion* people would have to move from the subtropics or die."

"My God," said the PM, "how did we get to this stage?"

"Through lack of concern by people, governments, and industry," said David quietly, "and by complete focus on the dollar as the gauge of human success."

"I fully agree," said the PM. After a brief pause, "I notice, Dr. Nicholson, that you did not provide us with a scenario for 10°C warming and beyond. I presume we don't want to talk about that."

"You're absolutely correct Prime Minister. We don't want to go there at all."

"Is there anything at all positive with regard to the methane problem?" Environment Minister Webb Andrews asked.

"About the only positive thing is the residency time of CH₄ in the atmosphere. We consider carbon dioxide to have atmospheric residency measured in centuries; for methane, it's more like decades."

"Eric, tell us what needs to happen and we'll do it."

"First off, as my late-colleague Prof. Mazurenko warned last February, we need an immediate moratorium on all offshore drilling in the Arctic, at least until we have better data. But that involves a lot of international cooperation."

"Damn it all," said the PM. "Then we have to get that too."

"The next thing we desperately need," David threw in, "is a northern observing network for methane and research to determine potential reserves of methane for both the melting peat lands and from the offshore areas."

"You shall have that too," PM Thomas replied.

The prime minister and his ministers discussed a few more points. Then, the PM said, "Eric, could you please get some of your colleagues together, national and international, and be ready to attend a meeting of heads of state by early July? We need the support of your international colleagues on this to convince all countries involved in Arctic drilling. Mr. Andrews and our aides will be available to start other things happening, but the moratorium on drilling that you are suggesting seems to be a critical first step. A second step, which may prove more difficult, but it absolutely must happen, is to obtain international agreement to immediately reduce carbon emissions, significantly and permanently.

"You have my utmost cooperation, Sir. I will contact my colleagues immediately. Just let us know of a date and location, and we'll be there."

"Good. Now, let's get that weather update. Carol, I understand you are briefing us on this?"

"Yes, sir. First, let me give you the east coast situation, as that seems most immediate and the most serious." Pointing to the 500 hPa analysis, "This shows the air flow and controlling features in the upper troposphere that dictate the development and motion of surface features, the lows and highs. The controlling feature in this instance is this high-amplitude trough that lies northwest to southeast across the continent. It is driving very warm moist air and higher-level heat energy from southwest of California in across the southern part of the

US and supports this low pressure system that you see off Cape Hatteras on the surface chart here. That low has deepened dramatically over the last 15-20 hours and is now dragging relatively cool surface air southward into its southwest sector. From there, it will move out over the very warm waters off Hatteras. When you move low-level cold air over much warmer water, the water evaporates quite readily and rapidly, which on condensing and forming cloud, injects a lot of latent heat energy into the system. That's caused the more rapid deepening in the past six hours, and the result is what we call in our profession a weather *bomb*. As it intensifies, that system is now moving more slowly northward and is already battering the Washington-Baltimore area with flooding rains and high winds. Those conditions will spread all the way into the Maritimes and as far west as Toronto and Ottawa."

"But take note of Hurricane *Barry*, which has already broken records for damage and deaths in the Caribbean and the Bahamas, because it's now moving into that mix. It's still a Category 5 hurricane, has blasted through the Bahamas and will shortly catch up and merge with that low. The result will be … well … very nasty, shall we say."

"What kind of precipitation amounts?" Webb Andrews asked.

"The models are all predicting widespread amounts exceeding 125 mm within the next 24 hours throughout the northeastern US and the Maritimes, with local amounts up to 250 mm! Even Toronto and Ottawa can anticipate well over 100 mm."

Prime Minister Thomas cut in with, "Eric, are you still there?"

"Yes sir!"

"Are we seeing an impact of global warming in this? I mean, this is the second bout of this kind of weather in just a couple of weeks. Is this what we can look forward to in the future?"

"No climate scientist would blame a storm solely on global warming, but surely we are experiencing the impacts, with more frequent, more intense storms of all kinds. Prior to now, we've observed only an increase in severe tropical storm intensities in the subtropics. It's now coming to us at mid-latitudes, coming home to roost, you might say, where the cause of global warming is rooted. So, yes, we can look forward to more of this in the future. I believe I can say that without fear of contradiction from most of my colleagues."

"Carol, please go on."

"That's the worst of it for the east coast. For the west coast, we have a developing situation over the northeast Pacific." She pointed to that area on the surface analysis. "This low has been racing eastward while it deepens. The precipitation and winds from this will start affecting southern BC by early this evening. We're expecting winds exceeding 100 kph and rainfall amounts of 50-100 mm, both record values, throughout southern BC. That will tie down evening traffic on the ground and certainly air traffic out of the Vancouver-Seattle area."

"Another glaring impact from global warming, Eric?"

"Possibly, but the major impact to southern BC has been the intensification of the subtropical high, normally offshore California, expanding northward and bringing summer drought to BC, not this. However, the increased atmospheric energy has to go somewhere, so in this case, it's manifested into storms like this breaking through the subtropical high."

"Does that agree with your analysis, Carol?"

"Yes. Until today, that ridge of high pressure," she pointed to the ridge southwest of BC, "was building up into BC, but this storm has flattened it out and forced it southward. The numerical models predict it will build up again after tomorrow. But in the meantime, we get rain and winds for 24 hours."

"Have either of you, Carol or Eric, anything else to add?"

"No," they answered in unison.

"Then we'd best get on with our job. I'll be calling President Illyana Dinton first, then we'll see if we can convince Russia, the UK, and the Scandinavians to attend an emergency meeting. Eric, you'll hear soon from Minister Andrews and/or my aide. Meanwhile, go ahead and order whatever instrumentation, supplies, and aircraft support you need for your work in the Northwest Territories—and no limits! Perhaps it will be small compensation for the termination of CFCAS funds that the federal government should have continued to support a decade ago. Then maybe we would have had more warning for the mess we're in today."

"In terms of methane research, yes, we likely would be much further ahead", added Eric. "Thank you Mr. Thomas for your understanding. We will assuredly do the best we can to make up time."

"And if you require assistance with field technicians, then I'm sure Minister Andrews can help out there as well. Later today we'll be calling a media conference to let our country and the world know about the situation and what we plan to do about it."

* * *

The emergency meeting of all northern countries with claims to Arctic waters and drilling was arranged for July 10 in New York, at the United Nations headquarters. Eric and David were to be among several dozen climate scientists from around the globe, all contributing members of the IPCC, to give briefings on the major aspects of the problem. This time, politicians intended to listen. Their very survival as politicians depended on it, for their electorates would likely not tolerate any further foot-dragging.

18. Atmospheric Methane Continues to Rise

In Dease Lake, John and Tony had been intently watching the CBC coverage of the Prime Minister's media conference.

"I'm decided now," John said. "Dr. Pearce invited me this spring to join his department for a master's degree in applied climate science. I'm going to accept his offer and work on this permafrost/methane problem."

"Based on how intently you've been making those methane observations, I thought you might be thinking that way," said Tony. "I guess I should confess that I've been thinking of doing likewise, with a thesis based on data assimilation and processing."

"That would be fantastic, Tony."

"Somebody has to look out for you. By the way, I've been thinking about this methane sensor, and I think we could automate things even more."

"How do you mean?"

"It has an extra pair of I/O ports, along with a communications port. We could easily hook in a simple GPS and have a central computer, say back at UVan, call it up and download data automatically, as long as the GPS can access satellites."

"Good idea! Why don't you work on the communications software, and I can design the electronics for that? With the addition of GPS, we could distribute any number of these among reliable people travelling in the north and collect much more data."

"That's exactly what I was thinking. Let's start working on it in our spare time."

"I'll mention it to Sis and she might start thinking of people she is meeting as possible data collectors. And I'm sure Dad and Professor Pearce will be interested."

* * *

Julia and her friends watched the same media conference coverage that morning before they departed Aklavik for Inuvik, a flight time of only 30 minutes. As they flew across the Mackenzie Delta, Julia was amazed at the myriad tributaries. By 12:30, they were back at Great Bear's office to meet the fingerprint expert who had arrived the previous evening from Yellowknife. He accompanied Great Bear and Duane to the airport to see if fingerprints could be recovered from Duane's aircraft.

Julia, Nancy, and Paul completed witness forms while at the RCMP offices, and Julia was able to bring her notes up to date. She had made a methane check and recorded 3200 ppb, up slightly from two days before. She emailed a copy of her notes to her dad, along with a summary of methane readings collected to date. Some of the fingerprints from the aircraft cowlings matched Todd Barton's perfectly. They were all ecstatic at having one more variable removed from the mystery.

Over lunch, Great Bear reviewed the procedure that would be followed the next day at Barton's hearing. Once the hearing was over, Great Bear would be flying to Vancouver to debrief police officials there. Great Bear confided that Whitehorse RCMP had discovered the pilot's body in a gravel pit outside of Whitehorse the previous day. He had been strangled with a wire. Nolan Smith, possibly using several aliases, was now wanted for murder. The manhunt for Smith covered all of the Yukon, including Whitehorse, Dawson City, Haines Junction, and Watson Lake, but the consensus was that Smith (alias Savage) would likely have attempted to escape by crossing into Alaska. Still, the possibility of him still being at large and a danger to the girls disturbed Great Bear. Given Great Bear's schedule and their joint concerns about the girls being on their own in Watson Lake for a day, Julia and Nancy decided that they would take a side trip to Fort McPherson the day after the hearing. That provided an opportunity to interview Gwich'in First Nations people who figured prominently there. Paul could accompany them with a mutual interest in taking additional methane readings. They should then be safe flying on to Fort Liard the following day, while Great Bear would meet up with them in Watson Lake the day after that. Great Bear planned to arrive in Watson the evening before the girls to ensure their safety. Julia phoned her brother to let him know about the delays so far. John said that they could probably delay their trip by 4 or 5 days. Meanwhile, John told Julia about his latest methane readings, and that methane concentrations appeared to be rising as the days got warmer. He said he was doing a lot more reading about global warming causes and impacts, perhaps even rethinking his career plans a bit. "I'll talk to you later about that," he added.

* * *

Barton's hearing started at 9:30 AM the next day. After testimonies from Great Bear, Julia, Nancy, Paul and Duane, the clincher being Duane's positive identification of him as the one who had asked about the girls at Tuk Airport, Barton confessed to the sabotage of Duane's aircraft. He insisted that he had not intended them any harm, just wanted to slow them down. Barton stated that he had not been instructed by Keller or anyone else to carry out the sabotage. He claimed that when he had flown to Inuvik, two weeks previously, he thought that Nick Savage had headed back to Houston from Yellowknife. And he had never heard of any Nolan Smith. He had simply taken it upon himself to delay Ms. Nicholson's report because he thought that First Nations' claims were blown out of proportion. The judge declared that Barton would stand trial in Vancouver. Great Bear later suggested that some time in jail might convince Barton to change his mind and name his employer, especially if they could nail Nolan Smith and get him to confess.

* * *

Duane had to fly back to Tuktoyaktuk that evening with a paying passenger. The four friends promised to keep in touch.

Over dinner, Great Bear, Julia, Paul, and Nancy reviewed the events of the past two weeks. Julia and Nancy suggested that they should visit Fort McPherson and Fort Laird while Great Bear would be in Vancouver. They assured Paul and Great Bear that these two diversions would be useful and most likely safe. After all, Barton was in custody. The last they'd heard about Nolan Smith was that he had flown to Whitehorse and murdered the pilot. He had likely left the country via Alaska by now. Great Bear and Paul agreed as long as at least Paul could accompany them. The girls also promised to check in with local RCMP each day. They had already rented a vehicle for the trip.

Early the following morning, Julia, Nancy, and Paul headed south from Inuvik 130 km to the ferry crossing the Mackenzie at Tsiigehtchic, then a further 60 km west to Fort

McPherson. Methane readings were still around 3200 ppb in Inuvik, but increased to 3300 ppb on their way to Fort McPherson. Values around Fort McPherson were as high as 3900 ppb. Julia thought this might be significant and made a mental note to ask her dad about it.

Julia commented to Nancy on the beauty surrounding Fort McPherson, which sits on the banks of the Peel River overlooking the majestic Richardson Mountains. Fort McPherson itself was surrounded by beautiful birch, spruce, and pines trees, and the fresh waters of the Peel.

"If you're not careful, Julia, Nancy replied, "we may have to declare you an honorary Dene and you'll have to stay with us."

"In country like you've been showing me, that wouldn't be so bad."

Paul had arranged for Julia to meet with Chief John Salu of the Tetlit Gwich'in. Once again, Julia found the local First Nations people in general very much opposed to the Mackenzie pipeline. They desperately wanted jobs for their people, but they were not prepared to sacrifice their land, way of life, and culture for them. Chief Salu said, "When we stand shoulder to shoulder opposed to the pipeline, we're not at all looking for a better deal. We just want to protect our land and culture."

* * *

Late that evening back in Inuvik, Julia called home to speak with her dad. When he answered, she updated him first on the hearing for Todd Barton the previous day.

"I heard all about it from Great Bear this afternoon," Eric replied. "How are your methane readings.

"That's partly my reason for calling so late. We found a peak value of 3900 ppb around Fort McPherson, as high as at Tuktoyaktuk. I thought values might be lower away from the delta, and we were more than 100 km south of Inuvik. Any idea why they are so high there?"

"My gut feeling is that McPherson is close to the southern edge of the continuous permafrost zone. It's had more time to thaw and for the peat bogs to decompose, but I'll certainly ask Prof. Pearce about this tomorrow when we meet. Speaking of Prof. Pearce, has John told you about his plans for this fall?"

"Not specifically, but from the way he spoke the other day, I'm suspecting he may switch into applied climate science for his MSc. I hope so, because John has a very enquiring-type mind, and I think he is well-suited for a career in research."

"You guessed right, but that's not all. David tells me that Tony has also applied to enter climate science as a software specialist. He's almost certain to be accepted."

"I'm not too surprised. Those two are like peas in a pod."

"They've both made a good start already. John is tweaking the electronics of his methane sensor, identical to your own as you know, while Tony is writing some software so that all data are processed and automatically downloaded to our server. They are also working over the electronics to add a small GPS receiver so that it could possibly be used for mobile data collection by someone who doesn't even understand what is being measured. We're thinking that it might be useful to have a few dozen mobile units as well as a fixed network. And by the way, John indicated that methane concentrations around Dease Lake had gone up by 200-300 ppb from their readings last week. David and I will be looking at their data tomorrow, along with your readings, so perhaps you could email your latest data tonight?"

"Will do, right away."

"How is your own study going? Any further consensus coming out of your talks with First Nations people concerning the Mackenzie pipeline?"

"For the most part, they seem to be against the pipeline, everywhere we've visited anyway. They all want jobs, but not at the risk of their land and culture. I'm realizing too, that analyzing the legal implications of all this is going to be difficult. One of my biggest problems is that many First Nations bands have settled their land claims issues with the federal and territorial governments, but many more have not. Their legal status on the pipeline issue is quite different. Then, this is all complicated by Metis groups, who are treated differently in the Northwest Terrirories than Metis in southern Canada."

"I see you have your work cut out for you when you return. Your plans are to go on to Fort Liard tomorrow morning I gather?"

"Yes, Nancy and I have a flight to Fort Simpson at 8:30, about three hours, then a short hop to Fort Liard about noon, in to Liard about 2 PM. Nancy made a reservation for us at the Liard Valley Hotel."

"I've got that. Would you call your mother soon after you arrive to let her know? I may be tied up between the university and RCMP headquarters all day tomorrow."

"Will do, I promise. Is mom there?"

"No, she is on an evening shift, which also reminds me that there is another storm brewing. We expect heavy rain and very strong winds in Vancouver tomorrow. It will probably run itself down by the time it gets anywhere near you, but if not, snow is a possibility. If Great Bear's flight gets delayed, I expect you and Nancy will manage okay for an extra day in Watson Lake?"

"I'm sure we will, and besides, John and Tony should arrive there around the same time."

"Look after yourselves then, and will you please check in with the RCMP in Watson Lake in case they have news about Mr. Smith?"

"Will do. Luv you, and give my love to Mom. Bye."

"Bye."

19. Kidnapping

Nick Savage, going by the alias, Nadair Sciarra, met with Joe Malone who had been with Savage during the Iraqi war and, after discharge from the army, had taken on various mining jobs in northern BC. They were both hardened by the war and well-suited to each other. Neither had any scruples about killing other human beings when it suited their purpose. They had spent almost two weeks in Watson Lake chumming and planning together, knowing that Julia planned to meet her brother there.

Savage had received a brief text from Todd Barton saying, *Close the web on B1 at 6,* meaning to kidnap Julia, and that he expected Julia to arrive in Watson Lake in a few days. All they needed to do was to take her while she was separated from Nancy. This had to be done cleanly with no observers. And they would have to leave Watson Lake unobserved immediately after.

Savage was discussing the planned kidnapping over a take-out dinner at a deserted cabin that Malone had found several miles from Watson Lake.

"If my information's correct, the Nicholson kid and her assistant should be here tomorrow. But my contact tells me the cop protecting her is in Vancouver and won't get here until the following day. That gives us a 24-hour period to trap the bitch. But we can't stay in this area with the cops already hot on my trail. Do you know of any deserted mining areas where we could hole up for a week or two, preferably a hundred kilometres or so from here?"

"Maybe. A couple of years ago I did some scouting around Cassiar in northern BC for a company interested in silicates after the asbestos mines closed for good in '99."

"How far away is this Cassiar? And are there any towns nearby? And is this company still working the mines?"

"Cassiar's about 150 km southwest of here, in BC, with nothing nearby. It's a ghost town. The company I worked for gave up. They were mostly interested in silicon agates that they could make jewelry from. They sometimes find these near asbestos sites, but we found nothing of interest to them."

"But are there still people there? Do the cops frequent the area?"

"Naw, just the odd hunter or hobo in there, but I'd recommend a deserted cabin I know of a few kilometres southwest of Cassiar. Nobody important ever goes near there."

"Sounds like what we need. All right, here's the plan. I'm too recognizable around here, so you'll do the shopping for supplies. We'll make up a list this evening."

* * *

Julia, Nancy, and Paul flew to Fort Simpson, and from there to Fort Liard. Julia took methane readings at the airport and near their hotel in Fort Liard, with both readings around 2800 ppb.

Nancy, being a Dene from Yellowknife, was able to arrange a meeting with the local Acho Dene Koe Band the following morning. Julia briefed the Council on her work, mentioned the two main offshore sources of new methane release and responded to their questions. While Fort Liard First Nations (Dene and Métis) were not anticipating any pipeline construction in the near future, they were just as opposed to the Mackenzie pipeline as all other First Nations bands that Julia and Nancy had encountered. Julia demonstrated the use of her methane sensor and was surprised to see that concentrations had risen to 2900 ppb. The band then invited the girls to a special lunch in their honour.

On calling home that evening, Julia spoke with her mother and found that Vancouver was shut down due to heavy rains and near hurricane-force winds.

"Your dad was still conferring with the RCMP, Hans Stahl, and Great Bear today," Carol mentioned. "They're hoping for a breakthrough on the case, but your dad couldn't elaborate. There's been an airline accident at Vancouver International with the high winds. All flights will be delayed for a day or two."

"Tell Dad I'm emailing some new data again while enroute from here. Nothing spectacular, but methane concentrations do seem to be rising everywhere in the north."

Nancy was able to contact Great Bear, who confirmed that he could not get a flight out of Vancouver for at least another 24 hours. He advised, "We may have some new answers by then, but meanwhile, you and Julia need to be extra careful around Watson Lake. While we think that this Nolan Smith, or whatever he calls himself right now, may have escaped into Alaska, but he just might still be in the Yukon. If so, he could be waiting for Julia if they know you are going to Watson Lake. You recall meeting Cst George Bergman back in Norman Wells?"

"Yes, of course," replied Nancy. "He was very helpful and gave us a wonderful swamp boat ride back to Norman Wells."

"Vancouver has given him a temporary assignment in Watson Lake to look after both of you. Promise me you'll check in with George at the local detachment as soon as you arrive there."

"I'll make certain we do," replied Nancy. Glancing over at Julia, she added, "Sometimes Julia does not take danger seriously enough. By the way, I miss you."

"Hey, me too. When this is all over, maybe you and I can sit down and talk about, well, future things"?

"I'd like that," said Nancy.

"Then you take care, right?"

"Bettcha!"

When Nancy had hung up, Julia said, "You two have something good going?"

"Umm, maybe," replied Nancy.

"I hope so. Great Bear obviously likes you, and he's really a great guy, I mean a great bear!"

"Speaking of which, Great Bear mentioned that Cst Bergman would look after us in Watson Lake. That should put a smile on your face."

"I have to agree. He is kinda cute. What do you think?"

"Oh, no argument there, and he was quite attentive to you back in Norman Wells."

"All part of the RCMP service I guess."

Julia then called John in Dease Lake.

John was ecstatic to hear from his sister. "Tony and I have to work late today, but we'll head up to Watson tomorrow morning. My boss insisted that we take a company truck and made up some excuse that he wanted me to pick up some forestry data for him at Watson Lake. The drive is just 3-4 hours, so we should see you girls by early-afternoon. I've got lots of news to tell you."

"I'm dying to hear how your job is going. And what kind of methane readings are you getting?"

"Nothing like you've been reporting, but values seem to be rising almost daily. Today we noted readings of 2600 ppb, where it was only 2500 a week ago."

"We're seeing increases wherever we go," said Julia.

"Sis, I hear this Smith character that shot at you at Fort Good Hope strangled a guy near Whitehorse and is still at large. You *will* be careful tomorrow, right?"

"Hey, don't worry, Baby Bro. Besides, Nancy is keeping close watch on me."

"All right, looking forward to seeing you tomorrow, Sis."

"Me too. Bye for now."

"Bye."

* * *

The girls took an Air Tindi flight to Watson Lake the next morning.

"The flight is less than 300 km, two hours max straight west, and the weather enroute is good," said Nancy.

"You seem particularly bubbly this morning. Good news?" asked Julia.

"Yeah, maybe. Actually, last night Great Bear asked if we could sit down and talk about the future when this adventure is over. Course, I said no."

"I heard differently."

"Knew I couldn't fool you. You know, I've always had, well, good feelings about Great Bear, but I didn't think he, you know, felt that way about me."

"Nancy, Great Bear is a wise bear and knows a great mama bear when he sees her!"

"I have to be honest. I'm so excited I could scream!"

"That makes me so happy. You know what, Nancy. I have lots of friends, but I feel like I've known you for years, that you're a best friend."

"Feeling's mutual, you know."

They smiled happily.

While waiting for their luggage at Watson Lake Airport, Julia and Nancy had no reason to suspect a supposed baggage handler who was watching their every move. However, Joe

Malone was careful not to draw attention from an RCMP constable who was waiting for the girls.

"Good morning, ladies. Constable George Bergman at your service again. I've been instructed by Vancouver RCMP headquarters to meet you and see that you reach your hotel okay. I hope I am not imposing on you in any way."

"Certainly not," said Julia quickly. "We're both glad to see you again. Has there been any news about this Nolan Smith?"

"Nothing new. In fact, we are doubtful that he is in the area at all. We're thinking he may have escaped to Alaska by way of Skagway, possibly caught one of the tour boats. They're checking passenger lists."

"I don't know if that's good news or bad," replied Julia. "I'm sure we would all like to see him reined in."

"We'll get him yet," answered the constable. "We always do, you know."

"Here are our bags," said Nancy. "We have reservations at the Air Force Lodge."

"Ah, good choice," said Constable Bergman. "I'm staying there myself. It's just over 15 km to the lodge, I'll have you there in less than 20 minutes."

Dropping the girls off to check in at the lodge, Cst Bergman said he needed to check in at his office and would be back within an hour, as his instructions were to accompany them everywhere.

Unbeknownst to the three, Malone followed at a distance, continuing by the Air Force Lodge as they pulled into the parking lot. Malone continued on to the cabin that he and Savage occupied outside of the town.

"They've booked into the Air Force Lodge," he said to Savage.

"We need to keep an eye on them and wait for our chance to get the little bitch. We don't want to be bothered with two of them, so we need to catch the Nicholson girl by herself. You can snoop around, I'll stay in the truck. Any cop comes around and I disappear. We can link up again by texting. While you were at the airport, I got the truck loaded up, ready to go at a moment's notice. Once we have her in tow, we leave immediately, head to this Cassiar place of yours."

After checking-in, Julia and Nancy made a quick methane reading. It indicated 2700 ppb.

"Why don't we call a local taxi and whip into town for lunch?" suggested Nancy. "We can leave a message for Cst Bergman to meet us there. We could also check out Kaska Dena Council who have an office in the town."

"Good plan, then later we can have a quick look around. I want to see this Signpost Forest that's mentioned on the town's website. Apparently some homesick US GI started it during the war years, placing a sign from his hometown there. Now people bring signs from all over the world."

They had a quick lunch, then the waitress directed them to the Kaska Dena Council office about 200 metres west of the restaurant. As they approached the office, Julia noticed a small shop on a side street and said, "I'm sure we're safe enough here. You go ahead and see if you can arrange a meeting. I'll just check out this store, see if I can pick something up for Mom and Dad."

"Okay, but don't be more than a couple of minutes."

As Julia turned down the side street, Savage and Malone saw what might be their only chance to catch her alone. Savage had noted all vehicle and foot traffic. It looked pretty clear. Malone stepped from their truck. As Julia passed between two trees, he called out, "Excuse me, Miss, I'm new in town and looking for the Big Horn Hotel. Can you tell me where I can find it?"

"My gosh, I don't really know, since this is the first time I've been here. Why don't you ask them at this store here—oh, it looks like it's shut down. Perhaps you can … what are …?"

Malone had pressed a cloth soaked in an anesthetic into Julia's face and she passed out. Savage had followed discreetly and now quickly brought the truck up. Malone hastily lifted Julia into the back seat and climbed in the front.

"Let's get outta here," said Malone.

"Get her onto the floor and put that blanket over her," replied Savage. And for God's sake, find her cell phone and take it. We don't need her advertising what has happened."

They drove west toward the Stewart-Cassiar Highway 20 km west of Watson Lake, then turned south toward Cassiar.

Two hours later, they arrived at the Cassiar turnoff and headed west. Savage noticed a truck parked at the turnoff and was immediately nervous and suspicious.

"Don't worry about it Savage. The sign on the door indicates it's just one of those highway maintenance trucks."

They stopped a few kilometres further on. Malone took the wheel and drove the remaining 15 km to Cassiar, then several kilometres past to where they took an old dirt trail south for several kilometres. Finally he turned in to a lane that led to a deserted cabin. They carried the unconscious Julia into the cabin and into a separate room in the back. The room had no windows and the door could be barred and padlocked from the outside. "Perfect," said Savage, once they had unloaded their truck. "Now to see about informing Mr. Professor Nicholson about what we want from him."

* * *

Back at Watson Lake, Nancy had arranged for a meeting with the head of Kaska Dena Council, Timothy Miller. She then walked toward the store where Julia had headed. She immediately noticed that the store was closed. Panicking, she looked around for Julia. There was no one in sight, so she headed back to the council office. She quickly explained her concerns and Timothy immediately called the RCMP offices. Cst Bergman arrived five minutes later with another RCMP officer, Cst Jane Anstey, in a second vehicle. The four quickly searched the immediate area.

Cst Bergman asked Nancy whether Julia might have gone back to the lodge.

"Not a chance, not without finding me first," she said.

Bergman sent Anstey on to the lodge in any event. A short while later she reported back in the negative.

"We'll continue the search obviously, but I'll be reporting her as missing, possibly a kidnapping, given the situation as you described."

Nancy was beside herself. "I shouldn't have left her alone for a single minute. This is my fault," she sobbed.

"You mustn't feel that way, Miss Wedzin. No blame can possibly be attributed to you. In fact, it's more my fault than anyone else's, since my instructions were to accompany you everywhere."

"I should have known better. We should have waited at the lodge as agreed. It was my suggestion to go ahead and just leave you a note. And please, just call me Nancy."

"All right, let's go back to the station. I'm going to call an all-points search for Julia within a 100 km radius to start, having officers flag down every vehicle and even check out their trunks. Then we'll report in to RCMP headquarters in Vancouver and to her parents."

"Please, let's hurry."

Chief Timothy Miller spoke up at this point, "I'll contact all our people as well. Have everyone on the lookout for Miss Nicholson or anyone suspicious," he said.

"That could be very helpful," replied Constable Bergman.

Two tense hours later, Nancy had finished speaking with Julia's mom and dad. She was beside herself, alternating between detailed explanations and quick sobs. She spoke with Great Bear as well, and he was equally distraught. Great Bear had a reservation to fly to Watson Lake at 2 PM. Hans decided that he needed to go as well, and this was quickly arranged, along with one other RCMP crime expert from the Vancouver office. "If the flight is full, we'll simply pull rank for you,"

"You're the ultimate target in this, Eric," he said. "There's no point in making it easier for this bunch by exposing yourself. At this stage, I doubt whether they would hesitate at all to assassinate you. Your daughter, at this stage, is an essential bargaining chip, so they won't really harm her. We need to play along until we hear further from them. I'll be in frequent contact with you. You and Carol will need police protection. We don't want either of you going anywhere on your own just now. Understood?

"I suppose you're right. I'll trust your judgment on this. Meanwhile, you realize that our son, John, and his friend, Tony, are already headed to Watson Lake, not knowing about this latest situation with Julia."

"That is a concern, and another reason Great Bear and I both need to get there A-S-A-P. You'll be able to reach us at any time on our satellite phone. We'll need to know immediately if they contact you."

* * *

Later that afternoon, Eric received an untraceable email with the following message:

You will stop all northern research on methane immediately. Your results and all data must be turned over to us within three days if you want to see your daughter alive again. We will inform you by tomorrow evening how the turnover will take place. Do not fail to follow these instructions, and do not be so foolish as to think you can discover her whereabouts. If police come within 20 km of our location, she will be disposed of immediately and you will never find her body.
Nadair Sciarra

David was present, along with Eric's RCMP bodyguard. Eric tensed when he read the message. His two hands went to his forehead with his elbows on the desk.

"I can hardly believe this is happening," he said to David.

"They won't get away with it. Hans has handled threats like this before."

"I'd best contact him immediately. They left on a 2 PM flight, so they should be in Watson by now."

He dialed Hans' cell phone number. Hans immediately picked up.

"Yes," said Hans. "Go ahead."

"Eric here, Hans. I just received a note from the kidnappers, our fiend friend, Nadair Sciarra." Eric read the note to Hans.

Hans said, "Don't worry yet. This is a typical threat for kidnappings. They risked this much and they're not going to do anything like that message threatens. We just arrived. We're still at Watson Airport in fact. Wait until we have a chance to assess what went on here. Play along with them when they call you again, and delay in any reasonable way. Then call me immediately afterward, before you do anything at all."

"Okay. Please look out for John and Tony. They should arrive there and meet Nancy this afternoon. Don't let them do anything rash either. We don't want any other kidnappings."

"Absolutely Eric. You just look after yourself and Carol right now. I can't tell you not to worry of course. That's understood. Just remember that we have the best experts in the country working on this case. We *will* get these guys, and Julia *will* be safe. I promise you."

* * *

190

"Do you have any details, have we received a note for ransom, or …?" Carol asked Eric later. She instinctively knew that this did not involve money, at least not as a ransom.

Eric replied, his voice faltering, "The note states that I have to turn over all our data and results on the Arctic Ocean project and stop all research there, or we will never see Julia alive again. The police examined the email, but they say it's not traceable."

Carol broke down sobbing.

After a few moments, Eric went on, "Dear, this has to do with Dr. Mazurenko's project on the Arctic Ocean sea-floor. As I told you the other evening, Hans thinks Mazurenko was murdered because of it. These people will stop at nothing it seems, although we don't really know who *these people* are."

"Didn't you say that Matthew Keller may be a suspect?"

"Yes, but if he is involved, he's just small potatoes. Somebody, or some very large corporate organization is at the core of this. Between you and me, I don't think for a minute that CUUON is innocent. I have to admit that I've been concerned about something like this happening, but I didn't want to worry you unnecessarily."

"Eric, you know me better than that! I knew you were worried about something, but I didn't want to cause you even more stress by pressing you on it."

"I guess we're alike that way, but now we have much more to concern us. God, you don't know how many times this week I've wished I never got involved in climate problems."

"But you also know deep down that nothing would stop you, and neither are you going to quit now. We'll get through this." Carol's voice cracked, and she suddenly broke down sobbing again.

"Carol, listen to me. We must trust Hans and the RCMP. They have their best intelligence working on this case. One other concern I have is that John is headed to Watson Lake, not knowing what has happened. But Hans and Great Bear will soon link up with him and make sure he and Tony, plus Nancy, are safe. Meanwhile, we each have a bodyguard. Neither of us should venture outside without them accompanying us."

20. Rescue

John and Tony had left about 10 AM that morning. They were held up for more than an hour by road maintenance, then stopped for a quick break during the early-afternoon right at the turnoff to Cassiar. While they munched on a sandwich, a black GMC Yukon turned off from the north, headed for Cassiar.

"Wonder what they're up to, given that Cassiar has been shut down for decades," mused John.

"Probably just some hunters," replied Tony.

"Perhaps," said John, "but they didn't look like hunters to me. I didn't see any rifles, quad or any hunting equipment."

"Fishing or photography, perhaps?"

They quickly forgot about the black truck and drove on, arriving in Watson Lake in mid-afternoon. John called Julia's cell number, but it rang until her message manager cut in, so John left a message, "Hi Sis, we've just arrived in Watson. You're not answering your cell, but I expect we'll see you within the hour. I'll try the number you gave me for Nancy the other day."

John then dialed Nancy's number. Nancy answered on the first ring, "Hello."

"Hi Nancy, this is John, we just …."

Nancy cut him off immediately, "John, something terrible has happened. Julia has disappeared. We think she's been kidnapped."

"Oh Lord," John replied. "We just arrived, we're on the west side of town. Where can we find you?"

"I'm at the RCMP office. It's right on the corner of 8th Street and the highway. Great Bear is here now too, along with your Dad's Interpol contact, Hans Stahl, and two other RCMP officers."

Five minutes later, John and Tony were at the Watson Lake RCMP detachment.

After introductions to Nancy, Great Bear and the other RCMP officers, John and Tony were given a detailed update of all events of the past few days, and were briefed on what Hans and the Vancouver office had determined so far. Hans mentioned, "We're fairly certain that Julia's kidnapper is Nick

Savage, who also goes by the alias Nolan Smith, believed to be the one who shot up their canoe at Fort Good Hope, then persuaded or forced their pilot to fly him to Whitehorse, where he murdered him after getting him stone drunk. He's using the alias Nadair Sciarra, which he used to rent a vehicle in Whitehorse. We believe he has picked up another accomplice, who is probably doing all their purchasing and other work; otherwise Constable Bergman and his crew would have nabbed him by now. I also have reason to believe that he was responsible for murdering your father's Russian colleague in Bonn. There he used the alias Nils Scheer. You'll note that all his aliases have the initials NS, which seems somewhat dumb, as it is the one clue tying all these names together. If we're right on this, it puts the nail in the coffin for linking him to Matthew Keller, an old colleague of your dad, who also works with CUUON, the really big fish."

"I remember Dad telling me about Keller. And Julia mentioned that Keller's son, Malcolm I believe his name is, works out of Yellowknife with Nancy."

"That's right," said Nancy.

"Malcolm's been estranged from his father ever since his parents went through a nasty divorce about 10 years ago," Hans added.

"All of this is starting to make some sense, isn't it," said John.

"We think the case is ready to be broken. We just need to know where your sister is being kept."

"Any ideas which way they may have gone?"

"With no public transport, they have to have used a vehicle of some sort. And there are a limited number of roads they can take up here. Surely you should be able to trace that rental vehicle?"

"That's true," said Constable Bergman, "but so far we've come up blank. Right now we're stopping every vehicle we see within 100 km of here."

"What kind of vehicle did this culprit rent in Whitehorse? Is there any chance he ditched it and stole another vehicle?" John asked.

"It's unlikely that he would steal a vehicle without us knowing within hours," said Bergman. "He rented a black GMC Yukon in Whitehorse on May 30th."

John and Tony immediately looked at each other. John blurted, "Bingo! We might have him!"

"What do you mean?" said Hans.

"We stopped for a break on the way up here at the turnoff to that ghost mining town of Cassiar. While we were there, a black Yukon turned off from the north and headed toward Cassiar."

Hans lit up. "That's the most fortuitous clue that I've heard yet. We may very well have them trapped, then. However, we can't endanger Julia. The note your dad received warns that they will kill her if they think any police are within 20 km of their location."

"First we have to find out their exact location," said John.

"Constable Bergman, would you like to demonstrate some magic on our version of Google Earth?" asked Hans.

"I sure would. Right this way, ladies and gentlemen," he said as he walked over to his desk. "What we have access to is real-time satellite imagery at much higher resolution than the public sees on the Internet."

"That's awesome," spoke up Tony for the first time, always interested in any new technology.

"Here's the Cassiar area. Hans, would you expect Savage and his accomplice more likely to hide out somewhere east or west of Cassiar?"

"I'd suggest west of Cassiar," interjected Hans, "because they want to remain hidden from all observers. Try looking at some area a few kilometres west of Cassiar."

Bergman zoomed in to the west side of the ghost town. "Let's move slowly west looking for any side-roads or off-road trails."

"There," spoke up Hans. "There's a trail leading south, follow it down. That's what, about 3½ km southwest of the town site?"

"Yes," replied Constable Bergman.

"The imagery is extremely good over this region," said John.

"Google seems to favour large towns and industrial or mining areas, even deserted ones," replied Hans.

"There's an open area, looks like a cabin on the east side of the road. Is that smoke coming from a chimney?" asked Tony.

"It sure is," said Hans, "and unless I miss my guess altogether, that black rectangle within the trees is our GMC Yukon."

"So, how do we deal with this?" asked Constable Bergman. "We can't just rush in there."

"We need to position ourselves so that Savage and his accomplice are separated from Julia," said Hans. John and Tony, are you two sure there were only two guys in that truck? We need to know if there are more than two."

"There were definitely only two people visible in the truck."

"We have to assume then that there wasn't a third person in the cabin waiting for Savage and the other guy."

Taking charge, Hans said "We need to map out the whole area, choose who we want, then plan our attack. And we need to get this completed tomorrow, people. We can't afford to let these guys get wind of us and get them trigger happy."

* * *

Meanwhile, Savage had heard Julia's phone ring and saw that it was from someone called John.

Julia was just regaining consciousness when Savage came to check on her. Although still groggy, Julia immediately recognized Savage as the man with the scar she observed on the flight to Fort Simpson.

"So, Mr. Savage, alias Mr. Smith. How many other aliases do you have?"

"Enough to keep you lot confused," Savage answered. "We're well hidden in the wilderness. None of your friends can find you, and you'd better do exactly what we say."

"Where are we?"

"Uh uh, that's a secret. By the way, you had a call from John, I imagine that's your brother, which I didn't answer, needless to say, but your phone indicates that he left a message. Where was he at the time? Was he going to meet you at Watson Lake?"

"I've no idea," lied Julia.

"In that case, you will access your message manager."

"I don't remember my password," said Julia.

Savage backhanded her across the face and said, "That should shake your memory. Here, the lovely lady on your message manager wants your password."

Julia noted the time on her iPhone to be 7:15 PM. She input the code and Savage grabbed the phone.

"He'll see you within the hour, he thinks" said Savage. "That was a few hours ago. So he *was* headed to Watson Lake. Where was he coming from?"

Julia sensed a trap here, so she answered quickly, "We were originally going to meet in Whitehorse, but then he decided to come to Watson. I guess you ruined that plan."

"We intend to change a few plans, including those of your daddy."

Julia bristled, but decided not to take the bait. "Look, I really gotta go to the bathroom. Please?"

"The bathroom is an outdoor privy. We're a long way from any civilization. We'll take you out, but don't try anything funny."

Julia carefully noted the location of windows as she moved through the cabin. Outside she saw the dirt road to the left, their truck under some trees straight ahead, the privy off to the right and nothing but heavy brush and trees in all other directions. She had no idea where they could be. Her initial guess was somewhere within 20-30 km of Watson Lake, but then realized that the net had been closing on them, so Savage would want to be as far away as possible. Savage had said John called a few hours ago, so maybe three or four hours. She guessed they may have driven a couple of hours. She had been out for at least another hour, so they could be 100-200 km from Watson Lake.

* * *

Hans and Great Bear had decided that Nancy would be safe with an RCMP bodyguard at Watson Lake, but John was too tempting a target in case there was a third kidnapper. John would be best under Hans' and Great Bear's protection. Two more RCMP officers had been brought in, Cst Robison, from Vancouver who had expertise in forensic analysis, and Farrel from Whitehorse. They were both expert sharpshooters, as were Great Bear and Hans. Farrel had discovered the pilot's body south of Whitehorse. They all headed to Andrea's Restaurant and a private room for dinner and planning.

Hans took charge and decided that they would drive to Cassiar in two vehicles, hide the vehicles in the ghost town then move ahead through the bush on foot. The cabin faced north. Hans selected positions and contact call signs for each team rescue member. Hans (R1) and Great Bear (R2) directly facing the front door, off to either side, about 45 degrees to the cabin door; Constable Bergman (R3) to their right closest to the dirt road, Farrel (R4) to the left. The trick was for each team member to have an unobstructed view of the cabin while remaining completely concealed. The fifth member, Constable Robison (R5) would guard the rear, provide backup and attempt rescue if Julia (J) was visible through a window. John (R6) was to back up Bergman closest to the road. The plan was to wait for both men to appear outside and away from the door. It was inevitable that one or both would move away from the cabin at some point, since the cabin would not have toilet facilities. The two members on either side, Bergman and Farrel, would concentrate on the man closest to the door (A), Hans and Great Bear on whomever moved away from the cabin (B). They would signal Hans when (A) was at least six feet from the door. Both had to indicate that they had a clear shot if it was necessary to shoot.

Hans would order Savage and his accomplice to immediately drop to the ground or be shot. If either of them attempted to dash back to the cabin, they would be taken down. Hans was taking no chances on the kidnappers carrying out their threat against Julia. He was also aware that Savage was a trained sniper and assassin. He would most likely be the one who stayed close to the cabin, except when using the outdoor toilet off to their left. This was all predicated on Julia remaining locked in the cabin, although Hans allowed for the possibility that they just might bring Julia out with them.

Sunrise in Cassiar was about 4:25 AM. It would take them just under two hours to reach Cassiar and hide their vehicles. Depending on the terrain, they would need at least another hour to hike off the road about 5 km to the cabin and get set up. Robinson had arranged to have everyone in camouflage outer clothing. Farrel had been in the area several times over the past five years. He indicated that it was heavily wooded west of Cassiar, so the approach to the cabin on foot would be rough going. Hans wanted everyone in place before 6 AM, hopefully before the kidnappers were up and about. He decided they would depart from Watson Lake at 3 AM, arriving in Cassiar half an hour after sunrise so as not to attract attention with headlights, then make their way on foot to the cabin by 6 AM. That allowed everyone 6-7 hours to catch some sleep before they left Watson. All team members were fully aware that complete surprise was essential, that they could not risk the kidnappers suspecting that they might be in the area. By 8 PM they had completed their plans.

* * *

By 2:55 they were on the road in two vehicles. They arrived at the turnoff for Cassiar at 4:30, and by 5:00 they had hidden the vehicles in Cassiar inside an abandoned warehouse.

Great Bear, deferring to Hans, said, "All right, Chief, are we sticking to the same plan?"

"Yes, but there's one what-if. What if they bring Julia out with them? If she's exposed, we have to maintain cover. If they notice either one of us, the game plan changes and you three have to take them down, as long as Julia is not in the line of fire."

"That makes me very uncomfortable."

"I know. Me too, but we can't allow them one second to shoot down Julia. We have to shoot first, no other choice."

"That's the best plan. I'm glad you thought of that what-if," said Constable Bergman

"We must all have a well-concealed location. That's crucial for this operation. John, you're the odd man in this. I want you to the right with Constable Bergman, closest to the road. George, I want you to instruct John on the use of your gun just in case you go down, just as a precaution. I know it's against regulations, but this whole operation is too crucial to worry about that."

"I agree," said Bergman. "We just won't say anything about it later."

"Any other questions, anybody?"

Everyone shook their head in the negative.

"One last point," said Hans. "If at all possible, we need to take Savage alive, if only to make the link with others later. But if anyone is in any danger at all, don't hesitate to take him down. Okay, let's get on with it. I'll do a radio check with all of you as soon as we spread out and again when we're in position."

Hans sent Great Bear ahead, given his northern expertise in tracking wildlife. As they made their way to the cabin, they checked out their radio protocols, going over all plans once more. Along the way, Constable Bergman gave John the basic pointers of how to fire his gun, without any practice shooting.

"Rescue squad units 2, 3, 4, 5, 6, this is R-1. Please confirm copy in order.

"This is R-2, copy 10-4."

"R-3, 10-4."

"R-4, 10-4."

"R-5, 10-4."

"R-6, 10-4."

"All units, this is R1, all copy fine. Out."

* * *

Back at the cabin, Malone had just heated up some beans and bacon, plus a pot of coffee. The three unlikely companions ate in silence. They set Julia to cleaning up the dishes, then Savage said, "It's about time I contacted your daddy again. And just to be nice, and to make sure he knows we're not bluffing, I'll use your phone Miss Julia. If you give your daddy even a hint of your whereabouts, then you're as good as dead. Got that?"

"I've got it," Julia replied curtly.

Savage dialed Eric's cell number.

Eric answered, "Hello."

"Good evening Professor Nicholson," Savage replied. "This is your friend, Nadair Sciarra again, calling on your daughter's cell phone. Listen carefully and take notes." Waiting a few moments while Eric retrieved pen and paper, he went on, "Tomorrow you are to put your computer drives, anything with your data on it, in a red plastic bag then take a flight alone to Calgary. There's a direct flight leaving Vancouver at 9 AM. When you arrive at the Calgary airport, take a taxi, alone, to downtown. You will get out at the corner of 9th Avenue southwest and 1st Street southwest. Wait until 1 PM Calgary time, then walk two blocks east to the Calgary Tower. Outside its main doors you will see a garbage container alongside two flower pots. Deposit the red bag with your hard drives there, continue east to the next block where you will hail another taxi back to the airport. Take the next flight back to Vancouver. You will be monitored at each point along the way. You will not talk to or meet anyone else at any time before you arrive back in Vancouver. DO NOT keep any copies of the data. Your daughter will be held for several days or weeks yet, while we check that you have followed these instructions to the letter."

"I have those instructions, but let me speak with Julia."

"Why, sure thing. Here you go darling, talk to your daddy."

"Dad, I'm fine, so don't worry."

"Okay, dear. Just do as they say. I'm sure things will work out."

"Give my love to …."

"That's enough dearie," said Savage as he grabbed the phone away again. "One last warning: if we find later that you have another copy of these data, our next target will be rather direct. Do you get my drift?"

"Clearly," said Eric.

"You will be contacted once again after my agents pick up the drop and check it out. Any attempt to interfere with them will be considered fatal. Bye." Savage clicked off the phone.

Eric immediately called Hans, who was just leaving Cassiar on foot for the cabin. They quickly exchanged notes. Hans reassured Eric that they had everything in hand and his daughter would be safe, somewhat more assuredly than he felt himself, not knowing all the variables. However, the threat given to Eric re-emphasized the need for care in the operation just started, so he warned his team once more of what was at stake.

* * *

They arrived several hundred metres from the cabin.

"R-1 to all units, you all know the plan," Hans broadcast. "We each need to move quietly into position from here. I don't need to tell you that invisibility and silence are essential. You're all experienced trackers. Good luck. We'll keep radio talk to a minimum, but everyone keep an eye on the cabin door and any windows. Be careful of any reflection off your guns. Report any movement you see to the rest of us, identifying yourselves by number. They went over positions and call signs one more time, then each man headed into position. Constable Robison crossed the road to move through the trees on the west side, crossing back south of the cabin. Ten minutes later they were all in position and reported in one by one to Hans. R1 through R4 all had good visibility to the front door of the cabin, while Robison (R5) at the rear was in good backup position to Farrel (R4).

* * *

"I need to use the privy," Julia complained from her room.

Joe, would you accompany the lady to our first class facility outside."

"Absolutely," replied Malone. "This way, your highness." He opened the door and went ahead of Julia, Savage following Julia, but staying back, as if nervous of something.

"All units, R-1," suspects are coming out."

"R-1, R-3 here, have perfect bead."

"R-1, R-4, likewise."

"R-4, R-5 here, I have your back."

Malone moved to the right toward the outdoor privy, his rifle in his right hand, followed by Julia. Savage (alias Sciarra) remained on the deck near the door, his rifle up, not aimed, but on the ready. Hans took a tense swallow, knowing that Savage may be the best marksman among all of them. He looked nervous and ready, as if suspecting something was up. Hans waited until Julia was inside the privy. Then, using a megaphone, he called out, "Drop your guns immediately and get down on the ground—now! You are surrounded and there's no escape."

Malone stood there stupefied, then reluctantly dropped his gun and went down on the ground. Savage, however, jumped to his left behind some trees. There he was in his element. All his marine training came back into force. He quickly moved into heavy brush. With all the noise, no one could tell his position as he worked his way toward the road and then toward the truck where Cst Bergman and John waited. A shot rang out. John stared in horror as Cst Bergman went down. John ducked before the next shot, then instinctively raised his gun and fired as Savage came crashing through the brush toward him. There was then an eerie silence. By then, Great Bear had moved up to the truck and was covering behind John. "John, stay down," he called out.

Seconds passed as Cst. Robison (R-5) came up behind Savage's track, then called out, "Suspect is down. John got him." He kept his gun on Savage as he approached, then kicked Savage's gun aside. Savage grunted as Robison turned him over. Robison then noticed Bergman sitting up with blood coming from a wound in his right arm. "Suspect is immobilized. George is wounded but okay," he called out.

Meanwhile, Cst Farrel (R-4) had secured Malone. Hans called out to Julia. "Julia, this is Hans, Great Bear, and your brother John here. You're safe, thanks to your brother."

"I'll be out in a few moments," Julia called back. Five minutes later, Julia and John were hugging and shedding a few tears. Julia immediately called her parents to tell them that everyone was safe. Eric and Carol decided to fly to Whitehorse the following evening where they could all reunite and share stories. Julia replied that she and Nancy still planned to do some pipeline research at the Yukon archives in Whitehorse.

Great Bear called Watson Lake RCMP for an ambulance while Cst Bergman and Savage were being bandaged up. They made three trips in Savage's truck to transport everyone back to the deserted town of Cassiar. Two hours later, two ambulances arrived to take Cst Bergman and Savage back to Watson Lake, Farrel accompanying Savage. Robison and Hans took charge of Malone in one vehicle, Great Bear drove with Julia, while John drove the kidnappers' truck.

Just before leaving Cassiar, John said, "Wait one minute, I want to get a methane reading here." He reported, "Lower than at Watson Lake, 2300, but still pretty high."

"You're awfully keen about that," Julia observed, "after what's happened this last couple of days."

"I've been doing a lot of thinking and I'm changing my profession, just slightly," John responded.

"That's one of the worst kept secrets around here."

"I guess so, but I'm making it official."

* * *

That evening, Julia, Nancy, Great Bear, John, and Tony had an enjoyable and tearful meeting. They all visited Cst Bergman in the local hospital. "Doc tells me he'll release me tomorrow," said Bergman. "Told me the town can't afford to keep me here long, I need to be back on patrol by tomorrow evening," he laughed.

"I feel partly responsible for you getting shot," said Julia, "not much thanks for you ferrying Nancy and me down the Mackenzie."

"I'm just happy that you're safe and sound."

Julia gave him a big hug, thanked him and promised to see him again.

"I would like that very much," Bergman replied.

They all headed to the Big Horn Hotel restaurant where they had reserved a private room for dinner. There were toasts all around. Hans stood up and said: "I want to first congratulate *Single-shot John*, who took down our most notorious wanted man with just one shot," chuckling all around, "undoubtedly saving all our lives. What will you do for an encore, John?"

"I'm retiring from all guns, Hans. Besides, with one shot, one down, I want to keep my perfect record." Everyone laughed again, and Julia gave her brother a big bear hug.

Then Hans added, "Now I think Great Bear has something special to say."

Great Bear stood and said, "Ladies and gentlemen, I have a very important announcement to make." When everyone was quiet, Great Bear continued, "These two ladies," pointing to Julia and Nancy, "have complicated my life in the past few weeks, with me trying to keep track of them and keep them safe. I decided that I had to take more drastic measures with at least one of them. "So …," he hesitated, "I've asked Nancy if she will marry me. I'm shocked that she agreed right away."

Julia squealed, jumped up and hugged Nancy. "I just knew you'd take my advice and marry that wonderful man." They stood there wrapped around one another. Then Julia jumped at Great Bear and gave him a huge bear hug. "You have just made me as happy as Nancy is," she said. "Now I have two best friends together. And don't think we don't appreciate how hard you've worked to keep Nancy and me out of trouble. And Nancy, you're just the best. What else can I say? You've been looking after me for a month."

"My boss ordered me to look after you. As for what else you can say, you can promise me you'll be at our wedding in late July, as soon as we work out the details."

"Nothing will keep me away."

By the next day, Julia, Nancy, Great Bear, John, Tony, and Hans had all decided to drive to Whitehorse.

"I'm still required to watch over you two," said Great Bear, "and besides, I called the rental agency in Whitehorse. They're giving us a freebee if we drive Savage's Yukon back there. Savage and Malone will get special RCMP accompaniment on their flight to Vancouver tomorrow. I also have to accompany Julia back to Vancouver after they finish up in Whitehorse. Nancy might as well join us."

John and Tony called their supervisor in Dease Lake, who suggested that they use the company vehicle to drive to Whitehorse, before heading back to Dease Lake two days later. Julia and Hans elected to drive with John and Tony, giving Great Bear and Nancy some time alone. Along the route, Julia and John alternated taking methane readings, noting the concentrations climbing up to 2900 ppb in Whitehorse.

When they met Eric and Carol at Whitehorse Airport that evening, they were surprised to see Professor Pearce with them. "I want to see these methane concentrations for myself," David commented. But Julia suspected that something else was motivating Professor Pearce as well, something to do with John.

That evening in a private restaurant room, they all had a chance to review what had happened over the past month. When it came to John's turn, he said "First, I want to make an announcement, not as important as Great Bear's last evening, and probably the worst-kept secret among you all. But I've been talking with Prof. Pearce and he has agreed to risk taking me on as a graduate student in climate field research this fall." Julia, who was sitting next to her brother, immediately stood up, embraced him, and kissed him on the cheek.

"I'm so proud of you, Bro," she said. There was applause all around.

"Ah, but Tony is also joining the group as an IT specialist in software and electronics development," John replied, "and he has some great ideas for methane data collection and assimilation."

Professor Pearce got up and shook John's hand, then Tony's. "Welcome to the climate group, you two." Then to the whole gathering he said, "With John and Tony's engineering knowledge, we plan to start looking more seriously at the dynamics of permafrost, so this represents more of an addition rather than a change in John's career. And we have some key data to start with, given what these two have started," nodding toward John and Julia.

"Plus, we have government support for this important aspect of climate research," added Eric.

The next day, most of the group spent time relaxing and planning. Julia, Nancy, and Carol took several hours to research pipeline information at the Yukon College archives. Great Bear and Hans were busy writing up reports to the RCMP and Interpol, while Eric, David, John, and Tony discussed field research plans.

David and Eric both approved John and Tony's suggestion of distributing a certain number of methane sensors to volunteers travelling throughout the north.

"I suspect that Great Bear, Nancy, and Julia have enough contacts who would make reliable volunteers for this," said John.

"Okay," replied Professor Pearce, "can we leave the selection of volunteers to you two to arrange?"

"You bet," said John and Tony together.

"Next, we need to decide how many fixed and mobile units we'll need to get the job done. We need to be thinking of both the permafrost and offshore methane sources," said Professor Pearce, as he unrolled a large gridded map.

Two days later, John and Tony set out for Dease Lake, while the others flew back to Vancouver. Eric and David had barely a month to prepare for the emergency meetings in New York on July 10th. The primary agenda item was to negotiate a full moratorium on all drilling in the Arctic until further results were available.

21. Emergency International Meeting

During early July, between the Canadian and US national holidays, Canada's Prime Minister Mulligan Thomas and US President Illyana Dinton had met and agreed on the necessity for the immediate moratorium on Arctic drilling. Extensive briefings followed, with ambassadors from Russia, Finland, Sweden, Denmark, Norway, and Iceland, all northern countries with borders within the Arctic. These countries, along with the US and Canada, claimed rights to Arctic Ocean waters. The emergency meeting was arranged for July 10th, chaired by the Secretary-General of the United Nations. All government leaders received prior briefings on the reality of the methane risks and impacts from their own climate scientists. For this emergency meeting, Eric, David, and other climate scientists from each of these Arctic nations only needed to update the leaders on the findings of the past year, starting with Mazurenko's discoveries in the Barents Sea, up to the most recent results from methane measurements in Canada's north.

Leading the presentations at the U.N., Eric described how atmospheric carbon dioxide concentrations now exceeded 420 ppm, which was threatening enough. He explained how methane, mass for mass, has almost 30 times the potential of carbon dioxide for warming the climate, although it has a much shorter residency time in the atmosphere. While concentrations of methane were under 2 ppm in 2012, they had risen sharply over Arctic regions during the past year because of two factors—rapid permafrost melt over the Arctic tundra, with resulting decay of peatland bogs and methane released from beneath the permafrost, plus the release of methane from offshore drilling for oil, and from methane clathrates. Values of up to 4 ppm were being recorded all around the Arctic Ocean and for hundreds of kilometres inland. The ice island measurements that Dr. Mazurenko had made in the Barents Sea suggested that this could easily exceed 10 ppm within five years, the equivalent of increasing CO_2 from its present 420 ppm to over 650 ppm, which would guarantee a shocking and catastrophic increase in global temperature. The threat didn't stop there, because there had been recent discoveries of enormous quantities of naturally occurring methane trapped in ice-like structures in the cold northern muds at the bottom of the seas. These structures, called clathrates, could potentially increase atmospheric methane concentrations by a factor of 5 or 10 times.

"And here's the scary part," warned Eric. "A temperature increase of merely a few more degrees could cause these gases to volatilize and burp into the atmosphere, which would further raise temperatures. That would release yet more methane, heating the Earth and seas further, and so on. What we are threatened with is a runaway greenhouse effect, and possibly the eventual extinction of mankind and virtually every other creature on Earth!"

The Russian President attempted some reverse reasoning, "So we are talking global warming. Isn't all that extra heat spread out over the whole globe? How can another temperature rise of a degree or so make all that difference?"

"It is heat energy we are considering," Eric replied. "If all that heat were spread out evenly across the Earth's surface, there might not be any major change. But the point is that heat is a system which flows, and some of it cannot help but pile up somewhere. When that happens, something big occurs. One pile-up is the very unusual number of intense hurricanes we've seen in the Atlantic this year. Another is the heating of the Arctic Ocean. Once these offshore clathrates start releasing methane in a serious way, all bets will be off. We simply will not be able to control it. And make no mistake—it may already be too late, but that should not stop us from trying to stem the tide."

Even Russia's President could not mount any further argument for delay. He gave in. With the recent results revealed, all the leaders agreed and signed a binding agreement to take effect immediately, with energy companies ordered to cap all Arctic wells safely until further notice. In his closing remarks, the Secretary-General praised the work of Dr. Mazurenko in particular, and congratulated the Russian President on behalf of the global community for providing the opportunity for Mazurenko's research, even though most were aware of the clandestine nature of that research. He also congratulated Eric and David for their work and collaboration with Mazurenko. He acknowledged Eric's children for their contributions to this international agreement by independently collecting methane data.

The following day, the U.N. Security Council met and endorsed the motion, such that it became international law. The UN could now impose complete trade embargoes on any country that did not comply without the risk of a veto.

* * *

While these emergency meetings were going on, Hans, working through the RCMP, Interpol, and the CIA, had produced overwhelming evidence linking Savage to the murders of both Dr. Mazurenko (in Germany) and the Norman Wells pilot in Whitehorse. Through plea bargaining, Savage was promised a reduced sentence for testifying that Matthew Keller was the brains behind these killings, with the full knowledge of key management within CUUON, including Tom Bolton. Both were arrested immediately. Keller, Bolton, Barton, Savage, and Malone were headed for long prison terms, while other heads, including that of CEO David Brown, were rolling at CUUON in Houston, as well as in Moscow. Subsequent investigations through Interpol revealed that CUUON had been channeling millions to climate denialists in several countries for the previous two decades. Further arrests followed in the US, Canada, the UK, Germany, and Russia.

Immediately following the U.N. meetings in mid-July, Eric and David spent a week with their graduate students, planning and preparing instrumentation and supplies for the necessary field work to be conducted in the Arctic over the next few months. Scientists from Russia, the US, and Sweden also contributed to this effort, so that the UVan Department of Climate became a very busy place that week. Technical and professional assistance were also provided by the Canadian and US governments.

During this time, Eric and David's colleague, Kelvin Nordsen from Geophysics, dropped by the Climate Department. "It's hard not to notice what's going on here," Kelvin said to them, "so I've been giving some extra thought to a possible connection between the methane emissions from offshore drilling and the methane release from your permafrost south of the Arctic Ocean."

"Have you come up with any theory relating the two yet?" Eric asked.

"Possibly ...," he hesitated. "I'd like to join your team and take some seismic measurements along the Mackenzie."

"What do you think could be the connection?" asked David.

Kelvin opened a map of the Arctic Ocean. "You're all familiar with the Mid-Atlantic Ridge on a divergent fault line, which extends northward through Iceland and was formed by the sea floor spreading 200-300 million years ago. And it's still spreading."

"I understand that," replied Eric. "After all, Alfred Wegener, a meteorologist, first proposed continental drift in 1915," he added amusingly.

"Touché, Eric! This convergent fault line," Kelvin pointed to the map, "extends northward east of Greenland, then right across the Arctic Ocean, through the East Siberian Sea, southward through eastern Russia, where it becomes a transform fault, then out across the northern part of the Kamchatka Peninsula. From there, the fault is convergent, which created the Aleutian chain, south of Alaska. It then extends down the west coast of North America and includes the San Andres fault. All of this," drawing a figurative circle, "forms the North American plate."

"I see," said Eric. "How does any connection between the methane emissions from offshore drilling and the methane release from the permafrost south of the Arctic Ocean come into this?"

"This is all untested theory, but what we do know is that much of the Northwest Territories, Alberta, and further south, was once an inland sea, in other words, separating eastern North America from what we refer to as the Rocky Mountains and the Coastal range, all of British Columbia in fact."

"Where are we going from here?" asked David.

"Some geophysicists have speculated that there was also a secondary fault running south across the Arctic Ocean, then down through what we know today as the Mackenzie River Basin, and further south, possibly even the Athabasca River, which flows into the Mackenzie by way of Great Slave Lake."

"Ah" Eric exclaimed. "You're thinking that the fossil fuels and methane of the Arctic Ocean and the methane peat bogs of the Northwest Territories could be physically linked through this fault line, including the oil known to be around Norman Wells, and possibly even the oil sands along the Athabasca near Fort McMurray?"

"It's all theory at this stage, but yes, that's about it."

"I'm not sure how much this complicates our methane problem, but if it's true, we certainly need to know as soon as possible," added David.

"That's why I'd like to join your team, initially to get some additional seismic data, although given the territory, it would involve some dedicated helicopter work and lots of funding."

"The Prime Minister has told us there are no limits on funding," said Eric, "within reason. And as David says, we certainly need to know if there is such a connection. It would be great if you would join the team, Kelvin. If you can prove this connection, it might shed some light on how to mitigate methane emissions. The problem is that, even with this moratorium on drilling, the Arctic Ocean is still heating up. There is a huge risk that a whole cascade of methane could be released from the offshore clathrates at some point, if it hasn't already happened. The same applies to permafrost melt. Both continue to be sources of methane. But if there's some physical connection between the two, perhaps something positive could come from that. What, I'm not sure, but we can hope."

Kelvin replied, "My knowledge of the Mackenzie geology is weak, my expertise being major faults offshore the west coast of Canada. However, I've been doing lots of reading on the Mackenzie Valley geology this summer. As soon as I heard of this moratorium on offshore drilling, I wondered if you have authority to gain some access to information on drilling results from both Esso and CUUON in the Arctic offshore. They may already have data on any fault line that runs toward the Mackenzie Delta. I'd like to explore that for starters."

"We've been given access to all data that they collected," said David. "We weren't sure what use we could make from that access, but I'm thinking you may have an answer for that."

Kelvin continued, "They drill many holes before they decide which ones to pursue further. I'd like to see those data, then do some other critical seismic tests along the Mackenzie and Athabasca."

"This could be a game-breaker for us," added Eric. "Incidentally, I've also been in touch with a chap from North American Pipelines Incorporated in Yellowknife, Calvin Hollsworth, their chief of field operations. He knows a fair amount about the seismic tests that have been done in the Northwest Territories. With the moratorium on offshore drilling, the northern pipeline is also on hold, so he tells me that he can be available to help interpret any data related to that. The Sierra Club in Canada has offered him a job heading up a northern branch of the club, given his knowledge of the northern environment. He would make a good contact for you. Can you work up a budget for funding your field tests, as soon as possible?"

"You've read my mind exactly," said Kelvin. "I'll get in touch with Hollsworth right away. I have two new grad students interested in taking on the seismic data already available. We'll need to contract for at least a hundred hours of helicopter time, possibly two choppers working out of Inuvik, whatever that costs, plus a few hundred thousand in supplies, manpower, and travel."

"Consider it done! Welcome to the team. Come back to our field prep lab and meet the other team members."

"Good idea."

Hans stayed on in Vancouver for a long overdue holiday, then attended Nancy and Great Bear's wedding in Yellowknife in late July, followed by a week-long canoe holiday with the Nicholson family in the Northwest Territories. It was a glorious week for all, short because all members had serious business to return to, but long enough to create lifelong bonds. Hans accompanied Eric's research team back to the Northwest Territories in early August, helping out where he could. Constable George Bergman, fully recovered and back on duty in Norman Wells, took time off to visit Yellowknife while Julia was there for the wedding. The two enjoyed each other's company for two days. George told Julia that he would be transferred to Vancouver in September and asked if he could see her there. Julia readily agreed.

22. The Methane Time Bomb
and New Research

By late July, the UVan team, with technical assistance from the Canadian Department of Environment and Climate Change, had completed installations for 50 fixed methane sites. John and Tony, using recommendations from Great Bear and Paul Anawak, made arrangements with northern residents for another 50 mobile methane units. Data was being downloaded directly to UVan daily. By early September, Kelvin, using seismic data from offshore drilling and working with Earthquake Canada and USGS seismologists, confirmed the existence of the secondary fault lying within or near the Mackenzie and Athabasca river valleys. Other teams were working at establishing the potential risks from offshore and permafrost methane under the tutelage of Professor Pearce. The Northwest Territories, the Yukon, Alaska, and northern Alberta had suddenly become the world's hotbed of environmental research. A Russian-American team was carrying out related research over northern Russia.

Pockets of atmospheric methane exceeding 4000 ppb were routinely being recorded, although these were confined to the Arctic and sub-Arctic regions so far. All data were made readily available in real time, and all major global climate research centres were updating their model inputs as data were obtained. The IPCC announced that the global mean temperature had increased by almost 0.5°C in just the previous five years. No one could predict when the infamous tipping point in climate might occur, but all agreed that it could not be far off. Most results suggested that it would occur within 10-15 years, and certainly before 2040 if a significant reversal in carbon emission rates could not be achieved soon.

During July, concern over disastrous climate change impacts had finally become the major global concern virtually overnight. This prompted a number of positive outcomes, including huge investments in renewable energy sources, solar, wind, tidal, and nuclear. Ironically, Alberta became an instant leader in these endeavours, centred in, of all places, Fort McMurray. Even terrorist activities had lessened as the new reality of global warming sank in.

The global warming impacts were many. Lake Chad in the Sahel was officially declared dry in July. Virtually all crops had failed across the Sahel, with rampant starvation requiring massive emergency aid. Second waves of climate refugees from desertification in both the Sahel and Middle East regions had already started, with Syria declared virtually a full desert by early July. The Fertile Crescent, so-called from before biblical times, in the Middle East had been reduced to a few pockets of agriculture along the four major rivers—the Tigris, Euphrates, Jordan, and Nile—where irrigation was still possible.

Similar desertification was widespread in South Africa, Mexico, the southwest US, and Australia. Parts of the Canadian prairies and the US High Plains were experiencing an intensely dry summer, while adjacent parts suffered violent thunderstorms, hail, tornadoes, and flooding. An F5 tornado with a one-kilometre-wide funnel ripped through Saskatoon in late July, destroying a whole subdivision of homes and killing more than 100 people, a new Canadian record. Yellowknife had experienced a severe thunderstorm in mid-July with golf ball-size hail for the very first time, while lightning from the same storm set off widespread fires throughout the Northwest Territories in the excessively dry forests.

Atlantic hurricanes were at an all-time high, with storm names running through the alphabet by mid-September. A record eight Category 4/5 hurricanes were tracked. Five of these, including the earlier *Aletta* and *Barry* storms, hit the US east coast. Combined insurance losses from storms and drought were already in the hundreds of billions of dollars by the end of August, with thousands of deaths from the hurricanes alone. Hurricane *Winnie* hit Halifax in early September, destroying ancient trees that had survived the Halifax explosion more than a century before, wrecking many vessels and causing more than 100 deaths. Two hurricanes even made it to European shores as tropical storms. It seemed that Gaia was truly having its revenge.

Despite all the havoc and predictions of doom, the northern studies prompted by the methane threat were being carried out with unprecedented speed and cooperation from all concerned. Teams had gathered in the Northwest Territories, Alaska, and Siberia. The team led by Eric, David, Kelvin Nordsen and Calvin Hollsworth, together with scientists and graduate students from all over the globe, were seriously grappling with the methane problem.

John and Tony were monitoring daily methane data from all over the Northwest Territories. It soon became apparent that the concentrations not only varied with time, in pulses, but that the pulses from near-shore and from tundra permafrost were virtually simultaneous. David, their thesis supervisor, recognized the importance of this without yet having a clear definition of the physical connections. He had them write up a brief article for the Canadian Journal of Climate Change to document their findings. Despite the statistical connection, the physical connection between the two sources of methane remained a puzzle. The answer would eventually come from Dr. Nordsen's research.

* * *

Eric took a two-week break in late August to travel to Durban again for Nelson Tutu's PhD defense. Arrangements were then made for Nelson to join his team the following month as a post-doctoral fellow at UVan, studying the social and economic consequences of global warming in Arctic regions. Nelson found an immediate interest in and link to Julia's preliminary work on the legal aspects of the pipeline controversy.

Mahmoud Wassouf started a teaching-research position in Saskatoon in September, investigating climate impacts on prairie drought.

* * *

While all this climate research progressed, Julia was busy compiling results from her adventures in the north. In order to gauge legal implications, Julia needed to be familiar with all First Nations, Inuit, and Metis land claims in the Northwest Territories, and this occupied much of her time that fall. Professor Samson was elated with her preliminary findings, which were described in their final report to NAPI. This report, combined with the methane results, convinced NAPI to terminate their agreement with CUUON to build the northern pipeline. To their credit, NAPI provided the report to the federal Department of Environment and Climate Change. It was instrumental in the federal government cancelling all permits pertaining to oil and gas in Arctic and sub-Arctic Canada. With public opinion solidly behind the science, the US quickly followed suit. Interestingly, NAPI found another use for pipeline construction, to bring water to northern communities.

Despite her blossoming romance with Cst George Bergman, Julia's PhD thesis followed smoothly that winter. She graduated in record time the following summer. Many requests for speaking engagements, as well as TV and radio interviews, followed upon her graduation. She was doubly delighted when Great Bear was transferred to the RCMP crime investigation unit in Vancouver that year, and her friendship with Nancy grew stronger.

Carol also gained recognition, as the federal government frequently called upon her and Eric to brief them on weather and climate events in the months that followed. The whole family was featured on several television interviews.

For Eric and all his team, it was troubling not knowing whether a tipping point in global climate was imminent. Perhaps nature was already starting the process of restoring equilibrium in a relatively rapid but catastrophic way. If so, then would civilization survive in some form? Would mankind survive at all? At least the effort to drastically reduce atmospheric carbon emissions was finally in progress for real, where previously no genuine attempt had been made.

By late September that year, almost every nation on the globe was finally cooperating. Most countries immediately invested billions in solar, wind, and tidal power projects, along with other non-fossil fuel endeavours, while embarking on ambitious carbon fee and dividend programs. Carbon footprinting quickly became part of virtually every human endeavour, including educational programs.

The big question was whether carbon emissions and global warming could be curtailed in time. Eric thought, *Time enough to worry about the final outcome. For now, we have a huge task ahead of us, and for once we have the backing of most governments. Let's get on with it. No more convenient mistruths. And God help us all if the climate has already reached a tipping point.*

END

APPENDIX I: MAIN CHARACTERS

Dr. Eric Nicholson – internationally-known climate scientist, Climate Department, University of Vancouver (UVan), BC, expertise in climate modelling and impacts.

Carol Nicholson – Eric's spouse of 28 years, meteorologist/forecaster in Vancouver.

Julia Nicholson – Eric's daughter, 25, BSc, MA, doctoral candidate in environmental law, UVan.

John Nicholson – Eric's son, 21, 3rd year environmental engineering student at the UVan, with expertise in computer technology.

Tony Bradley – computer software geek at the University of Vancouver and close friend of John, from Dallas, Texas.

Dr. David Pearce – department head at the UVan Climate Department, mentor of Eric Nicholson and acclaimed for his work on the northern permafrost melt threat.

Thelma Pearce – David's wife of 50 years, chemist.

Melanie Wood – Climate Department secretary at UVan.

Dr. Kelvin Nordsen – Dept. of Geophysics, University of Vancouver and colleague of Eric and David.

Dr. Kane Samson – Faculty of Law, University of Vancouver, Julia's PhD supervisor.

Dr. Ivan Mazurenko – climate scientist from the Department of Atmospheric Chemistry, University of Moscow, and working colleague of Eric Nicholson and David Pearce.

Nania Mazurenko – Ivan's wife in Moscow, scientist and teacher.

Dr. Klarno – Director of the Russian Science Ministry, Moscow.

Viktor Gruboff – Officer of the Russian FSS (Federal Security Service), Moscow.

Dr. Henry Jackson – eminent climate scientist at the University of Maryland.

Dr. Ching Dao – climate scientist, Bejing University, China, uncle of Chi-Min Chang, with expertise on climate modelling and impacts on weather systems, close friend and colleague of Eric.

Chi-Min Chang – Chinese PDF and research assistant of Eric Nicholson, nephew of Dr. Ching Dao.

Hans Stahl – German detective in the Bonn police force, former naval officer in security, former member of Interpol.

Cpl Garan Liebermann – police officer assigned to protect Eric in Germany.

Tom Bolton – member of the climate denialist organization, for Climate Stability (CCS).

Matthew Keller – former climate scientist colleague of Eric's (now a climate denialist), with financial ties to CUUON (China-Uzbekistan-US Oil Network), and a founding member of CCS.

David Brown – Chief of Environmental Engineering, CUUON, Houston, TX.

Todd Barton – works closely with Matthew Keller and Nick Savage within CUUON.

Nick Savage – henchman for Malcolm Keller and Todd Barton Uses several aliases: Nils Scheer while in Germany, Nolan Smith or Nadair Sciarra while in the Northwest Territories.

Andrew Vinson – student in Nicholson's Climate Change 201 class at the University of Vancouver, planted by Matthew Keller to spy on Nicholson's work.

Ted O'Brien – computing expert working on computer security systems at the University of Southern Alberta (UnSA); working for Matthew Keller and funded through the Companions for Climate Stability (CCS) with CUUON funds. He secretly contracts other villains involved, including student Andrew Vinson (in Eric's climate course) and Joe Malone, Savage's henchman.

Joe Malone – drifter hired by Nick Savage.

Professor Kane Samson – Julia's PhD supervisor in the Faculty of Law, University of Vancouver.

Dr. Samuel Zwane – head of Atmospheric Science Department, University of KwaZulu-Natal, Durban, South Africa.

Nelson Tutu – climate graduate student of Dr. Zwane, studying impacts of global warming on the African Sahel. (Related to Archbishop Tutu and Nelson Mandela).

Nancy Wedzin – member of the Yellowknives, a band of the Dene First Nations, and administrative employee of NAPI (North American Pipelines Inc.) in Yellowknife whom

Julia befriends in Yellowknife, and who accompanies Julia
on the remainder of her Northwest Territories-Yukon
investigative trip.

Dr. Andrew Long – Executive Vice President, NAPI, Canadian
operations.

Calvin Hollsworth – Chief of field operations for NAPI,
Yellowknife.

Malcolm Keller – estranged son of Matthew, field technician
with NAPI in Yellowknife.

Chief Margaret Roche – Deh Cho First Nations, Fort Simpson.

Chief Daniel Mackenzie – of the Dene Nation, Norman Wells.

Tim (Light Foot) Wedzin –Nancy's uncle, lives with his wife
Betty and family in Norman Wells, hunts and fishes out of
Fort Good Hope and runs a guiding service there.

Betty Wedzin – Tim Wedzin's wife

Constable George Bergman – RCMP Detachment, Norman
Wells, temporary assignment to Watson Lake, later to
Vancouver.

Cpl Bob (Great Bear) Jackson – RCMP, Inuvik, Northwest
Territories.

Paul Anawak – Inuvialuit graduate student studying
environmental engineering impacts of northern climate
change at the University of Vancouver; a close friend of
John; from Inuvik, Northwest Territories.

Duane Day – Paul's pilot friend, operates a five-passenger
aircraft service out of Inuvik serving Tuktoyaktuk and
Aklavik.

Chief Patrick Elias – Inuvialuit Land Administration office
manager, Tuktoyaktuk.

John Anawak – Paul Anawak's uncle, an Inuvialuit visionary
in Aklavik.

Mulligan Thomas – NDP Prime Minister of Canada.

Webb Andrews – Environment/Energy Minister in Canada's
NDP-Green Party coalition government.

Illyana Dinton – President of the US.

Timothy Miller – Chair Kaska Dena Council, Watson Lake.

Constable Tom Farrel – Whitehorse YT RCMP detachment.

Constable Michael Robison – Vancouver RCMP Crime
Detection.

APPENDIX II: Chronology of Climate Change Science

While this story is a work of fiction, it is helpful to review relevant facts about climate change. Key historical events in this science, and other events relevant to this novel, are quoted as accurately as possible in what follows. They are presented in chronological order to place our story into a proper context.

1712   *Thomas Newcomen* was an English inventor who built what he called the atmospheric engine, often referred to simply as a Newcomen engine, the first practical device to harness the power of steam to produce mechanical work.

1775   *James Watt*, a Scottish inventor and mechanical engineer, vastly improved the Newcomen engine, fuelled by fossil fuels (wood and coal at that time). It was then rapidly developed to provide power to pumps for pumping water out of mines. Starting in the 1780s, it was also applied to power other types of machines. The steam engine enabled rapid development of efficient, semi-automated factories on a previously unimaginable scale in places where water power was not available. Some interpret this as the beginning of the *Industrial Revolution*. While coal had been in use for heating and cooking for thousands of years, its use increased exponentially with the steam engine. With it came an increase in carbon dioxide (CO_2) emissions to the atmosphere.

1788   *Alexander Mackenzie* noted bituminous oil in the Athabasca region, which later became the oil sands we know today; the following year he noted oil on the banks of the Mackenzie River at what is now known as Norman Wells, NWT.

1815   *Jean-Pierre Perraudin* described for the first time how glaciers might be responsible for the giant boulders seen in alpine valleys.

1824   French scientist and mathematician, *Joseph Fourier* described a warming effect by various gases in the atmosphere, which he theorized was keeping the planet warmer than what it would be otherwise.

1837   *Louis Agassiz*, a Swiss-American biologist and geologist, was the first to scientifically propose that the Earth had been subject to a past ice age. This became widely accepted in the 1870s.

1854   *Ignacy Łukasiewic*, a Polish pharmacist, constructed the world's first oil well, followed in 1856 by the world's first oil refinery; related achievements included distillation of kerosene from oil, invention of the kerosene lamp, and the first modern street lamps.

1856   *Eunice Newton Foote* studied the warming effect of the sun, including how this warming was increased by the presence of carbonic acid gas (carbon dioxide), and suggested that the surface of an Earth, with an atmosphere rich in this gas, would have a higher temperature.

1861   *John Tyndall* was an Irish physicist who demonstrated that small amounts of water vapour and hydrocarbons like methane (CH_4) and carbon dioxide (CO_2) were able to absorb and emit amounts of radiant heat sufficient to control the heat budget of the planet.

1896   *Svante Arrhenius* was a Swedish scientist who examined the effects of different levels of atmospheric CO_2 concentration on the temperature of the planet, accounting for solar and terrestrial radiation, including the fourth-power relationship between temperature and radiation, and estimated the absorption of terrestrial radiation by water vapour and carbon dioxide. He calculated that doubling atmospheric CO_2 would raise global temperatures by 3-3.5°C, while reducing CO_2 by one-third would lower temperatures by roughly the same amount. He reasoned at that time that this would not be a concern for 1000 years.

1908   *Henry Ford* and the Ford Motor Company introduced the Model T, generally regarded as the first affordable automobile. Within two years, there were more than one million motor vehicles. The numbers grew exponentially from there, as did atmospheric CO_2, despite Arrhenius' opinion that it would not be a problem for a thousand years.

1911   Prospector *JK Cornwall* investigated the oil seeps at Norman Wells and discovered that they consisted of high quality crude oil. Imperial Oil subsequently drilled and struck oil in 1920.

1920   Serbian scientist *Milutin Milankovic* published an explanation of Earth's long-term climate changes caused by variations in eccentricity, axial tilt and precession of the Earth's orbit, which he claimed determined climatic patterns on Earth through orbital forcing changes in the position of the Earth in comparison to the Sun, now known as Milankovitch cycles. This explained the ice ages occurring in the geological past of the Earth, as well as climate changes on the Earth that can be expected in the future on time scales of ~100,000 years.

1923   Large oil reservoirs discovered in Texas.

1926   Dr. Karl Clark began work on the oil sands for the Alberta Research Council and the University of Alberta.

1929   American astronomer *Andrew Douglass* discovered strong indications of climate change in tree rings, noting that rings were thinner in dry years, and subsequently founded the discipline of dendrochronology, a method of dating wood by the growth ring pattern.

1937   Imperial Oil built an oil refinery at Norman Wells to supply local NWT markets.

1938   *Guy Callendar* was an English steam engineer and amateur climatologist, born in Montreal, who compiled available statistics on atmospheric CO_2 measurements and demonstrated continuously rising concentrations from 290 ppm (1866) to 310 ppm in 1934. He was the first scientist to document that the planet had warmed from atmospheric CO_2 emissions.

1942   The U.S. military built the Alaska Highway and connected a pipeline to the Norman Wells oilfilelds; it was abandoned a year later.

1947   Tremendous oil reserves were discovered near Leduc, Alberta.

1953   The Trans Mountain Pipeline was completed, transporting oil from Edmonton, Alberta to Burnaby, British Columbia.

1956   *Charles Keeling,* an American scientist of the Scripps Institution of Oceanography, began continuous measurements of atmospheric CO_2 at Mauna Loa and alerted the world to the possibility of an anthropogenic contribution to the greenhouse effect and global warming. Keeling showed that atmospheric CO_2 concentrations had exceeded 310 ppm by 1956 and were continuing to rise. [Note: there is a discontinuity in the concentration of 310 ppm claimed by Callendar in 1934 and Keeling in 1956, with Keeling's value accepted as correct.]

1960   *Keeling* confirmed that annual increases in atmospheric CO_2 roughly matched the amount of global fossil fuels being burned annually.

1962   Development of Alberta oil sands commenced.

1963   *The Clean Air Act* was enacted by the US Congress to control air pollution on a national level and requires the Environmental Protection Agency (EPA) to develop and enforce regulations to protect the general public from exposure to airborne contaminants that are known to be hazardous to human health. The Act was passed in 1963 and significantly amended in 1970, 1977 and 1990 (e.g., the 1977 amendment allowed certain environmental improvements, or offsets, that a company could make to help meet its targets).

1965   The US President's Scientific Advisory Committee warned of global warming from CO_2 and that continued emissions *will modify the heat balance of the atmosphere to such an extent that marked changes in climate, not controllable through local or even national efforts, could occur.*

1967   *Syukuro Manabe* and *Richard Wetherald* made a convincing calculation that doubling CO_2 would raise world temperatures by 2°C.

1968   American glaciologist *John Mercer* pointed out that the West Antarctic Ice Sheet is in a delicate balance; shelves of ice float at its rim and these shelves could disintegrate under a slight warming, collapsing the ice sheet and raising global sea levels by up to 5 m.

1968   *Paul Ehrlich* wrote that the enhanced greenhouse effect caused by burning fossil fuels is being countered by manmade aerosols of dust and other contaminants.

1972   Countries attending the UN Conference on Human Development in Stockholm signed a declaration with 26 principles, which was the starting point for internationally cohesive attempts to understand the issues related to the stratospheric ozone layer depletion and climate change.

1977   *The Berger Report*, commissioned by the Canadian Government and headed by Justice Thomas Berger, recommended that no pipeline be built through the northern Yukon and that a pipeline through the Mackenzie Valley should be delayed for 10 years.

1979   The first World Climate Conference on climate change was held in Geneva and led to the establishment of the World Climate Program. It called on governments *to foresee and prevent potential man-made changes in climate.*

1982   Imperial Oil constructed six artificial islands on the Mackenzie River at Normal Wells, and an 870-km pipeline to Zama, Alberta.

1985   The first major international conference on the greenhouse effect was held in Villach, Austria. Scientists warned that greenhouse gases will, *in the first half of the next century, cause a rise of global mean temperature and a rise of sea levels,* and that gases other than CO_2, such as methane, ozone, chlorofluorocarbons and nitrous oxide also contribute to global warming.

1985   A Franco-Soviet team at the Vostok Station in Antarctica showed that CO_2 and temperature had gone up and down together in wide swings through past ice ages, confirming the CO_2-temperature relationship in a manner entirely independent of computer climate models, strongly reinforcing the emerging scientific consensus.

1987   The Montreal Protocol of the Vienna Convention imposed international restrictions on the emission of ozone-destroying gases.

1988   *James Hansen*, head of the NASA Goddard Institute for Space Studies, gave testimony on climate change to congressional committees that helped raise broad awareness of global warming, along with his advocacy of action to avoid dangerous climate change. In recent years, Hansen has become an activist for action to mitigate the effects of climate change, which on a few occasions has led to his arrest.

1988   *The Intergovernmental Panel on Climate Change* (IPCC) was set up by the World Meteorological Organization (WMO) and by the United Nations Environment Program (UNEP). The IPCC is mandated to provide reports based on scientific evidence which reflect existing viewpoints within the scientific community.

1988   Atmospheric CO_2 concentrations had reached 350 ppm and were increasing by 1.5 ppm/yr.

1990   The *IPCC* released its *First Assessment Report* (AR-1), stating that the planet had warmed by 0.5°C in the past century, and at business as usual emission rates, there would be an effective doubling of CO_2 in the atmosphere sometime between 2025 and 2050, resulting in an increase in global mean temperature of 1.5-4.5°C. The distribution of this increase would be unequal, with a smaller increase of half the global mean in tropical regions and twice the global mean in polar regions. Impacts would include a sea-level rise of about 0.3-0.5 m by 2050 and about 1 m by 2100.

1991   Mt. Pinatubo exploded, and *James Hansen* predicted a short-term cooling pattern, verified in 1995 using computer models of aerosol effects.

1991   Studies from 55 million years ago suggested that clathrate ices, frozen in layers spread through sea floor muds, might hold more carbon compounds than all the world's coal and oil. Warming of the oceans could cause some of the deposits to disintegrate in a landslide-like chain reaction, which would vent enough methane and CO_2 into the atmosphere to redouble global warming.

1992   The United Nations Earth Summit took place in Rio de Janeiro attended by 172 countries. *The United Nations Framework Convention on Climate Change* from the Summit was signed by 154 nations, in which they agreed to prevent dangerous warming from greenhouse gases and set an initial target of reducing emissions from industrialized countries to 1990 levels by the year 2000. This led to negotiations which resulted in the Kyoto Protocol several years later.

1995   The *IPCC* released its *Second Assessment Report* (AR-2), in which it warned that carbon emissions had accelerated current warming, which *is unlikely to be entirely natural in origin* and that *the balance of evidence suggests a discernible human influence on global climate.* For the mid-range IPCC emission scenario, climate models projected an increase in global mean surface air temperature relative to 1990 of about 2°C by 2100, along with a sea level rise of about 50 cm by 2100. The IPCC also warned of potential unexpected future behaviours in the climate system due to the non-linear nature of the climate.

1997   *The Kyoto Protocol* was initially adopted on December 11, 1997 in Kyoto, Japan and entered into force on February 16, 2005. As of April 2010, 191 states had signed and ratified the protocol, with notable exceptions such as the US and China. Signatories agreed to legally binding emissions cuts for industrialized nations, averaging 5.4%, to be met by the 2008-2012 commitment period. The protocol also adopted a series of flexibility measures, allowing countries to meet their targets partly by trading emission permits, establishing carbon sinks such as forests and by investing in other countries.

1997   Toyota introduced the Prius in Japan, the first mass-market electric hybrid car.

1998   A super *El Niño* made 1998 an exceptionally warm year, equaled in later years but not clearly exceeded until 2014.

1999   *Harvey* and *Huang* (in J.Geophys.Res.) estimated that a release of 24,000 Gt of methane clathrates in marine sediments and 800 Gt in terrestrial sediments could increase global warming by 10-25%.

2000   According to Mauna Loa measurements, atmospheric CO_2 values had reached 369 ppm, and concentrations were increasing by 1.6 ppm/yr since 1990.

2001   The *IPCC* released its *Third Assessment Report* (AR-3). This report concluded that *There is new and stronger evidence that most of the warming observed over the last 50 years is attributable to human activities.* The global average surface temperature had increased over the 20th century by about 0.6°C. Average global surface temperature is projected to increase by 1.4-5.8°C by 2100, while sea level is projected to rise by 0.1-0.9 m over the same period; the wide range in predictions is based on scenarios that assume different levels of future CO_2 emissions.

2002   The UK Emissions Trading Scheme (ETS) commenced. It was the first cross-industry, national greenhouse gas emissions trading scheme in the world.

2003   Atmospheric CO_2 concentrations reached 375 ppm and had accelerated to 2 ppm/yr.

2005   The Kyoto Protocol came into force in Feb. 2005. Kyoto signatories were required to discuss emissions targets for the second compliance period beyond 2012, while countries without targets, including the US and China, agreed to a non-binding dialogue on their future roles in curbing emissions. Canada, which ratified the legally-binding accord in parliament in 2002, opted out in December 2011.

2005   Hurricane *Katrina* and other major tropical storms spurred debate over the impact of global warming on storm intensities.

2006   Former Vice President *Al Gore's* documentary film, *An Inconvenient Truth*, directed by Davis Guggenheim, opened in New York and Los Angeles and raised international public awareness of climate change. The documentary was aimed at alerting the public to an increasing planetary emergency due to global warming. The film included segments intended to refute critics who say that global warming is unproven, or that warming will be insignificant. It was a critical box office success, winning two Academy Awards for Best Documentary Feature and Best Original Song, and resulted in Gore receiving the Nobel Peace Prize in 2007.

2007   The Nobel Peace Prize 2007 was awarded jointly to the Intergovernmental Panel on Climate Change (IPCC) and to Albert (Al) Gore, Jr. *for their efforts to build up and disseminate greater knowledge about man-made climate change, and to lay the foundations for the measures that are needed to counteract such change.*

2007   Following changes in governments, Australia joined the 174 nations in ratifying the Kyoto Protocol, while Canada, under Conservative PM Harper, unofficially opted out.

2007   *IPCC Fourth Assessment Report* (AR-4). This report concluded that there was *very high confidence that the global average net effect of human activities since 1750 has been one of warming* and warns that the *warming of the climate is unequivocal*. Furthermore:

- Most of the observed increase in globally averaged temperatures since the mid-20th century is very likely (>90%) due to the observed increase in anthropogenic (human) greenhouse gas concentrations.
- Anthropogenic warming and sea level rise would continue for centuries due to the timescales associated with climate processes and feedbacks, even if greenhouse gas concentrations were to be stabilized, although the likely amount of temperature and sea level rise varies greatly depending on the fossil intensity of human activity during the next century.
- The probability that this is caused by natural climatic processes alone is < 5%.
- World temperatures could rise by between 1.1 and 6.4°C during the 21st century and: sea levels will probably rise by 18 to 59 cm.
- There is a confidence level >90% that there will be more frequent warm spells, heat waves, and heavy rainfall.
- There is a confidence level >66% that there will be an increase in droughts, tropical cyclones, and extreme high tides.
- Both past and future anthropogenic CO_2 emissions will continue to contribute to warming and sea level rise for more than a millennium.
- Global atmospheric concentrations of CO_2, methane, and nitrous oxide have increased markedly as a result of human activities since 1750 and now far exceed pre-industrial values over the past 650,000 years.

2008   *James Hansen* warned that because of global warming that has already occurred, positive feedbacks have been set in motion, and the additional warming has brought us to the precipice of a planetary *tipping point*. We are close to that tipping point because the climate state includes large, positive feedbacks provided by the Arctic sea ice, the West Antarctic ice sheet, and much of Greenland's ice. Little additional forcing is needed to trigger these feedbacks and magnify global warming. If we go over the edge, we will transition to an environment far outside the range that has been experienced by humanity, and there will be no return within any foreseeable future generation.

2008   The US Geological Survey reported that the Arctic Ocean contains more than a fifth of the world's unexploited, recoverable oil and gas resources.

2009   Several months prior to the Copenhagen Conference on Climate Change in December, there was a notable increase in writings and rhetoric by the climate denialist community. This culminated in the so-called *Climategate* in November, a completely contrived climate controversy that began with the illegal hacking of email files at the University of East Anglia's Climatic Research Unit (CRU), one of several major research centres that constructs various global temperature and precipitation analyses. Six government-appointed independent committees subsequently investigated the allegations during 2010, and all scientists involved were completely absolved of any fraud or scientific misconduct. The contrived allegations involved rewording and taking email comments completely out of context, a practice common with the denialist community. However, the incident was a public relations disaster for climate science and the damage was done for the Copenhagen meeting in December 2009, resulting in a much watered-down Copenhagen Accord, salvaged only by last-minute efforts by US President Obama.

2009   The Copenhagen Conference on Climate Change resulted in the *Copenhagen Accord*, a non-binding agreement by signatories. While the Accord was a disappointment to many, countries did agree to the goal of keeping increases in global average temperatures below 2°C. For the first time, both China and India made non-binding pledges to reduce their emissions intensities (rather than the much more desirable Total emissions, but at least it was a small start).

2010   The 2010 United Nations Climate Change Conference in Cancun resulted in the Cancun Agreements, which consolidated and extended the Copenhagen Accord and included a Green Climate Fund of $100 billion a year by 2020 to assist poorer countries in financing emission reductions and adaptation, albeit with no agreement for the source of these funds. Cancun was seen by some as a new beginning for international climate change efforts, particularly bringing large emitters such as China, the US, and India into the community.

2010   Atmospheric CO_2 values had reached 390 ppm, and concentrations had accelerated by 2.1 ppm/yr since 2000.

2011   Australia announced a framework for introducing a fixed carbon price for Australia as of 01 July 2012 (subject to parliamentary approval), followed in 3-5 years by an emissions trading scheme.

2011   Following the Climate Change Conference in Durban, South Africa, the Harper government of Canada officially withdrew its commitments to the Kyoto Accord, a setback to scientists involved in climate research and utter embarrassment and bitter disappointment for Canadian scientists.

2012   Energy giant Total (in the British newspaper *Financial Times*) warned against drilling for crude oil in Arctic waters because damage caused by a potential oil spill would be disastrous in such an environmentally sensitive area.

2013   *IPCC Fifth Assessment Report* (AR-5). This fifth assessment report was, as in past reports, very conservative and concluded:

- Warming of the atmosphere and ocean system is unequivocal. Many of the associated impacts such as sea level change (among other metrics) have occurred since 1950 at rates unprecedented in the historical record.

- There is a clear human influence on the climate.
- It is extremely likely that human influence has been the dominant cause of observed warming since 1950, with the level of confidence having increased since the fourth report.
- IPCC pointed out that the longer we wait to reduce our emissions, the more expensive it will become.

2014   Atmospheric concentrations of CO_2 reached 400 ppm (March 2014) and continued to accelerate by 2.2 ppm/yr (since 2000)

2015   *Pope Francis* released his second encyclical, *Laudato sI*, in June 2015, which critiqued consumerism and irresponsible development, lamented environmental degradation and global warming, and called on all people of the world to take *swift and unified global action.*

2015   The 21st session of the Conference of the Parties (COP-21) to the UNFCCC, December 2015, in Paris, France, set a goal of limiting global warming to less than 2°C compared to pre-industrial levels, agreed to *pursue efforts to* limit the temperature increase to 1.5 °C, and called for zero net anthropogenic greenhouse gas emissions to be reached during the second half of the 21st century.

2016   In January, 2015 was declared the warmest year ever on Earth.

2016   The highest ever daily average atmospheric CO_2, 409.44 ppm, was recorded at the Mauna Loa Observatory in Hawaii on April 9.

2016   On Earth Day, April 22, 174 countries signed the COP-21 agreement in New York and began adopting it within their own legal systems through ratification, acceptance, approval, or accession.

2016   A paper by *James Powell* in the Bulletin of Science, Technology & Society in July showed 99.99% consensus of 69,406 authors of peer-reviewed articles in 2013-14 agreeing on the truth of anthropogenic global warming.

2016   Canada and the European Union approved the Paris Agreement ratification on October 5, effectively accepting UN enforcement of the COP-21 global agreement.

2016   *James Hansen* reported on October 17 that September 2016 was the 17th straight month of record monthly global mean temperatures, confirmed by NOAA, NASA, and the Japan Meteorological Association. He also predicted that 2016 would break, by a wide margin, the 2015 record warm year.

2016   Atmospheric CO2 concentrations had accelerated alarmingly in the last five years to 2.8 ppm/yr (from 391.6 to 405.4 ppm).

APPENDIX III

Acronyms, Abbreviations and Technical Terms

ADM — Assistant Deputy Minister (Canadian government)

AMS — American Meteorological Society

CCS — Companions for Climate Stability (a climate denialist organization)

CFCAS — Canadian Foundation for Climate and Atmospheric Sciences, a very successful research fund established by the federal government in 2000, but terminated in 2011.

CH_4 — Methane

CSIS — Canadian Security Intelligence Service

CMOS — Canadian Meteorological & Oceanographic Society

CO_2 — Carbon dioxide

COP — Conference of the Parties

CUUON — China-Uzbekistan-US Oil Network

DFO — Fisheries and Oceans Canada formerly Department of Fisheries and Oceans

FSS — Russian Federal Security Service

GPS — Global Positioning System

hPa — Atmospheric pressure unit; hecto-Pascal = millibar (mb)

I/O — Input/output

IPCC — Intergovernmental Panel on Climate Change, climate reporting body for the United Nations.

kph — Kilometres per hour

MSC — Meteorological Service of Canada, a division of Environment Canada

NAPI — North American Pipeline Incorporated

NASA — National Aeronautics and Space Administration

NOAA — National Oceanic and Atmospheric Administration in Washington, DC

RCMP — Royal Canadian Mounted Police

SST — Sea surface temperatures

UNFCCC — United Nations Framework Convention on Climate Change

UnSA — University of Southern Alberta

UTC   Coordinated Universal Time (same as GMT, Greenwich Mean Time)
USGS   United States Geological Survey (https://www.usgs.gov/)
UVan   University of Vancouver
WMO   World Meteorological Organization, part of the United Nations.

APPENDIX IV — About the Author

Geoff Strong's career started with teaching high school, then moving on to weather forecasting, to research on severe storm evolution, to prairie drought and water issues, to focusing on issues of climate change impacts, back to teaching at several universities, and finally this novel. He holds MSc and PhD degrees in atmospheric science from the University of Alberta, where he developed a lifelong passion for severe thunderstorms. He is a Fellow of and a former national President (2006-07) of the Canadian Meteorological & Oceanographic Society (CMOS) and has chaired several CMOS centres across Canada. He has also received several CMOS awards for his work over many years.

In retirement, Geoff devotes extensive volunteer time to environmental and church organizations, particularly on issues relating to climate change, and to emergency aid and development issues of the subtropics. Global warming has its most severe impacts in the subtropics where NGO aid agencies are hard-pressed to meet minimal demands caused by desertification and related water and food issues, sea level rise, ocean acidification, increased severity of tropical storms, and refugees resulting from global warming. It is these issues that also triggered this novel.

Geoff gives frequent public talks and courses and writes media articles on environmental issues, mostly focused toward public education on global warming and its impacts. He chairs or co-chairs several environmental groups on Vancouver Island, as well as an environmental committee called Creation Matters within the Anglican Church. For leisure, Geoff enjoys nature walks, with his wife and dogs, and gardening, and is an avid reader (of mystery and action novels). While Geoff has written numerous scientific papers throughout his career, this is his first foray into writing a novel.

Contact Geoff Strong at geoff.strong@shaw.ca.